Edgar Fawcett

The Adventures of a Widow

A Novel

Edgar Fawcett

The Adventures of a Widow
A Novel

ISBN/EAN: 9783337225520

Printed in Europe, USA, Canada, Australia, Japan

Cover: Foto ©Andreas Hilbeck / pixelio.de

More available books at **www.hansebooks.com**

THE

ADVENTURES OF A WIDOW

A Novel

BY

EDGAR FAWCETT

AUTHOR OF "A GENTLEMAN OF LEISURE," "A HOPELESS
CASE," "AN AMBITIOUS WOMAN," "TINKLING
CYMBALS," ETC.

BOSTON

JAMES R. OSGOOD AND COMPANY

1884

THE ADVENTURES OF A WIDOW.

I.

IT is not long ago that the last conservative resident of Bond Street, proud of his ancient possessorship and no doubt loving the big brick structure with arched doorway and dormer windows in which he first saw the light, felt himself relentlessly swept from that interesting quarter by the stout besom of commerce. Interesting the street really is for all to whom old things appeal with any charm. It is characteristic of our brilliant New York, however, that few antiquarian feet tread her pavements, and that she is too busy with her bustling and thrifty present to reflect that she has ever reached it through a noteworthy past. Some day it will perhaps be recorded of her that among all cities she has been the least preservative of tradition and memorial. The hoary antiquity of her transatlantic sisters would seem to have made her unduly conscious of her own youth. She has so long looked over seas for all her history and romance, that now, when she can safely boast two solid centuries of age, the habit yet firmly clings, and she cares as little for the annals of her fine and stately growth as though, like Troy, she had risen, roof and spire, to the strains of magic melody.

It might be of profit, and surely it would be of pleasure, were she to care more for the echoes of those harsh and sometimes tragic sounds that have actually blent their serious music with her rise. As it is, she is rich in neglected memories; she has tombs that dumbly reproach her ignoring eye; she has nooks and purlieus that teem with reminiscence and are silent testimonials of her indifference. Her Battery and her Bowling Green, each bathed in the tender glamour of Colonial association, lie frowned upon by the grim scorn of recent warehouses and jeered at by the sarcastic shriek of the neighboring steam-tug. She can easily guide you to the modern clamors of her Stock-Exchange; but if you asked her to show you the graves of Stuyvesant and Montgomery she might find the task a hard one, though thousands of her citizens daily pass and re-pass these hallowed spots. Boston, with its gentle ancestral pride, might well teach her a lesson in retrospective self-esteem. Her own harbor, like that of Boston, has had its "tea-party," and yet one whose anniversary now remains a shadow. On Golden Hill, in her own streets, the first battle of our Revolution was fought, the first blood in the cause of our freedom was spilled; yet while Boston stanchly commemorates its later "massacre," what tribute of oratory, essay or song has that other momentous contest received? This metropolitan disdain of local souvenir can ill excuse itself on the plea of intolerance toward provincialism; for if the great cities of Europe are not ashamed to admit themselves once barbaric, Hudson in fray or traffic with the swarthy Manhattans, or old Van Twiller scowling at the anathemas of Bogardus, holds at least a pictorial value and significance.

Bond Street has always been but a brief strip of thoroughfare, running at right angles between the Bowery and Broadway. Scarcely more than thirty years ago it possessed the quietude and dignity of a patrician domain; it was beloved of our Knickerbocker social element; it was the tranquil stronghold of caste and exclusiveness. Its births, marriages and deaths were all touched with a modest distinction. Extravagance was its horror and ostentation its antipathy. The cheer of its entertainments would often descend to lemonade and sponge-cake, and rarely rise above the luxury of claret-punch and ice-cream. Its belles were of demurer type than the brisk-paced ladies of this period, and its beaux paid as close heed to the straight line in morals as many of their successors now bestow upon it in the matter of hair-parting. Bond Street was by no means the sole haunt of the aristocracy, but it was very representative, very important, very select. There was even a time when to live there at all conferred a certain patent of respectability. It was forgiven you that your daughter had married an obscure Smith, or that your son had linked his lot with an undesirable Jones, if you had once come permanently to dwell there. The whole short, broad street was superlatively genteel. Nothing quite describes it like that pregnant little word. It dined at two o'clock; it had "tea" at six; its parties were held as dissipated if they broke up after midnight; its young men "called" on its young women of an evening with ceremonious regularity, never at such times donning the evening-coat and the white neck-tie which now so widely obtain, but infallibly wearing these on all occasions of after-noon festivity with an unconcern of English usage that would keenly shock many of their descend-ants.

But by degrees the old order changed. Commerce pushed northward with relentless energy. Its advance still left Bond Street uninvaded, but here and there the roomy brick dwellings received distinctly plebeian inmates. One night, in this street formerly so dedicated to the calm of refinement, a frightful murder occurred. No one who lived in New York at that time can fail to remember the Burdell assassination. It was surrounded by all the most melodramatic luridness of commission. Its victim was a dentist, slaughtered at midnight with many wounds from an unknown hand. The mysterious deed shook our whole city with dismay. For weeks it was a topic that superseded all others. To search through old newspapers of the excited days that followed is to imagine oneself on the threshold of a thrilling tale, in which the wrong culprits are arraigned and the real offender hides himself behind so impregnable an ambush that nothing but a final chapter can overthrow it. Yet in this ghastly affair of the stabbed dentist a protracted trial resulted in a tame acquittal and no more. The story ended abruptly and midway. It lies to-day as alluring material for the writer of harrowing fiction. It still retains all the ghastly piquancy of an undiscovered crime.

The vast surrounding populace of New York have long ago learned to forget it, but there would be truth in the assertion that Bond Street recalls it still. Its garish publicity scared away the last of her fine-bred denizens. The retreat was haughty and gradual, but it is now absolute. Where Ten Eyck and Van Horn had engraved their names in burly letters on sheeny door-plates, you may see at present the flaunting signs of a hair-dresser, a beer-seller, a third-rate French *restaurateur*, a furrier, a flower-maker, and an intercessor between despairing authors and obdurate publishers. The glory of Bond Street has departed. Its region has become lamentably "down town." The spoilers possess it with undisputed rule. It is in one sense a melancholy ruin, in another a sprightly transformation.

But several years before its decadence turned unargued fact (and now we near a time that almost verges upon the present), Mr. Hamilton Varick, a gentleman well past fifty, brought into perhaps the most spacious mansion of the street a bride scarcely eighteen. Mr. Varick had lived abroad for many years, chiefly in Paris. He was a tall, spare man, with a white jaunty mustache and a black eye full of fire. He was extremely rich, and unless remote relations were considered, heirless. It was generally held that he had come home to end his days after a life of foreign folly and gallantry. This may at first have seemed wholly true, but it also occurred that he had chosen to end them in the society of a blooming young wife.

His Bond Street house, vacant for years, suddenly felt the embellishing spell of the upholsterer. Mr. Varick had meanwhile dropped into the abodes of old friends not seen in twenty years, had shaken hands, with a characteristic lightsome cordiality, right and left, had beamingly taken upon his lap the children of mothers and fathers who were once his youthful comrades in dance and rout, had reminded numerous altered acquaintances who he was, had been reminded in turn by numerous other altered acquaintances who they were, had twisted his white mustache, had talked with airy patriotism about getting back to die in one's native land, had deplored his long absence from the dear scenes of youth, had regretted secretly his transpontine Paris, had murmured his bad, witty French *mots* to whatever matron would hear them, had got himself re-made a member of the big, smart Metropolitan Club which he thought a mere tiresome sort of parochial tavern when he last left it, and had finally amazed everyone by marrying the young and lovely Miss Pauline Van Corlear.

Pauline herself had very little to do with the whole arrangement. She was the only child of a widowed mother who had long ago designed to marry her notably. Mrs. Van Corlear lived upon a very meagre income, and had been an invalid since Pauline was eight. But she had educated her daughter with a good deal of patient care, and had ultimately, at the proper age, relegated her to the chaperonage of a more prosperous sister, who had launched her forth into society with due *élan.* Pauline was not a good match in the mercenary sense; she was perfectly well aware of the fact; she had been brought up to understand it. But she was fair to see, and perhaps she understood this a little too well.

New York was then what so many will remember it to have been about twelve years ago. The civil war had left few traces of disaster; it was the winter of seventy-one. Wall Street was in a hey-day of hazardous prosperity; sumptuous balls were given by cliques of the most careful entertainers; a number of ladies who had long remained unfashionable, yet who had preserved an inherited right to assert social claim when they chose, now came to the front. These matrons proved a strong force, and resisted in sturdy confederacy all efforts of outsiders to break their dainty ranks. They shielded under maternal wings a delightful bevy of blooming young maidens, among whom was Pauline Van Corlear.

It was a season of amusing conflict. Journalism had not yet learned to fling its lime-light of notoriety upon the doings and mis-doings of private individuals. Young girls did not wake then, as now, on the morning after a ball, to read (or with jealous heart-burning *not* to read) minute descriptions of their toilets on the previous night. The "society column" of the New York newspaper was still an unborn abomination. Had this not been the case, a great deal of pungent scandal might easily have found its way into print. The phalanx of assertive matrons roundly declared that they had found society in a deplorable condition. The balls, receptions and dinners were all being given by a horde of persons without grandfathers. The reigning belles were mostly a set of loud, rompish girls, with names that rang unfamiliarly. The good old people had nearly all been drowsing inactive during several winters; one could hardly discover an Amsterdam, a Spuytenduyvil, a Van Schuylkill, among this unpleasant rabble. There had been quite too many of these spurious pretenders. Legitimacy must uplift its debased stand-ards.

Legitimacy did so, and with a will. Some very fine and spacious mansions in districts bordering or approximate to Washington Square were hos-pitably thrown open, besides others of a smarter but less time-honored elegance in " up-town " en-vironments. The new set, as it was called, carried things by storm. They were for the most part very rich people, and they spent their wealth with a lavish freedom that their lineage saved from the least charge of vulgarity. No display of money is ever considered vulgar when lineage is behind it. If you are unblessed with good descent you must air your silver dishes cautiously and heed well the multiplicity of your viands; for though your cook possess an Olympian palate and your butler be the ex-adherent of a king, the accusation of bad taste hangs like a sword of threat in your banquet hall.

Among all the winsome *débutantes* of that sea-son, Pauline Van Corlear was the most comely. She had a sparkling wit, too, that was at times mercilessly acute. Most of the young friends with whom she had simultaneously " come out " were heiresses of no mean consideration; but Pauline was so poor that an aunt would present her with a few dozens of gloves, a cousin would donate to her five or six fresh gowns, or perhaps one still more distant in kinship would supply her with boots and bonnets. The girl sensitively shrank, at first, from receiving these gifts; but her plaintive, faded mother, with her cough and querulous temper, would always eagerly insist upon their acceptance.

"Of course, my dear," Mrs. Van Corlear would say, in her treble pipe of a voice, while she rocked to and fro the great chair that bore her wasted, shawl-wrapped body — "of course it is quite right that your blood-relations should come forward. They all have plenty of money, and it would be dreadful if they let you go out looking shabby and forlorn. For my part, I 'm only surprised that they don't do more."

"I expect nothing from them, mamma," Pauline would say, a little sadly.

" *Expect*, my dear? Of course you don't. But that does n't alter the *obligation* on their part. Now please do not be obstinate; you know my neuralgia always gets worse when you 're obstinate. You are very pretty — yes, a good deal prettier than Gertie Van Horn or Sallie Pough-keepsie, with all their millions — and I have n't a doubt that before the winter is over you 'll have done something really handsome for yourself.   If you have n't, it will be your own fault."

Pauline clearly understood that to do something handsome for herself meant to marry a rich man. From a tender age she had been brought up to believe that this achievement was the goal of all hopes, desires and aims.   Everybody expected it of her, as she grew prettier and prettier; everybody hinted or prophesied it to her long before she "came out."   The little contracted and conventional world in which it was her misfortune to breathe and move, had forever dinned it into her ears until she had got to credit it as an article of necessitous faith.   There are customs of the Orient that shock our Western intelligences when we read of women placidly accepting their tyrannies; but no almond-eyed daughter of pasha or vizier ever yielded more complaisantly to harem-discipline than Pauline now yielded to the cold, commercial spirit of the marriage decreed for her.

She was popular in society, notwithstanding her satiric turn.   She always had a nosegay for the German, and a partner who had pre-engaged her. It was not seldom that she went to a ball quite laden with the floral boons of male admirers. Among these latter was her third cousin, then a gentleman of thirty, named Courtlandt Beekman.

Courtlandt had been Pauline's friend from childhood. She had always been so fond of him that it had never occurred to her to analyze her fondness now, when they met under the festal glare of chandeliers instead of in her mother's plain, dull sitting-room. Nor had it ever occurred to any of her relations to matrimonially warn her against Courtlandt. He was such a nice, quiet fellow; naturally he was good to his little cousin; he was good to everybody, and now that Pauline had grown up and begun to go to places, his devotion took a brotherly form. Of course he was poor, and, if sensible, would marry rich. He had been going about for an age in "that other set." He knew the Briggs girls and the Snowe girls, and all the *parvenu* people who had been ruling at assemblies and dancing-classes during the dark interregnum. Perhaps he would marry a Briggs or a Snowe. If he did, it would be quite proper. He was Courtlandt Beekman, and his name would sanctify nearly any sort of Philistine bride. But no one ever dreamed of suspecting that he might want to marry the cousin, twelve years his junior, who had sat on his knee as a school-girl, munching the candies he used to bring her and often pelting him with childish railleries at the same ungrateful moment.

In person Courtlandt was by no means prepossessing. He had a tall, brawny figure, and a long, sallow face, whose unclassic irregularities might have seemed dull and heavy but for the brown eyes, lucid and variant, that enlivened it. He was a man of few words, but his silences, though sometimes important, were never awkward. No one accused him of stupidity, but no one had often connected him with the idea of cleverness. He produced the impression of being a very close observer, you scarcely knew why. Possibly it was because you felt confident that his silences were not mentally vacuous. He had gone among the gay throngs almost since boyhood; if he had not so persistently mingled with ladies (and in the main very sweet and cultured ones, notwithstanding the denunciations hurled against "that other set") it is probable that he would continuously have merited the title of ungainly and graceless. But ease and polish had come to him unavoidably; he was like some rough-shapen vessel that has fallen into the hands of the gilder and decorator. It would have been hard to pick a flaw in his manners, and yet his manners were the last thing that he made you think about. He was in constant social demand; his hosts and hostesses forgot how valuable to them he really was; he almost stood for that human miracle, a man without enemies. He made a kind of becoming background for nearly everybody; he had no axe to grind, no ladder to climb, no prize to win; he stood neither as debtor nor creditor toward society; he was, in a way, society itself. There were very few women who did not enjoy a chat with him *à deux;* and in all general conversation, though his attitude was chiefly that of listener, the talkers themselves were unaware how often they sought the response of his peculiar serious smile, or the intelligent gleam of his look.

Pauline had not been greatly troubled, on her advent among the merry-makers, with that timidity which is so keen a distress to so many callow maids. Bashfulness was not one of her weak points; she had borne the complex stare levelled at her in drawing-rooms with excellent *aplomb.* Still, she could not help feeling that her kinsman, Courtlandt, had comfortably smoothed her path toward an individual and secure foothold. Those early intervals, dire to the soul of every novice like herself, when male adherence and escort failed through meagreness of acquaintanceship, Court-landt had filled with the supporting relief of his presence and his attentions. There had been no *mauvais quart d'heure* in Pauline's evenings; her cousin had loyally saved her from even the momentary chagrin of being left without a courtier. Later on, his kindly vigilance had become needless; but he was always to be trusted, nevertheless, as a safeguard against possible desertion.

The occasion on which Mr. Hamilton Varick first saw Pauline was at a ball given in the February of her first season, two full months after she had modestly emerged with her little sisterhood of rosebud damsels. It was a very beautiful ball, given in a stately and lovely house adjacent to the Park, and by a lady now old and wrinkled, who had held her own, forty years ago, as a star in our then limited firmament of fashion. The dancers, among whom was her fair and smiling granddaughter of eighteen, chased the jolly hours in a spacious apartment, brilliant with prismatic candelabra and a lustrous floor of waxed wood. The rosy-and-white frescoes on the ceiling, the silver-fretted delicacy of frieze and cornice, the light, pure blues and pinks of tapestries, the airy and buoyant effects in tint and symmetry, made the whole quick-moving throng of revellers appear as if the past had let them live again out of some long-vanished French court-festival.

" These young people only need powdered heads to make it look as if Louis Quinze were entertaining us in dead earnest," said Mr. Varick, with his high-keyed, nonchalant voice. He addressed an elderly matron as he spoke, but he gave a covert glance at Pauline, to whom he had just received, through request, the honor of a presentation.

" I think it would be in very dead earnest if he did," said Pauline, speaking up with a gay laugh; and Mr. Varick laughed, too, relishing her pert joke. He paid her some gallant compliments as he stood at her side, though she thought them stiff and antique in sound, notwithstanding the foreign word or phrase that was so apt to tinge them. She found Mr. Varick pleasantest when he was asking after her sick mother, and telling her what New York gayeties used to be before the beginning of his long European absence. He had a tripping, lightsome mode of speech, that somehow suited the jaunty upward sweep of his white mustache. He would oscillate both hands in a graceful style as he talked. Elegant superficiality flowed from him without an effort. It needed no keenness to tell that he had been floating buoyantly on the top crest of the wave, and well amid its froth, all his life. He made no pretense to youth; he would, indeed, poke fun at his own seniority, with a re-lentless and breezy sort of melancholy.

" Did you ever hear of a French poet named

François Villon," he said to Pauline, dropping into a seat at her side that some departure had just left vacant. " No, I dare say you 've not. He was a dreadful chap — a kind of *polisson*, as we say, but he wrote the most charming ballads; I believe he was hanged afterward, or ought to have been — I forget which. One of his songs had a sad little refrain that ran thus: '*Où sont les neiges d'antan?*' — 'Where are the snows of last year?' you know. Well, mademoiselle — no, Miss Pauline, I mean — that line runs in my head to-night. *Ça me gêne* — it bothers me. I want to have the good things of youth back again. I come home to New York, and find my snow all melted. Everything is changed. I feel like a ghost — a merry old ghost, however. *Tenez* — just wait a bit. Do you think those nice young gentlemen will have anything to say to you after they have seen you a little longer in my company? I 'm sure I have frightened four or five of them away. They 're asking each other, now, who is that old *épourvantail* — what is the word? — scarecrow. Ah! *voilà* — here comes one much bolder than the rest. I will have mercy on him — and retire. But before my *départ* I have a favor to request of you. You will give mamma my compliments? You will tell her that I shall do myself the honor of calling upon her? Thanks, very much. We shall be ghosts together, poor mamma and I; you need not be *chez vous* when I call, unless you are quite willing — that is, if you are afraid of ghosts."

"Oh, I 'm not," laughed Pauline. "I don't believe in them, Mr. Varick."

"That is delightful for you to say!" her companion exclaimed. "It means that you will listen for a little while to our spectral conversation and not find it too *ennuyeuse*. How very kind of you! Ah! we old fellows are sometimes very grateful for a few crumbs of kindness!"

"You can have a whole loaf from me, if you want," said Pauline, with an air of girlish diversion.

Not long afterward she declared to her cousin, Courtlandt: "I like the old gentleman ever so much, Court. He 's a refreshing change. You New York men are all cut after the same pattern."

"I 'm afraid he 's cut with a rather crooked scissors," said Courtlandt, who indulged in a sly epigram oftener than he got either credit or discredit for doing.

"Oh," said Pauline, as if slowly understanding. "You mean he is *French*, I suppose."

"Quite French, they report."

Mr. Varick made his promised visit upon Pauline and her mother sooner than either of them expected. Mrs. Van Corlear was rather more ill than usual, on the day he appeared, and almost the full burden of the ensuing conversation fell upon her daughter.

The next evening, at the opera, he dropped into a certain box where Pauline was seated with her aunt, Mrs. Poughkeepsie. On the following day Pauline received, anonymously, an immense basket of exquisite flowers. Twice again Mr. Varick called upon her mother, in the charmless up-stairs sitting-room of their boarding-house. As it chanced, Pauline was not at home either time.

An evening or two afterward she returned at about eleven o'clock from a theatre-party, to find that her mother had not yet retired. Mrs. Van Corlear's usual bed-time was a very exact ten o'clock.

The mother and daughter talked for a little while together in low tones. When Pauline went into her own chamber that night, her face was pale and her heart was beating.

At a great afternoon reception which took place two days later, Courtlandt, who made his appearance after five o'clock, coming up town from the law-office in which he managed by hard work to clear a yearly two thousand dollars or so, said to his cousin, with a sharpened and rather inquisitive look:

" What's the matter? You don't seem to be in good spirits."

Pauline looked at him steadily for a moment. It was a great crush, and people were babbling all about them. " There's something I want to speak of," the girl presently said, in a lingering way.

A kind of chill stole through Courtlandt's veins at this, — he did not know why; he always afterward had a lurking credence in the truth of presentments.

" What is it?" he asked.

Pauline told him what it was. He grew white as he listened, and a glitter crept into his eyes, and brightened there.

" You're not going to *do* it?" he said, when she had finished.

She made no answer. She had some flowers knotted in the bosom of her walking-dress, and she now looked down at them. They were not the flowers Mr. Varick had sent; they were a bunch bestowed by Courtlandt himself at a little informal dance of the previous evening, where the cotillon had had one pretty floral figure. She regarded their petals through a mist of unshed tears, now, though her cousin did not know it.

He repeated his question, bending nearer. It seemed to him as if the sun in heaven must have stopped moving until she made her answer.

"You know what mamma is, Court," she faltered.

"Yes, I do. She has very false views of many things. But you have not. You can't be sold without your own consent."

"Let us go away from here together," she murmured. "These rooms are so hot and crowded that I can hardly breathe in them."

He gave her his arm, and they pushed their way forth into a neighboring hall through one of the broad yet choked doorways.

Outside, in Fifth Avenue, the February twilight had just begun to deepen. The air was mild though damp; a sudden spell of clemency had enthralled the weather, and the snow, banked in crisp pallor along the edge of either sidewalk, would soon shrink and turn sodden. At the far terminus of every western street burned a haze of dreamy gold light where the sun had just dropped from view, but overhead the sky had that treacherous tint of vernal amethyst which is so often a delusive snare to the imprudent truster of our mutable winters. Against this vapory mildness of color the house-tops loomed sharp and dark; a humid wind blew straight from the south; big and small sleighs were darting along, with the high, sweet carillons of their bells now loud and now low; through the pavements that Courtlandt and Pauline were treading, great black spots of dampness had slipped their cold ooze, to tell of the thaw that lay beneath. Yesterday the sky had been a livid and frosty azure, and the sweep of the arctic blast had had the cut of a blade in it; to-day the city was steeped in a languor of so abrupt a coming that you felt its peril while you owned its charm. Courtlandt broke the silence that had followed their exit. He spoke as if the words forced themselves between his shut teeth.

"I can't believe that you really mean to do it," he said, watching Pauline's face as she moved onward, looking neither to right nor left. "It would be horrible of you! He is over sixty if he's a day, besides having been mixed up in more than one scandal with women over there in Paris. I think it must be all a joke on your part. If it is, I wish for God's sake that you'd tell me so, Pauline!"

"It isn't," she said. She turned her face to his, then, letting him see how pale and sad it was.

"I must do it, Court," she went on. "It 's like a sort of fate, forcing and dragging me. I had no business to mention mamma in the matter, I suppose. She could n't *make* me consent, of course, although, if I did not, her lamentations would take a most distracting form for the next year or two. No; it 's not she; it 's myself. I don't live in a world where people held very high views of matrimony. And I hate the life I 'm living now. The other would be independence, even if bought at a dear price. And how many girls would envy me my chance? What am I at present but a mere pensioner on my wealthy relatives? I can't stay in; I 've started with the whirl, and I can't stop. Everybody whom I know is dancing along at the same pace. If I declined invitations; if I did n't do as all the other girls are doing; if I said 'No, I 'm poor and can't afford it,'—then mamma would begin tuning her harp and sending up her wail. And I should be bored to death, besides." Here Pauline gave a hollow laugh, and slightly threw back her head. "Good Heavens!" she continued, "there 's nothing strange in it. I 've been brought up to expect it; I knew it would probably come, and I was taught, prepared, warned, to regard it when it did come in only one way. If he had n't been old he might have been shocking. What a piercing pertinence there is to my case in that little proverb, 'Beggars must n't be choosers!' I 'm a beggar, you know: ask Aunt Cynthia Poughkeepsie if she does n't think I am. And *he 's* quite the reverse of shocking, truly. His hair may be rather white, but his teeth are extremely so, and I think they 're indigenous, aboriginal; I hope if they 're not he will never tell me, anyway."

She gave another laugh, as mirthless as if the spectre of herself had framed it. She had turned her face away from him again, and slightly quickened her walk.

"You mean, then, that your mind is really made up!" said Courtlandt, with an ire, a fierceness, that she had never seen in him before. "You mean that for a little riches, a little power, you 'll turn marriage, that should be a holy usage, into this wicked mockery?"

Pauline bit her lip. Such a speech as this from her equanimous cousin was literally without precedent. She felt stung and guilty as she said, with cool defiance, —

"Who holds marriage as a holy usage? I 've never seen anyone who did."

"I do!" he asseverated, with clouding face. "You do, too, Pauline in your heart."

"I have n't any heart. They 're not worn nowadays. They 're out of fashion. We carry purses instead — when we can."

"I think 1 will tell Mr. Varick you said that," he answered, measuring each word grimly.

"Oh, do!" Pauline exclaimed. A weary and mournful bravado filled her tones. "How he would laugh! Do you fancy he thinks I care a button for him? Why, nearly the first sentence he spoke to mamma on this weighty subject concerned the number of yearly thousands he was willing to settle upon me."

"So, it is all arranged?"

"It only awaits your approval."

"It can only get my contempt!"

"That is too bad. I thought you would anticipate some of the charming little dinners I intend to give. He has dreadful attacks of the gout, I have learned, and sometimes I 'll ask you to preside with me in his vacant chair. That is, if you"—

But he would hear no more. He turned on his heel and left her. He bitterly told himself that her heart was ice, and not worth wasting a thought upon. But he wasted a good many that night, and days afterward.

Whether ice or not, it was a very heavy heart as Pauline went homeward. Just in proportion as the excuses for her conduct were ready on her lips, so they were futile to appease her conscience.

And yet she exulted in one justifying circumstance, as she herself named it. "If I *loved* anybody — Court, or anybody else," she reflected, "I never *could* do it! But I don't. It's going to make a great personage of me. I want to find out how it feels to be a great personage. I want to try the new sensation of not wearing charity gloves."

. . . She had almost a paroxysm of nervous tears, alone in her own room, a little later. That evening Mr. Varick once more presented himself. . . .

At about eleven o'clock he jumped into a cab which he had kept waiting an interminable time, and lighted a very fragrant cigar as he was being driven off.

"*Elle est belle à faire peur*," he muttered aloud. And the next moment a thought passed through his mind which would resemble this, if put into English, though he always thought in French: —

"I will write to Madeleine to-morrow, and send her ten thousand francs. That will end everything — and if the gout spares me five years longer I shan't see Paris while it does."

He had not by any means come home to die. He had said so because it had a neat sound, throwing a perfume of sentiment about his return. And he was always fond of the perfume of sentiment. In reality he had come home to look after his affairs, which had grown burdensomely prosperous, and then sail back with all the decorous haste allowable.

Perhaps he had come home with a few other trifling motives. But of every conceivable motive, he had *not* come with one. That one was — to marry. And yet he had to-night arranged his alliance (satisfactorily on both sides, it was to be hoped) with Miss Pauline Van Corlear.

He leaned back in the dimness of the speeding cab, and reflected upon it. His reflections made him laugh, and as he laughed his lip curled up below his white mustache and showed his white teeth, with the good, dark cigar between them — the teeth of which Pauline had said that if they were false she did not wish to know it.

II

THE marriage was a quiet one, and took place in the early following spring. Pauline made a very lovely bride, but as this comment is delivered upon a most ample percentage of all the brides in Christendom, it is scarcely worth being recorded. The whole important constituency of her kindred were graciously pleased at the match, with a single exception. This was Courtlandt Beekman, who managed to be absent in Washington at the time of the wedding. Pauline's presents were superb; the Poughkeepsies, Amsterdams, and all the rest, came forth in expensive sanction of the nuptials. After a brief Southern tour the wedded pair took up their abode in the newly appointed Bond Street mansion. Mrs. Van Corlear, already ensconced there, welcomed them with as beaming a smile as her invalid state would permit. Pauline, as she kissed her, wondered if those same bloodless lips would ever have any further excuse for querulous complaint. It was pathetic to note the old lady's gratified quiver while her thin hand was gallantly imprinted, as well, by the kiss of her new son-in-law. She had surely reached the goal of all her earthly hopes. She had a silken chair to rock in, and a maid as her special attendant, and a doctor to be as devoted and exorbitant as he chose. Her neuralgia, her asthma, her rheumatism, her thousand and one ailments, were henceforth to wreak their dolorous inflictions among the most comfortable and sumptuous surroundings. And yet, as if in mockery of her new facilities for being the truly aristocratic invalid, this poor lady, after a few weeks of the most encouraging opportunity, forsook all its commodious temptations and quietly died in her bed of a sudden heart-seizure.

On the occasion of her death Pauline's husband, who had thus far been scrupulously polite, made a remark which struck his wife as brutal, and roused her resentment. He was a good deal more brutal, in a glacial, exasperating way, as Pauline's anger manifested itself. But shortly after the funeral he was prostrated by a sharp attack of his gout, during which Pauline nursed him with forgiving assiduity.

The young wife was now in deep mourning. Her husband's attack had been almost fatal. His recovery was slow, and a voyage to Europe was urgently recommended by his physicians. They sailed in latter June. Courtlandt was among those who saw Pauline off in the steamer. He looked, while taking her hand in farewell, as if he felt very sorry for her. Pauline seemed in excellent spirits; her black dress became her; she was so blonde that you saw the gold hair before you marked the funereal garb; and then she had her smile very ready, which had always won nearly everybody. Perhaps only Courtlandt, in his wise, grave taciturnity, saw just how factitious the smile was.

Mr. Varick quite recovered from this attack. Pauline's letters said so. They had soon left London, near which the Cunarder had brought them, and gone to Paris; Mr. Varick was feeling so much better from the voyage, and had always felt so at home in Paris. For several months afterward Pauline's letters were sent oversea in the most desultory and irregular fashion. And what they contained by no means pleased their recipients. She appeared to tell nothing about herself; she was always writing of the city. As if one couldn't read of the Tuileries and Nôtre Dame in a thousand books! As if one hadn't been there oneself! Why did she not write *how they were getting on together?* That was the one imperative stimulus for curiosity among all Pauline's friends and kindred — how they were getting on together. All, we should add, except Courtlandt, who seemed to manifest no curiosity of whatever sort. Of course one could not write and ask her, point blank! What was one to do? Did rambling essays upon the pleasures of a trip to Versailles, or the recreation of a glimpse of Fontainebleau, mean that Mr. Varick had or had not broken loose in a mettlesome manner from his latter-day matrimonial traces?

"We are prepared for anything, you know," Mrs. Poughkeepsie, Pauline's aunt and former patron, had once rather effusively said to Courtlandt. "Now that Hamilton Varick is well, he might be larking over there to any dreadful extent. And Pauline, from sheer pride, might n't be willing to tell us."

"Very cruel of her, certainly," Courtlandt had responded, laconic and not a little sarcastic as well.

But as months went by, Pauline's correspondents forgot, in the absorption engendered by more national incentives for gossip, the unsatisfactory tone of her letters. Once, however, Pauline wrote that she wished very much to return, but that her husband preferred remaining in Paris.

"He won't come back!" immediately rose the

cry on this side of the water. "He's keeping her over there against her will! How perfectly horrible! Well, she deserves it for marrying a *vieux galant* like that! Poor Pauline! With her looks she might have married somebody of respectable age. But she would n't wait. She was so crazy to make her market, poor girl! It's to be hoped that he does n't beat her, or anything of that frightful sort!"

One auditor of these friendly allusions would smile at them with furtive but pardonable scorn. This auditor was Courtlandt; and he remembered how the same compassionate declaimers had been the first to applaud Pauline's astounding betrothal.

After two years of absence on the part of Mr. and Mrs. Varick, certain rumors drifted to America. This or that person had seen them in Paris. Pauline was still pretty as ever, but living quite retired. It was said she had taken to books and general mental improvement. No one ever saw her with her husband. She never alluded to him in any way. There were queer stories about his goings on. It was hard to verify them ; Paris was so big, and so many men were always doing such funny things there.

The conclave on these shores heard and sympathetically shuddered. The "new set" had now healed all its old feuds. New York society was in a condition of amicably cemented factions. The Briggs girls and the Snowe girls had married more or less loftily, and had proved to the Amsterdams and others that they were worthy of peaceable affiliation. "Poor Pauline Varick" began to be a phrase, though a somewhat rare one, for without anybody actually wakening to the fact, she had been living abroad four whole years. And then, without the least warning, came the news that she was a widow.

She was universally expected home, then, after the tidings that her husband was positively dead had been confirmed beyond the slightest doubt. But perhaps for this reason Pauline chose to remain abroad another year. When she did return her widowhood was an established fact. Her New York *clientèle* had grown used to it. Mr. Varick had left her all his fortune; she was a very wealthy young widow. Aggressive queries respecting his death, or his deportment during the foreign sojourn that preceded his death, were now quite out of order. She had buried him, as she had married him, decently and legally. He slept in Père la Chaise, by his own *ante mortem* request. No matter what sort of a life he had led her; it was nobody's business. She returned home, two years later, to take a high place and hold a high head. Those merciful intervening years shielded her from a multitude of stealthy interrogatories. She did not care to be questioned much regarding her European past as the wife of Mr. Varick, and she soon contrived to make it plain that she did not. There was no dissentient voice in the verdict that she had greatly changed. And in a physical sense no one could deny that she had changed for the better.

Her figure, which had before been quite too thin despite its pliant grace, was now rounded into soft and charming curves. Her gray eyes sparkled less often, but they glowed with a steadier light for perhaps this reason; they looked as if more of life's earnest actualities had been reflected in them. Her face, with its chiselled features all blending to produce so high-bred and refined an expression, rarely broke into a smile now, but some unexplained fascination lay in its acquired seriousness, that made the smile of brighter quality and deeper import when it really came. She wore her copious and shining hair in a heavy knot behind, and let it ripple naturally toward either pure temple, instead of having it bush low down over her forehead in a misty turmoil, as previously. Her movements, her

walk, her gestures, all retained the volatile brisk-
ness and freedom they had possessed of old; there
was not even the first matronly hint about her air,
and yet it was more self-poised, more emphatic,
more womanly.

"I really must move out of this dreadful Bond
Street," she said to Courtlandt, rather early in the
conversation which took place between them on
the day of their first meeting. "I think I could
endure it for some time longer if that immense
tailor-shop had not gone up there at the Broadway
corner, where such a lovely, drowsy old mansion
used to stand. Yes, I must let myself be compli-
antly swept further up town. There is a kind of
Franco-German tavern just across the way that
advertises a 'regular dinner'—whatever that is —
from twelve o'clock till three, every day, at twenty-
five cents."

"I see you have n't forgotten our national cur-
rency," said Courtlandt, with one of his inscrutable
dispositions of countenance.

Pauline tossed her head in a somewhat French
way. "I have forgotten very little about my own
country," she said.

"You are glad to get back to it, then?"

"Yes, very. I want to take a new view of it
with my new eyes."

" You got a new pair of eyes in Europe? "

" I got an older pair."   She looked at him earnestly for a moment. " Tell me, Court," she went on, " how is it that I find you still unmarried? "

He shifted in his chair, crossing his legs. " Oh," he said, " no nice girl has made me an offer."

Pauline laughed. " As if she 'd be nice if she had! Do you remember how they used to say you would marry in the other set? Is there another set now? ".

" There is a number of fresh ones. New York is getting bigger every day, you know. Young men are being graduated from college, young girls from seminaries. I forget just what special set you mean that you expected me to marry into."

" No, you don't! " cried Pauline, with soft positiveness. She somehow felt herself getting quietly back into the old easy terms with Courtlandt. His sobriety, that never echoed her gay moods, yet always seemed to follow and enjoy them, had readdressed her like a familiar though alienated friend. " You recollect perfectly how Aunt Cynthia Poughkeepsie used to lift that Roman nose of hers and declare that she would never allow her Sallie to know those fast Briggs and Snowe girls, who had got out because society had been neglected by all the real gentry in town for a space of at least five years?"

Courtlandt gave one of his slow nods. "Oh, yes, I recollect. Aunt Cynthia was quite wrong. She's pulled in her horns since then. The Briggses and the Snowes were much too clever for her. They were always awfully well-mannered girls, too, besides being so jolly. They needed her, and they coolly made use of her, and of a good many revived leaders like her, besides. Most of the good men like them; that was their strong point. It was all very well to say they had n't had ancestors who knew Canal Street when it was a canal, and shot deer on Twenty-Third Street; but that would n't do at all. No matter how their parents had made their money, they knew how to spend it like swells, and they had pushed themselves into power and were not to be elbowed out. The whole fight soon died a natural death. They and their supporters are nearly all married now and married pretty well."

"And you did n't marry one of them, Court?"

Courtlandt gave a slight, dry cough. "I'm under the impression, Pauline," he said, "that I did not."

"How long ago it all seems!" she murmured, drooping her blond head and fingering with one hand at a button on the front of her black dress. "It's only four years, and yet I fancy it to be a century." She raised her head. "Then the Knickerbockers, as we used to call them, no longer rule?"

Courtlandt laughed gravely. "I don't know that they ever did," he answered.

"Well, they used to give those dancing-classes, you know, where nobody was ever admitted unless he or she had some sort of patrician claim. Don't you recollect how Mrs. Schenectady, when she gave Lillie a Delmonico Blue-Room party (do they have Delmonico Blue-Room parties, now?), instructed old Grace Church Brown to challenge at the Fourteenth Street entrance (where he would always wait as a stern horror for the coachmen of the arriving and departing carriages) anybody who did not present a certain mysterious little card at the sacred threshold?"

"Oh, yes," returned Courtlandt ruminatively.

"And how," continued Pauline, "that democratic Mrs. Vanderhoff happened to bring, on this same evening, some foreign gentleman who had dined with her, and whom she meant to present with an apologetic flourish to the Schenectadys, when suddenly the corpulent sentinel, Brown, desired from her escort the mysterious card, and finding it not to be forthcoming sent a messenger upstairs? And how Mr. Schenectady presently appeared and informed Mrs. Vanderhoff, with a cool snobbery which had something sublime about it, that he was exceedingly sorry, but the rule had been passed regarding the admission of any non-invited guest to his entertainment?"

"Oh, yes; I remember it all," said Courtlandt. "Schenectady behaved like a cad. Nobody is half so strict, now-a-days, nor half so grossly uncivil. You'll find society very much changed, if you go out. You'll see people whose names you never heard before. I sometimes think there's nothing required to make one's self a great swell now-a-days except three possessions, all metallic — gold, silver, and brass."

"How amusing!" said Pauline. "And yet," she suddenly added, with a swift shake of the head, "I'm sure it will never amuse *me!* No, Court, I have grown a very different person from the ignorant girl you once saw me!" She lowered her voice here, and regarded him with a tender yet impressive fixity. "When I look back upon it all now, and think how I used to hold the code of living which those people adopt as something that I must respect and even reverence, I can scarcely believe that the whole absurd comedy

did not happen in some other planet. You don't
know how much I 've been through since you met
me last. I 'm not referring to my husband. It
is n't pleasant for me to talk about *that* part of the
past. . I would n't say even this much to any one
except you; but now that I have said it, I 'll say
more, and tell you that I endured a good deal of
solid trial, solid humiliation, solid heart-burning.
. . . There, let us turn that page over, you and
myself, and never exchange another word on the
subject. You were perfectly right; the thing I
did *was* horrible, and I 've bought my yards of
sackcloth, my bushels of ashes. If it were to do
over again, I 'd rather beg, starve, die in the very
gutter. There 's no exaggeration, here; I have
grown to look on this human destiny of ours with
such utterly changed vision — I 've so broadened in
a mental and moral sense, that my very identity of
the past seems as if it were something I 'd moulted,
like the old feathers of a bird. Feathers make a
happy simile; I was lighter than a feather, then —
as light as thistledown. I had no principles; I
merely had caprices. I had no opinions of my
own; other people's were handed to me and I
blindly accepted them. My chief vice, which was
vanity, I mistook for the virtue of self-respect,
and kept it carefully polished, like a little pocket-

mirror to look at one's face in. I was goaded by an actually sordid avarice, and I flattered myself that it was a healthy matrimonial ambition. I swung round in a petty orbit no larger than a saucer's rim, and imagined it to have the scope of a star's. I chattered gossip with fops of both sexes, and called it conversation. I bounced and panted through the German for two hours of a night, and declared it to be enjoyment. I climbed up to the summit of a glaring yellow-wheeled drag and sat beside some man whose limited wit was entirely engrossed by the feat of driving four horses at once; and because poor people stopped to sigh, and silly ones to envy, and sensible ones to pity, as we rumbled up the Avenue in brazen ostentation, I considered myself an elect and exceptional being. Of course I must have had some kind of a better nature lying comatose behind all this placid tolerance of frivolity. Otherwise the change never would have come; for the finest seed will fail if the soil is entirely barren."

"You have taken a new departure, with a vengeance," said Courtlandt. He spoke in his usual tranquil style. He considered the sketch Pauline had just drawn of her former self very exaggerated and prejudiced. He had his own idea of what she used to be. He was observing her with an excessive keenness of scrutiny, now, underneath his reposeful demeanor. But he aired none of his contradictory beliefs. It is possible that he had never had a downright argument with any fellow-creature in his life. Somehow the brief sentence which he had just spoken produced the impression of his having said a great deal more than this. It was always thus with the man; by reason of some unique value in his silence any terse variation of it took a reflected worth.

Pauline's hands were folded in her lap; she was looking down at them with a musing air. She continued to speak without lifting her gaze. " Yes," she went on, " the reformatory impulse must have been latent all that time. I can't tell just what quickened it into its present activity. But I am sure, now, that it will last as long as I do."

" What are the wonders it is going to accomplish ? "

" Don't satirize it," she exclaimed, looking up at him with a start. " It is a power for good."

" I hope so," he said.

" *I* know so ! Courtlandt, I 've come back home to live after my own fashion. I 've come back with an idea, a theory. Of course a good many people will laugh at me. I expect a certain amount of ridicule. But I shall despise it so heartily that it will not make me swerve a single inch. I intend to be very social — yes, enormously so. My drawing-rooms shall be the resort of as many friends as I can bring together — but all of a certain kind."

" Pray, of what kind ? "

" You shall soon see. They are to be men and women of intellectual calibre; they are to be workers and not drones; they are to be thinkers, writers, artists, poets, scholars. They can come, if they please, in abnormal coats and unconventional gowns; I sha'n't care for that. They can be as poor as church mice, as unsuccessful as talent nearly always is, as quaint in manner as genius incessantly shows itself." Here Pauline rose, and made a few eloquent little gestures with both hands, while she moved about the room in a way that suggested the hostess receiving imaginary guests. " I mean to organize a *salon*," she continued — " a veritable *salon*. I mean to wage a vigorous crusade against the aimless flippancy of modern society. I 've an enthusiasm for my new undertaking. Wait till you see how valiantly I shall carry it out."

" Am I to understand," said Courtlandt, without the vestige of a smile, "that you mean to begin by cutting all your former friends?"

She glanced at him as if with a suspicion of further satire. But his sedate mien appeared to reassure her. "Cutting them?" she repeated. "No; of course not."

"But you will not invite them to your *salon?*"

She tossed her head again. "They would be quite out of place there. They are not in earnest about anything. Everybody whom I shall have must be in earnest. I intend to lay great stress upon that one requirement. It is to be a passport of admission. My apartments are to be at once easy and difficult of entrance. I shall not object to the so-called aristocratic class, although if any applicant shall solicit my notice who is undoubtedly a member of this class, I shall in a certain way hold the fact as disqualifying; it shall be remembered against him; if I admit him at all I shall do so in spite of it and not because of it. —Is my meaning quite clear on this point?"

"Oh, excessively," said Courtlandt; "you could not have made it more so. All ladies and gentlemen are to be received under protest."

He let one of his odd, rare laughs go with the last sentence, and for this reason Pauline merely gave him a magnificent frown instead of visiting upon him more wrathful reprimand. At the same time she said: "It's a subject, Court, on which I am unprepared for trivial levity. If you can't treat it with respect I prefer that you should warn me in time, and I will reserve all further explanations of my project."

He gave a slight, ambiguous cough. "If I seem disrespectful you must lay it to my ignorance."

"I should be inclined to do that without your previous instructions." Here she regarded him with a commiseration that he thought delicious; it was so palpably genuine; she so grandly overlooked the solemn roguery that ambuscaded itself behind his humility.

"You see," he went on, "I have n't learned the vocabulary of radicalism, so to speak. I think I know the fellows you propose to have; they wear long hair, quite often, and big cloaks instead of top-coats, and collars low enough in the neck to show a good deal of wind-pipe. As for the women, they"—

"It is perfectly immaterial to me how any of them may dress!" she interrupted, with majestic disapproval. "I ought to be very sorry for you, Courtlandt, and I am. You're clever enough not to let yourself rust, like this, all your days. I don't believe you've ever read one of the works of the great modern English thinkers. You're sluggishly satisfied to go jogging along in the same old ruts that humanity has worn deep for centuries. Of course you never had, and never will have, the least spark of enthusiasm. You're naturally lethargic; if a person stuck a pin into you I don't believe you would jump. But all this is no reason why you should n't try and live up to the splendid advancements of your age. When my constituents are gathered about me — when I have fairly begun my good work of centralizing and inspiriting my little band of sympathizers — when I have defined in a practical way my intended opposition to the vanities and falsities of existing creeds and tenets, why, then, I will let you mingle with my assemblages and learn for yourself how you've been wasting both time and opportunity."

"That is extremely good of you," murmured Courtlandt imperturbably. "I supposed your doors were to be closed upon me for good and all."

"Oh, no. I shall insist, indeed, that you drop in upon us very often. I shall need your presence. You are to be my connecting link, as it were."

"How very pleasant! You have just told me that I was benighted. Now I find myself a connecting link."

"Between culture and the absence of it. I have no objection to your letting the giddy and whimsical folk perceive what a vast deal they are deprived of. Besides, I should like you to be my first conversion — a sort of bridge by which other converts may cross over into the happy land."

"You are still most kind. I believe that bridges are usually wooden. No doubt you feel that you have made a wise selection of your material. May I be allowed to venture another question?"

"Yes — if it is not too impudent."

She was watching him with her head a little on one side, now, and a smile struggling forth from her would-be serious lips. She was recollecting how much she had always liked him, and considering how much she would surely like him hereafter, in this renewal of their old half-cousinly and half-flirtatious intimacy. She was thinking what deeps of characteristic drollery slept in him — with what a quiet, funny sort of martyrdom he had borne her little girlish despotisms, before that sudden marriage had wrought so sharp a rupture of their relations, and how often he had forced her into unwilling laughter by the slow and almost sleepy humor with which he had successfully parried some of her most vigorous attacks.

"I merely wanted to ask you," he now said,

"where all these extraordinary individuals are to be found."

" Ah, that is an important question, certainly," she said, with a solemn inclination — or at least the semblance of one. " I intend to collect them."

" Good gracious! You speak of them as if they were minerals or mummies that you were going to get together for a museum. I have no doubt that they will be curiosities, by the bye."

" I am afraid *you* will find them so."

" Are they to be imported ? "

" Oh, no. That will not be necessary."

" I see ; they 're domestic products."

" Quite so. In this great city — filled with so much energy, so much re-action against the narrow feudalisms of Europe — I am very certain of finding them." She paused for a moment, and seemed to employ a tacit interval for the accumulation of what she next said. " I shall not be entirely unassisted in my search, either."

A cunning twinkle became manifest in the brown eyes of her listener. He drew a long breath. " Ah! now we get at the root of the matter. There 's a confederate — an accomplice, so to speak."

" I prefer that you should not allude to my assistant in so rude a style. Especially as, in the first place, you have never met him, and, in the second, he is a person of the most remarkable gifts."

"Is there any objection to my asking his name? Or is it still a dark mystery?"

She laughed at this, as if she thought it highly diverting. "My dear cousin," she exclaimed, "how absurd you can be at a pinch! What on earth should make the name of Mr. Kindelon a dark mystery?"

"Um-m-m. Somebody you met abroad, then?"

"Somebody I met on the steamer, while returning."

"I see. An Englishman?"

"A gentleman of Irish birth. He has lived in New York for a number of years. He knows a great many of the intellectual people here. He has promised to help me in my efforts. He will be of great value."

Courtlandt rose. "So are your spoons, Pauline," he said rather gruffly, not at all liking the present drift of the information. "Take my advice, and lock them up when you give your first *salon.*"

III

PAULINE had not been long in her native city again before she made the discovery that a great deal was now socially expected of her. The news of her return spread abroad with a rapidity more suggestive of bad than of good tidings; her old acquaintances, male and female, flocked to the Bond Street house with a most loyal promptitude. The ladies came in glossy *coupés* and dignified coaches, not seldom looking about them with *dilletante* surprise at the mercantile glare and tarnish of this once neat and seemly crossway, as they mounted Mrs. Varick's antiquated stoop. Most of them were now married; they had made their market, as Pauline's deceased mother would have said, and it is written of them with no wanton harshness that they had in very few cases permitted sentiment to enact the part of salesman. There is something about the fineness of our republican ideals (however practice may have determinedly lowered and soiled them) that makes the mere worldly view of marriage a special provocation to the moralist. Regarded as a convenient mutual barter in Europe, there it somehow shocks far less; the wrong of the grizzled bridegroom winning the young, loveless, but acquiescent bride bears a historic stamp; we recall, perhaps, that they have always believed in that kind of savagery over there; it is as old as their weird turrets and their grim torture-chambers. But with ourselves, who broke loose, in theory at least, from a good many tough bigotries, the sacredness of the marriage state presents a much more meagre excuse for violation. It was not that the husbands of Pauline's wedded friends were in any remembered instance grizzled, however; they were indeed, with few exceptions, by many years the juniors of her own dead veteran spouse; but the influences attendant upon their unions with this or that maiden had first concerned the question of money as a primary and sovereign force, and next that of name, prestige, or prospective elevation. These young brides had for the most part sworn a much more sincere fidelity to the carriages in which they now rode, and the pretty or imposing houses in which they dwelt, than to the important, though not indispensable, human attachments of such prized commodities.

Pauline found them all strongly monotonous; she could ill realize that their educated simpers and their regimental sort of commonplace had ever been potent to interest her. One had to pay out such a small bit of line in order to sound them; one's plummet so soon struck bottom, as it were. She found herself silently marvelling at the serenity of their contentment; no matter how gilded were the cages in which they made their decorous little trills, what elegance of filigree could atone for the absence of space and the paucity of perches?

The men whom she had once known and now re-met pleased her better. They had, in this respect, the advantage of their sex. Even when she condemned them most heartily as shallow and fatuous, their detected admiration of her beauty or of their pleasure in her company won for them the grace of a pardoning afterthought. They were still bachelors, and some of them more maturely handsome bachelors than when she had last looked upon them. They had niceties and felicities of attitude, of intonation, of tailoring, of boot or glove, to which, without confessing it, she was still in a degree susceptible.

But she did not encourage them. They were not of her new world; she had got quite beyond them. She flattered herself that she always affected them as being gazed down upon from rather chilly heights. She insisted on telling herself that they were much more difficult to talk with than she really found them. This was one of the necessities of her conversion; they must not prove agreeable any longer; it was inconsequent, untenable, that they should receive from her anything but a merely hypocritic courtesy. She wanted her contempt for the class of which they were members to be in every way logical, and so manufactured premises to suit its desired integrity. Meanwhile she was much more entertaining than she knew, and treated Courtlandt, one day, with quite a shocked sternness for having informed her that these male visitors had passed upon her some very admiring criticisms.

"I have done my best to behave civilly," she declared. "I was in my own house, you know, when they called. But I cannot understand how they can possibly *like* me as they no doubt used to do! I would much rather have you bring me quite a contrary opinion, in fact."

"If you say so," returned Courtlandt, with his inimitable repose, "I will assure them of their mistake and request that they correct it."

Pauline employed no self-deception whatever in

the acknowledgment of her real feelings toward
Courtlandt. She cherished for him what she liked
to tell herself was an inimical friendliness. In the
old days he had never asked her to marry him,
and yet it had been plain to her that under
favoring conditions he might have made her this
proposal. She was nearly certain that he no
longer regarded her with a trace of the former
tenderness. On her own side she liked him so
heartily, notwithstanding frequent antagonisms,
that the purely amicable nature of this fondness
blurred any conception of him in the potential
light of a lover.

But, indeed, Pauline had resolutely closed her
eyes against the possibility of ever again receiving
amorous declaration or devotion. She had had
quite enough of marriage. Her days of sentiment were past. True, they had never actually
been, but the phantasmal equivalent for them had
been, and she now determined upon not replacing
this by a more accentuated experience. Her path
toward middle life was very clearly mapped out
in her imagination; it was to be strewn with
nicely sifted gravel and bordered by formally
clipped foliage. And it was to be very straight,
very direct; there should be no bend in it that
came upon a grove with sculptured Cupid and

rustic lounge. The "marble muses, looking peace" might gleam now and then through its enskirting boskage, but that should be all. Pauline had read and studied with a good deal of fidelity, both during her marriage and after her widowhood. She had gone into the acquisition of knowledge and the development of thought as some women go into the intoxication of a nervine. Her methods had been amateurish and desultory; she had not been taught, she had learned, and hence learned ill. " The modern thinkers," as she called them, delighted her with their liberality, their iconoclasm. She was in just that receptive mood to be made an extremist by their doctrines, the best of which so sensibly warn us against extremes. Her husband's memory, for the sake of decency if for no other reason, deserved the reticence which she had shown concerning it. He had revealed to her a hollow nature whose void was choked with vice, like some of those declivities in neglected fields, where the weed and the brier run riot. The pathos of her position, in a foreign land, with a lord whose daily routine of misconduct left her solitary for hours, while inviting her, had she so chosen, to imitate a course of almost parallel license, was finally a cogent incentive toward that change which ensued. The whole falsity of the educational system which had resulted in her detested marriage was slowly laid bare to her eyes by this shocking and salient example of it.

There was something piteous, and yet humorous as well, in her present intellectual state. She was a young leader in the cause of culture, without a following. She believed firmly in herself, and yet deceived herself. Much in the world that it was now her fixed principle to shun and reprobate, she liked and clung to. These points of attraction were mostly superficialities, it is true, like the fashion of clothes or the conventionalism of accepted social customs. But even these she had more than half persuaded herself that she despised, and when she observed them in others they too often blinded her to attractions of a less flimsy sort. She had verged upon a sanguine and florid fanaticism, and was wholly unconscious of her peril. Some of Courtlandt's sober comments might effectually have warned her, if it had not been for a marked contrary influence. This was represented by the gentleman whom we have already heard her name as Mr. Kindelon.

She had been presented to him on the steamer during her recent homeward voyage, by an acquaintance who knew little enough regarding his antecedents. But Ralph Kindelon had been at once very frank with her. This was the most prominent trait that usually disclosed itself in him on a first acquaintance; he always managed to impress you by his frankness. He had a large head set on a large frame of splendid, virile proportions. His muscular limbs were moulded superbly; his big hands and feet had the same harmony of contour, despite their size; his grace of movement was extraordinary, considering his height and weight; the noble girth and solidity of chest struck you as you stood close to him — men found it so substantially, women so protectively, human. A kind of warmth seemed to diffuse itself from his bodily nearness, as if the pulse of his blood must be on some exceptionally liberal scale. But for those whom he really fascinated his real fascinations lay elsewhere. You met them in the pair of facile dimples that gave genial emphasis to his sunny smile; in the crisp, coarse curl of his blue-black hair, which receded at either temple, and drooped centrally over a broad, full brow; in the sensuous, ample, ruddy mouth, which so often showed teeth of perfect shape and unflawed purity, and was shaded by a mustache tending to chestnut in shade, with each strong crinkled hair of it rippling away to the smooth-

sloping cheeks; and lastly in the violet-tinted
Irish eyes, whose deep-black lashes had a beautiful length and gloss.

Kindelon spoke with a decided brogue. It was
no mere Celtic accent; it was the pure and original parlance of his native island, though shorn of
those ungrammatical horrors with which .we are
prone by habit to associate it. His English was
Irish, as one of his own countrymen might have
said, but it was very choice and true English,
nevertheless. Well as he spoke it, he spoke it
immoderately, even exorbitantly, when the mood
was upon him, and the mood was upon him, in a
loquacious sense, with considerable pertinacity.
He was the sort of man concerning whom you
might have said, after hearing him talk three minutes or so, that he talked too much; but if you
had listened to him five minutes longer, your
modified opinion would probably have been that
he scarcely talked too much for so good a talker.

It has been chronicled of him that he was extremely frank. Before he had enlivened during
more than an hour, for Pauline, the awful tedium
of an Atlantic voyage in winter, she discovered
herself to be in a measure posted concerning his
personal biography. His parents had been far-
mers in his native Ireland, and he was the fourth

of a family of eleven children. At the age of twelve years a certain benevolent baronet, whose tenant his father was, had sent him to school in Dublin with a view toward training and encouraging a natural and already renowned precocity. At school he had done well until seventeen, and at seventeen he had suddenly found himself thrown on the world, through the death of his patron. After that he had revisited his somewhat distant home for a brief term, and soon afterward had taken passage for America, aided by the funds of an admiring kinsman. He had even then developed evidence of what we call a knack for writing. After severe hardships on these shores, he had drifted into an editorial office in the capacity of printer. This had been a godsend to him, and it had fallen from the skies of Chicago, not New York. But New York had ultimately proved the theatre of those triumphs which were brilliant indeed compared with the humdrum humility of his more Western pursuits. Here he had written articles on many different subjects for the local journals; he had served in almost every drudging department of reportorial work; he had risen, fallen, risen, and at last risen once and for all, durably and honorably, as an associate-editor in a popular and prominent New York journal. He told Pauline the name of his journal—the New York "Asteroid"—and she remembered having heard of it. He laughed his affluent, mellow laugh at this statement, as though it were the most amusing thing in the world to find an American who had only "heard of" the New York "Asteroid."

In a political sense, and moreover in all senses, he was a zealous liberal. How he had managed to scrape together so remarkable an amount of knowledge was a mystery to himself. Everything that he knew had been literally "scraped together;" the phrase could not be apter than when applied to his mental store of facts. He read with an almost phenomenal swiftness, and his exquisite memory retained whatever touched it with a perfection like that of some marvellously sensitive photographic agent. He never forgot a face, a book, a conversation. He hardly forgot a single one of his newspaper articles, and their name was legion. His powers just stopped short of genius, but they distinctly stopped there. He did many things well — many things, in truth, which for a man so hazardously educated it was surprising that he did at all. But he did nothing superlatively well. It was the old story of that fatal facility possessed by numbers of his own countrymen who have migrated to these shores. Perhaps the

one quality that he lacked was a reflective patience
— and this is declared of his brains alone, having
no reference to his moral parts. He leaped upon
subjects, and devoured them, so to speak. It never
occurred to him that there is a cerebral digestion,
which, if we neglect its demands, inevitably entails
upon us a sort of dyspeptic vengeance. In crush-
ing the fruit with too greedy a speed we get to
have a blunted taste for its finer flavor.

Within certain very decided limits he had thus far
made an easy conquest of Pauline. She had never
before met any one whom he remotely resembled.
In the old days she would have shrank from him
as being unpatrician ; now, his fleet speech, his
entire lack of repose, his careless, unmodish,
though scrupulously clean dress, all had for her
an appealing and individual charm. After parting
on the arrival in New York, she and Kindelon had
soon re-met. He bore the change from oceanic surroundings admirably in Pauline's eyes. With characteristic candor he told her that he had come back
from the recent visit to his old parents in Ireland
(Pauline knowing all about this visit, of course)
to find himself wofully poor. She was wondering
whether he would resent the offer of a loan if she
made him one, when he suddenly surprised her by
a statement with regard to " present funds," that

certainly bore no suggestion of poverty. The truth was, he lacked all proper appreciation of the value of money. Economy was an unknown virtue with him; to have was to spend; he was incapable of saving; no financial to-morrow existed for him, and by his careless and often profuse charities he showed the same absence of caution as that which marked all other daily expenditures.

In her immediate purchase of a new residence she consulted with him, and allowed herself to be guided by his counsels. This event brought them more closely together for many days than they would otherwise have been. His artistic feeling and his excellent taste were soon a fresh surprise to her. "I begin to think," she said to him one day, "that there is nothing you do not know."

He laughed his blithe, bass laugh. "Oh," he said, "I know a lot of things in a loose, haphazard way. We newspaper men can't escape general information, Mrs. Varick. We breathe it in, naturally, and in spite of ourselves."

"But tell me," Pauline now asked, "are these other people to whom I shall soon be presented as clever as you are?"

He looked at her with merriment twinkling in his light-tinted eyes. "They're a good deal cleverer — some of them," he replied. "They could give me points and beat me, as we say in billiards."

"You make me very anxious to know them."

"When you talk like that I feel as if I might be tempted to postpone all introductions indefinitely," he responded. He spoke with sudden seriousness, and she felt that mere gallantry had not lain at the root of this answer.

As a matter of course, Kindelon and Courtlandt soon met each other in Pauline's drawing-room. Courtlandt was quite as quiet as usual, and the Irishman perhaps rather unwontedly voluble. Pauline thought she had never heard her new friend talk better. He made his departure before her cousin, and when he had gone Pauline said, with candid enthusiasm:

"Is n't he a wonderful man ? "

"Wonderful ? " repeated Courtlandt, a trifle drowsily.

She gave him a keen look, and bristled visibly while she did so. "Certainly ! " she declared. "No other word just expresses him. I did n't observe you very closely, Court," she went on, "but I took it for granted that you were being highly interested. I can't imagine your *not* being."

"He gave me a kind of singing in the ears," said Courtlandt. "I 've got it yet. He makes me think of one of those factories where there 's a violent hubbub all the time, so that you have to speak loud if you want to be heard."

Pauline was up in arms, then. "I never listened to a more scandalously unjust criticism ! " she exclaimed. "Do you mean to tell me, unblushingly, that you do not think him a *very* extraordinary person ? "

" Oh, very," said her cousin.

Pauline gave an exasperated sigh. "I am so used to you," she said, " that I should never even be surprised by you. But you need not pretend that you can have any except one *truthful* opinion about Mr. Kindelon."

"I have n't," was the reply. " He 's what they call a smart newspaper man. A Bohemian chap, you know. They 're nearly all of them just like that. They can talk you deaf, dumb, and blind, if you only give them a chance."

" I don't think the dumbness required any great effort, as far as *you* were concerned ! " declared Pauline, with sarcastic belligerence.

She never really quarrelled with Courtlandt, because his impregnable stolidity made such a result next to impossible. But she was now so annoyed by her cousin's slighting comments upon Kindelon that her treatment was touched with a decided coolness for days afterward.

Meanwhile her aunt, Mrs. Poughkeepsie, had undergone considerable discomforting surprise. Mrs. Poughkeepsie had been prepared to find Pauline changed, but by no means changed in her present way. On hearing her niece express certain very downright opinions with regard to the life which she was bent upon hereafter living, this lady at first revealed amazement and afterward positive alarm.

"But my dear Pauline," she said, "you cannot possibly mean that you intend to get yourself talked about?"

"Talked about, Aunt Cynthia? I don't quite catch your drift, really."

"Let me be plainer, then. If you remain out of society, that is one thing. I scarcely went anywhere, as you know, for ten years after my husband's death — not, indeed, until Sallie had grown up and was ready to come out. There is no objection, surely, against closing one's doors upon the world, provided one desires to do so — although I should say that such a step, Pauline, at your age, and after two full years of widowhood, was decidedly a mistake. Still" —

"Pardon me, Aunt Cynthia," Pauline here broke in. "Nothing is further from my wish than to close my doors upon the world. On the contrary, I want to open them very wide indeed."

Mrs. Poughkeepsie lifted in shocked manner both her fair, plump, dimpled hands. She was a stout lady, with that imposing, dowager-like effect of *embonpoint* which accompanies a naturally tall and majestic stature. Her type had never in girlhood been a very feminine one, and it now bordered upon masculinity. Her eyes were hard, calm and dark; her arching nose expressed the most serene self-reliance. She was indeed a person with no doubts; she had, in her way, settled the universe. All her creeds were crystallized, and each, metaphorically, was kept in cotton, as though it were a sort of family diamond. She had been a Miss Schenectady, of the elder, wealthy and more conspicuous branch; it was a most notable thing to have been such a Miss Schenectady. She had married a millionaire, and also a Poughkeepsie; this, moreover, was something very important and fine. She had so distinct a "position" that her remaining out of active participation in social pursuits made no difference whatever as regarded her right to appear and rule whenever she so chose; it had only been necessary for her to lift her spear, when Miss Sallie required her chaperonage, and the Snowes and Briggses had perforce to tremble.   And this fact, too, she held as a precious, delectable prerogative.

In not a few other respects she was satisfied regarding herself.   There was nothing, for that matter, which concerned herself in any real way, about which she did not feel wholly satisfied. Her environment in her own opinion was of the best, and doubtless in the opinion of a good many of her adherents also.   From the necklace of ancestral brilliants which she now wore, sparkling at ball or dinner, on her generous and creamy neck, to the comfortably-cushioned pew in Grace Church, where two good generations of Poughkeepsies had devoutly sat through many years of Sundays, she silently valued and eulogized the gifts which fate had bestowed upon her.

Pauline's present attitude seemed to her something monstrous.   It had not seemed monstrous that her niece should give the bloom and vital purity of a sweet maidenhood to a man weighted with years and almost decrepid from past excesses. But that she should seek any other circle of acquaintance except one sanctioned by the immitigable laws of caste, struck her as a bewildering misdemeanor.

"My dear Pauline," she now exclaimed, "you fill me with a positive fear! Of course, if you shut your doors to the right people you open them to the wrong ones. You have got some strange idea abroad, which you are now determined to carry out—to *exploiter*, my dear! With your very large income there is hardly any dreadful imprudence which you may not commit. There is no use in telling me that the people whom one knows are not worth knowing. If you have got into that curious vein of thought you have no remedy for it except to refrain from all entertaining and all acceptance of courtesies. But I beg, Pauline, that you will hesitate before you store up for yourself the material of ugly future repentance. Sallie and I have accepted the Effinghams' box at the opera to-night. Those poor Effinghams have been stricken by the death of their father; it was so sudden — he was sitting in his library and literally fell dead — he must certainly have left two millions, but of course that has nothing to do with their bereavement, and it was so kind of them to remember us. They know that I have always wanted a proscenium, and that there are no prosceniums, now, to be had for love or money. I have sent our box in the horse-shoe to cousin Kate Ten Eyck; she is so wretchedly cramped in her purse, you know, and still has Lulu on her hands, and will be so grateful — as indeed she wrote me quite gushingly that she *was*, this very afternoon. Now, Pauline, won't you go with us, my dear?"

Pauline went. A noted *prima donna* sang, lured by an immense nightly reward to disclose her vocal splendors before American audiences. But her encompassment, as is so apt to be the case here, was pitiably mediocre. She sang with a presentable contralto, a passable baritone, an effete basso, and an almost despicable tenor. The chorus was anachronistic in costume, sorry in voice, and mournfully undrilled. But the *diva* was so comprehensively talented that she carried the whole performance. At the same time there were those among her hearers who lamented that her transcendent ability should be burlesqued by so shabby and impotent a surrounding. The engagement of this famous lady was meanwhile one of those sad operatic facts for which the American people have found, during years past, no remedy and no preventive. The fault, of course, lies with themselves. When they are sufficiently numerous as true lovers of music they will refuse their countenance to even a great singer except with creditable artistic and scenic support.

Pauline sat in the Effinghams' spacious prosce-
nium-box, between Mrs. Poughkeepsie and her
daughter. Sallie Poughkeepsie was a large girl,
with her mother's nose, her mother's serenity,
her mother's promise of corpulent matronhood.
She had immense prospects; it was reported that
she had refused at least twenty eligible matrimonial offers while waiting for the parental nod of
approval, which had not yet come.

During the first *entr'acte* a little throng of admirers entered the box. Some of these Pauline
knew; others had appeared, as it were, after her
time. One was an Englishman, and she presently
became presented to him as the Earl of Glenartney. The title struck her as beautiful, appealing
to her sense of the romantic and picturesque; but
she wondered that it had done so when she subse-
quently bent a closer gaze upon the receding forehead, flaccid mouth and lank frame of the Earl
himself. He had certainly as much hard prose
about his appearance as poetry in his name. Mrs.
Poughkeepsie beamed upon him in a sort of sidelong way all the time that he conversed with
Sallie. A magnate of bountiful shirt-bosom and
haughty profile claimed her full heed, but she
failed to bestow it entirely; the presence of this
unmarried Scotch peer at her child's elbow was

too stirring an incident; her usual equanimity was in a delightful flutter; ambition had already begun its insidious whispers, for the Earl was known to be still a bachelor.

Pauline, who read her aunt so thoroughly, felt the mockery of this maternal deference. She told herself that there was something dreary and horrible about a state of human worldliness which could thus idolize mere rank and place. She knew well enough that so long as Lord Glenartney were not a complete idiot, and so long as his moral character escaped the worst depravity, he would be esteemed a magnificent match for her cousin.

The Earl remained at Sallie's side all through the succeeding act. When the curtain again fell he still remained, while other gentlemen took the places of those now departing. And among these, to her surprise and pleasure, was Ralph Kindelon.

She almost rose as she extended her hand to her friend. A defiant satisfaction had suddenly thrilled her. She pronounced Kindelon's name quite loudly as she presented him to her aunt. Instead of merely bowing to Mrs. Poughkeepsie, Kindelon, with effusive cordiality, put forth his hand. Pauline saw a startled look creep across her aunt's face. The handsome massive-framed

Irishman was not clad in evening dress. He towered above all the other gentlemen; he seemed, as indeed he almost was, like a creature of another species. His advent made an instant sensation; a universal stare was levelled upon him by these sleek devotees of fashion, among whom he had the air of pushing his way with a presumptuous geniality. He carried a soft "wide-awake" hat in one hand; his clothes were of some dark gray stuff; his neatly but heavily booted feet made dull sounds upon the floor as he now moved backward in search of a chair. There was no possible doubt regarding his perfect self-possession; he had evidently come to remain and to assert himself.

"Who on earth is he?" Mrs. Poughkeepsie found a chance to swiftly whisper in the ear of her niece. There was an absolutely dramatic touch in the agitation which went with her questioning sentence.

Pauline looked steadily at her aunt as she responded: "A very valued friend of mine."

"But, my dear!" faltered Mrs. Poughkeepsie. The fragmentary little vocative conveyed a volume of patrician dismay.

By this time Kindelon had found a chair. He placed it close to Pauline.

"I am so very glad that you discovered me," said Pauline. She spoke in quite loud tones, while everybody listened. Her words had the effect of a distinct challenge, and as such she intended them.

"I am flinging down a gauntlet," she thought, "to snobbery and conservatism. This slight event marks a positive era in my life."

"I saw you from the orchestra," now said Kindelon, in his heartiest tones. "The distance revealed you to me, though I cannot say it lent the least enchantment, for that would surely be impossible." He now looked towards Mrs. Poughkeepsie, without a trace of awe in his mirthful expression. "You must pardon my gallantry, madam," he proceeded. "Your niece and I, though recent friends, are yet old ones. We have crossed the Atlantic together, and that, in the winter season, is a wondrous promoter of intimacy, as you perhaps know. Perhaps Mrs. Varick has already done me the honor of mentioning our acquaintance."

"Not until now," said Mrs. Poughkeepsie, with a smile that had the glitter of ice in it.

IV.

THE orchestra had not yet re-commenced, and the curtain would not reascend for at least ten good minutes. A vigorous babble of many voices rose from the many upstairs boxes. In some of these Kindelon's appearance might not have created the least comment. Here it was a veritable bombshell.

The "Poughkeepsie set" was famed for its rigid exclusiveness. Wherever Miss Sallie and her mother went, a little train of courtiers invariably followed them. They always represented an ultra-select circle inside of the larger and still decidedly aristocratic one. Only certain young men ever presumed to approach Sallie at all, and these were truly the darlings of fortune and fashion — young gentlemen of admitted ascendency, whose attentions would have made an obscure girl rapidly prominent, and who, while often distinguished for admirable manners, always contrived to hover near those who were the sovereign reverse of obscure. They would carry only her bouquets, or those of other girls who belonged to the same special and envied clique; they would "take out in the German" only Sallie and her particular intimates. Bitter jealousies among the contemplating dowagers were often a result of this determined eclecticism. "Why *is* it that my Kate has to put up with so many second-rate men?" would pass with tormenting persistence through the mind of this matron. "Why can't my Caroline get any of the great swells to notice her?" would drearily haunt another. And between these two distressed ladies there might meanwhile be seated a third, whose daughter, for reasons of overwhelming wealth or particular attractiveness, always moved clad in a nimbus of sanctity.

Pauline was perfectly well aware that the coming of her friend had seemed an audacity, and that his unconventionally garrulous tongue was now regarded as a greater one. Courtlandt may have told her that the rival factions had cemented their differences and that all society in New York was more democratic than formerly. Still, it was unimaginable that her aunt Cynthia could ever really change her spots. Where she trod, there, too, must float the aroma of an individual self-glorification.

Pauline was as much delighted by Kindelon's easy daring as by the almost glacial answer of her stately kinswoman; and she at once hastened to say, while looking with a smile at the unembarrassed Kindelon himself, —

"I have scarcely had a chance to tell either my aunt or my cousin how good you were to me on the 'Bothnia.'" Then she lifted her fan, and waved it prettily toward Sallie. "This *is* my cousin, Miss Poughkeepsie," she went on; she did not wait for the slow accomplishment of Sallie's forced and freezing bow, but at once added: "and here is Lord Glenartney, here Mr. Fyshkille, here Mr. Van Arsdale, here Mr. Hackensack. Now, I think you know us all, Mr. Kindelon."

As she ended her little speech she met Mrs. Poughkeepsie's eyes fixed upon her in placid consternation. Of course this wholesale introduction, among the chance occupants of an opera box, was a most unprecedented violation of usage. But that was precisely Pauline's wish — to violate usage, if she could do it without recourse to any merely vulgar rupture. They had all stared at Ralph Kindelon, had treated him as if he were some curious animal instead of a fellow-creature greatly their own superior, and they should have a chance now of discovering just how well he could hold his own in their little self-satisfied assemblage.

Kindelon bowed and smiled in every direction. He appeared unconscious that everybody did not bow and smile with just the same reciprocal warmth.

"This is the most luxurious way of enjoying the opera," he exclaimed, with an upward gesture of both hands to indicate the walls of the commodious box. "But, ah! I am afraid that it possesses its drawbacks as well! One would be tempted to talk too much here — to discountenance the performance. Now, I am an irreclaimable talker, as Mrs. Varick can testify; she has hardly done anything but listen since the beginning of our acquaintance. And yet I should like to feel that I had my tribute of silence always ready for the great musical masters. Among these I rank the Italian composers, whom it has now become fashionable to despise. Pray, Mrs. Poughkeepsie, are you — or is your daughter? — a convert to what they term the new school?"

There was no ignoring the felicitous, rhythmic voice that pronounced these hurried and yet clearly enunciated sentences, unless by means of an insolence so direct and cruel that it would transgress all bounds of civil decency. Mrs. Poughkeepsie was capable of not a little insolence at a pinch; her ramparts were spiked, and could deal no gentle hurts to those who sought anything like the scaling of them. But here the overtures made were alike too suave and too bold. She felt herself in the presence of a novel civility — one that assumed her rebuff to be impossible.

"I have always preferred the Italian music," she now said. "But then my knowledge of the German is limited."

"Oh, German music is the most dreadful baw!" here struck in Lord Glenartney. He had taken an immediate fancy to Kindelon; he liked people who were in a different sphere from himself; he usually went with jockeys and prize-fighters, whenever the demands of his great position permitted such association, in his native country. Here in America he knew only the Poughkeepsie set, which had seized upon him and kept close watch over him ever since he had landed in New York.

"No, I don't at all agree with you there," said Kindelon. "Undoubtedly German music is based upon a grand idea. I should be sorry not to believe so."

"Bless my soul!" laughed his lordship; "I don't know anything about grand ideahs. The small ones are quite as much as I can manage comfortably."

"Mr. Kindelon will be shocked by such a confession, I'm sure," said the gentleman named Fyshkille, who was strikingly slim, who gazed at people condescendingly over a pale parapet of very stiff shirt-collar, and who considered himself to have a natural turn for satire. "He appears to be a person of such grand ideas himself."

This airy bit of impudence caused Mr. Van Arsdale to twirl one end of a dim, downy mustache and perpetrate a rather ambiguous. giggle. But Mr. Hackensack, who was stout, with a pair of large black eyes set in a fat, colorless, mindless face, whipped forth a silk pocket-handkerchief and gave an explosive burst of merriment within its soft folds.

"You seem to be very much amused at something," drawled Sallie, while she looked in her languid way toward her trio of admirers.

"We are," said the satirical Mr. Fyshkille, who prided himself on always keeping his countenance. His two friends, who thought him a devilish clever fellow, both produced another laugh, this time suppressed on the part of each.

Pauline felt keenly annoyed. She glanced at Kindelon, telling herself that he must surely see the pitiable ridicule of which he was being made the butt.

She had, however, quite miscalculated. The self-esteem of Kindelon as utterly failed to realize that he was an object of the slightest banter, whether overt or covert, as though he had been both near-sighted and deaf. He knew nothing of the idle autocracy with which accident had now brought him into contact. He was opposed to it on principle, but he had had no experience of its trivial methods of arrogance. He had come into the box to see Pauline, and he took it broadly for granted that he would be treated with politeness by her surrounders, and listened to (provided he assumed that office of general spokesman which he nearly always assumed wherever chance placed him) with admiring attention.

A few minutes later he had stripped his would-be foes of all sting by effectively and solidly manifesting unconsciousness that they had intended to be hostile. He talked of Wagner and his followers with a brilliant force that did not solicit heed and yet compelled it. He discoursed upon the patent absurdities of Italian opera with a nimble wit and an incisive severity. Then he justified his preference for Donizetti and Rossini with a readiness that made his past sarcasm on their

modes quickly forgotten. And finally he delivered a eulogy upon the German motive and ideal
in music which showed the fine liberality of a
mind that recognizes the shortcomings in its own
predilection, and foresees the inevitable popularity
of a more advanced and complicated system.

He had silenced everybody before he finished,
but with the silence of respect. He had forced
even these petty triflers who dwelt on the mere
skirts of all actual life, to recognize him as not
simply the comer from a world which they did
not care to know about, but from a world greater
and higher than any which they were capable of
knowing about. And finally, in the flush of this
handsome little triumph, he made his exit, just
as the curtain was again rising, after a few murmured words to Pauline regarding certain night-
work on the New York "Asteroid," which must
prevent him from seeing the remainder of the
performance.

Nobody heeded the opera for at least five minutes after his departure. He had left his spell
behind him. Pauline at first marked its cogency,
and then observed this gradually dissolve. The
flimsiness of their thinking and living returned
to them again in all its paltry reality.

"Of course," murmured Mrs. Poughkeepsie to

Pauline, " he is a person who writes books, of one sort or another."

" If they 're novels," said Lord Glenartney, "I 'd like awfully to know abaout 'em. I 'm fond of readin' a good novel. It 's so jolly if one 's lyin' daown and carn't sleep, but feels a bit seedy, ye know."

" I fancy they must be rather long novels," said Sallie, with a drowsy scorn that suited her big, placid anatomy.

" I wish he 'd not run off so; I wanted the address of his hatter," declared the envenomed Mr. Fyshkille.

" Or his tailor," amended Mr. Van Arsdale, with the auxiliary giggle.

" I guess you 'd find both somewhere in the Bowery," pursued the fleshy Mr. Hackensack, who always said " I guess," for " I fancy," and had a nasal voice, and an incorrigible American soul inside his correct foreign garments.

Pauline now swept a haughty look at Mr. Fyshkille and his two allies, and said, with open displeasure, —

" I suppose you think it an unpardonable sin for any gentleman to suit his own taste in dress, and not copy that of some English model. But your uncivil comments on Mr. Kindelon before myself, his admitted friend, show me that he might easily teach you a lesson in good manners."

All three of the offenders were now forced to utter words of apology, while Lord Glenartney looked as if he thought Mrs. Varick's wrath great fun, and Sallie exchanged a look of ironical distress with her mother, that seemed to inquire: "What uncomfortable absurdity will Pauline next be guilty of?"

But Mrs. Poughkeepsie and Sallie left their kinswoman at her Bond Street residence that night with very agreeable adieus. True, Lord Glenartney occupied a seat in their carriage, but even if this had not been the case, neither mother nor daughter would have vented upon Pauline any of the disapproval she had provoked in them. She was now a power in the world, and besides being near to them in blood, even her follies merited the leniency of a Poughkeepsie.

But after Sallie and her mother had said goodnight to his lordship and were alone at home together, the young lady spoke with querulous disgust of her cousin's behavior.

"She will lose caste horribly, mamma, if she goes on in this way. It's perfectly preposterous! If there is one thing on earth that is really *low*, it's for a woman to become strong-minded!"

Mrs. Poughkeepsie nodded. "You are quite right. But she's her own mistress, and there is no restraining her."

"People *ought* to be restrained," grumbled Sallie, loosening her opera cloak, "when they want to throw away their positions like that."

"Oh, Pauline can't throw hers away so easily," affirmed Mrs. Poughkeepsie with sapient composure. "No, not with her name and her big income. She will merely get herself laughed at, you know — *encanailler* herself most ludicrously; that is all. We must let her have her head, as one says of a horse. Her father was always full of caprices; he would n't have died a poor man if he had not been. She merely has a caprice now. Of course she will come to terms again with society sooner or later, and repent having made such a goose of herself. That is, unless " — And here Mrs. Poughkeepsie paused, while a slight but distinct shudder ended her sentence.

Sallie gave a faint, harsh laugh. "Oh, I understand you thoroughly, mamma," she exclaimed. "You mean unless some common man like that Mr. Kindelon should induce her to marry him. How awful such a thing would be! I declare, the very thought of it is sickening! With that superb fortune, too! I should n't be surprised if he had proposed already!   Perhaps she has only been preparing us gradually for the frightful news that she has accepted him!"

But no such frightful news reached the Poughkeepsies, as day succeeded day. Pauline went little into the fashionable throngs, which were at the height of their winter gayeties. She soon quitted her Bond Street residence for good, and secured a small basement-house on a side street near Fifth Avenue, furnishing it with that speed in the way of luxurious appointment which a plethoric purse so readily commands.

"I am quite prepared now," she said to Kindelon one morning, after having received him in her new and lovely sitting-room, where everything was unique and choice, from the charming chandelier of twisted silver to the silken Japanese screen, rich with bird and flower in gold and crimson. "Of course you understand what I mean."

He affected not to do so. "Prepared?" he repeated, with the gay gleam slipping into his eyes. "For what?"

"My *salon*, of course."

"Oh," he said. "I confess that I suspected what you meant, though I was not quite sure. I almost feared lest your resolution might have undergone a change of late."

"And pray, why?" asked Pauline, raising her brows, with a little imperious smile.

"You have not mentioned the project for surely a good fortnight," he returned. "I had wondered whether or no it had weakened with you."

"It is stronger than ever," Pauline asseverated. She folded her hands in her lap and tried to look excessively firm and resolute. She was always particularly handsome when she tried to look thus; she was just slender and feminine enough in type to make the assumption of strength, of determination, especially becoming.

"Ah, very well," replied Kindelon, with one of his richly expressive smiles. "Then I have a proposition to make you. It concerns an immediate course of action on your part. Have you ever heard of Mrs. Hagar Williamson Dares?"

Pauline burst into a laugh. "No. It sounds more like an affirmation than a name — 'Mrs. Hagar Williamson Dares.' One feels like saying, 'Does she?' Don't think me irredeemably trifling, and please continue. Please tell me, I mean, what remarkable things has this remarkably-named lady done?"

"Nothing."

Pauline's face, full of a pleased anticipation, fell. "Nothing! How tiresome!"

· "I mean nothing remarkable," Kindelon went on, "in the luminously intellectual sense. And yet she is a very extraordinary woman. At twenty-five she was divorced from her husband."

Pauline shook her head troubledly. "That does not sound at all promising."

"He was a dissolute wretch. The courts easily granted her a release from him. At this time she was almost penniless. The question, as she had two little children, naturally arose: 'How are we three to live?' She had been reared in a New England home; her dead father had been a man of extensive learning, and at one time the principal of a successful school. Hagar had always had 'a taste for writing,' as we call it. She began by doing criticisms for a New York journal of rather scholarly tendency, whose editor had combined pity for her almost starving condition with appreciation of her undoubted talents. But the prices that the poor struggling young mother received were necessarily very meagre. She became practical. She asked herself if there was no other way of earning money by her pen. She soon discovered a way; it did not require her to know about Diderot and Strauss and Spinoza, with all of whose writings (and with many classics more of equal fame) she was finely familiar; it simply required that she should lay aside every vestige of literary pride and write *practically.* Good Heavens! what a word that word 'practical' is in literature! You must tell the people how to bake a pie, to cure a headache, to bleach a shirt, to speak the truth, to clean silverware, to make a proposal of marriage. Mrs. Dares did it in country letters, in city letters, in newspaper editorials, in anonymous fine-print columns, in the back parts of fashion and household magazines— and she does it still. For a number of years past she has superintended a periodical of the popular sort, which I dare say you have never heard of. The amount of work that she accomplishes is enormous. A strong man would stagger under it, but this frail woman (you'll think her frail when you see her) bears it with wondrous endurance. Her life has been a terrible failure, looked at from one point of view—for it is scarcely exaggeration to say that had she not been handicapped by poverty in the beginning she might have swayed and charmed her generation with great books. But from another point of view her life has been a sublime success; she has trampled all aspiration under foot, forsworn every impulse of honorable egotism, and toiled for the maintenance of a home, for the education of her two daughters. They are both grown up, now — girls who are themselves bread-winners like their mother, and bearing their yoke of labor as cheerfully, though not with the same splendid strength, as she. One is a school-teacher in a well-known *kindergarten* here, and one has become an artist of no contemptible ability. Meanwhile Mrs. Dares has not merely established a pleasant and refined household; she has caused to be diffused from it, as a social centre, the warm radiations of a sweet, wholesome hospitality. Like some of the high-born Fifth Avenue leaders of fashion, she has her 'evenings.' But they are of a totally different character. They are not 'select;' I don't claim that grace for them. And yet they are very interesting, very typical. Some shabby people meet there — shabby, I mean, in mental ways no less than in character and costume. But the prevailing element is of a higher order than they. Anyone whom Mrs. Dares believes to be an earnest worker in the field of letters will have no difficulty about gaining her favor. I think she would rather greet in her rooms some threadbare young poet who had published at his own expense a slim little volume of poems possessing distinct merit and having received the snubs of both critics and public, than welcome some rich and successful writer whose real claim upon recognition she honestly doubted. And for this reason she makes mistakes. I have no doubt she is aware of making them. When we search the highways and hedges for cases of deserving charity, we cannot but light upon at least an occasional impostor — to put the matter as optimistically as possible. And now let me tell you that if my mighty explanatory outburst has roused your desire to meet Mrs. Dares, the opportunity to do so lies well within your reach."

" How ? " said Pauline. And then, as if abashed by the brusque abruptness of her own question, she added, with a little penitent nod : " Oh, yes ; you mean that she has kindly consented to let you bring her here."

" Not at all," said Kindelon. " It is true that she goes about a good deal. Her position as a journalist gives her, of course, the *entrée* to many theatres, and as she is passionately fond of the drama, her face is seldom missed on a *première* at any reputable house — Daly's, the Union Square, the Madison Square, or Wallack's. She takes delight, too, in appearing at the entertainments of her various friends, and she always does so clad elegantly, richly, but without a shadow of ostentatious display. On these occasions her society is eagerly sought. I have sometimes wondered why; for her conversation, though invariably full of sound sense and pithy acumen, lacks the cheerful play of humor which is so widely demanded to generate anything like popularity wherever men and women are socially met. But she is very popular, and I suppose it is her striking simplicity, her gift of always being sincerely and unaffectedly *herself*, which has made her so. Still, for all this gregarious impulse, if I may thus name it, I do not believe she would take the first step, where you are concerned, to establish an acquaintance."

" And for what reason?" asked Pauline. Her tones, while she put this query, were full of a hurt bewilderment. Kindelon seemed to muse for a brief space; and any such unconversational mood was rare, as we know, with his mercurial lightsomeness of manner. "She would be sensitive," he presently said, "about making an advance of this sort."

" Of this sort?" repeated Pauline, with a somewhat irritated inflection. "Of what sort?"

Her companion watched her with fixity for a moment. Then he raised his large forefinger, and slowly shook it, with admonitory comedy of gesture. "You must not tell me that you don't understand," he said. " Put yourself in this lady's place. Suppose that you, in spite of fine brains and noble character, lacked the social standing " —

Pauline broke in quite hotly at this. Her eyes had taken a quick sparkle, and the color was flying rosy and pure into her fair face. " Pshaw!" she exclaimed. " It is not any question of social standing. I want to know these people " — She suddenly paused, as though her tongue had betrayed her into some regrettable and unseemly phrase. "I want to pass," she continued more slowly, "from an aimless world into one of thought and sense. Mrs. Dares is prominent in this other world. From what you say I should judge that she is a very representative and influential spirit there. Why should she not be benign and gracious enough to seek me here? Why should she require that I shall emphatically pay her my court? Your description makes me glad and happy to know her. If she learned this, would she hold aloof from any absurd scruples about a disparity in social standing? — Well, if she did," declared Pauline, who by this time was quite excitedly flushed and fluttered, "then I should say that you had over-painted her virtues and too flatteringly concealed her faults!"

Kindelon threw back his head, as she finished, and laughed with such heartiness that more of his strong white teeth were transiently visible than would have pleased a strict judge of decorum.

"Oh, how amusing you are!" he cried. "You are really superb and don't perceive it!—Well," he proceeded, growing graver, "I suppose you would be far less so if you had the vaguest inkling of it. Now, pray listen. Does it enter your conscience at all that you are disguising a kind of royal patronage and condescension behind a gentle and saint-like humility? No— of course it does n't. But, my dear lady, this is unequivocally true. You scoff at social standing, and yet you complacently base yourself upon it. You want to desert all your old tenets, and yet you keep a kind of surreptitious clasp about them. You would not for the world be considered a person who cared for the aristocratic purple, and yet you wrap it round you in the most illogical fashion. Mrs. Dares has her evenings; to-night is one of them. You, as yet, have no evenings; your *salon* is still in embryo. You want to affiliate with her, to be one of her set, her surroundings, her *monde*. And yet you quietly bid her to your house, as though she were proposing your co-operation, your support, your intimacy, and not you hers!"

Pauline, with perhaps a deepened tinge of color in her cheeks, was staring at the floor when Kindelon ended. And from beneath her gown came the impatient little tap of a nervous foot. After an interval of silence, during which her friend's gaze watched her with a merry vivacity of expression, she slowly lifted her shapely blond head, and answered in grave, even saddened tones,—

"Then my *salon* is to be a failure? — an unrealizable castle in Spain?"

"Oh, no," promptly said Kindelon, with one of those sympathetic laughs which belonged among his elusive fascinations. "By no means — unless you so will it."

"But I don't will it," said Pauline.

"Very well. Then it will be a castle in — in New York. That sounds tangible enough, surely. It is the first step that counts, and you have only to take your first step. It will certainly look much better to know some of your courtiers before you ascend your throne. And meanwhile it would be far more discreet to cultivate an acquaintance with your probable prime minister."

"All of which means — ?" she said.

"That you had best let me accompany you to Mrs. Dares's house this evening."

"But I am not invited!" exclaimed Pauline.

"Oh yes, you are," said Kindelon, with easy security in the jocund contradiction. "Miss Cora, the youngest daughter of Mrs. Dares, told me last night that she and her mother would both be very glad to have you come."

There was a momentary intonation in Kindelon's voice that struck his listener as oddly unexpected. "So you have already spoken of me?" she said lingeringly, and looking at him with more intentness than she herself knew of.

"Yes," he replied, with a certain speed, and with tones that were not just set in an unembarrassed key. "I go there now and then."

"And you have mentioned me to Mrs. Dares?"

"Yes — more than once, I think. She knows that you may be induced to come this evening."

His glance, usually so direct, had managed to avoid Pauline's, which was then very direct indeed.

"Tell me," Pauline said, after another silence had somehow made itself felt between them. "Are you a very good friend of this girl — Miss Cora?"

He returned her look then, but with an un-

wonted vacillation of his own — or so she chose
to think.

"Yes," he responded, fluently frank, as it
seemed. "We are very good friends — excellent
friends, I may say. You will find her quite as
charming, in a different way, as her mother. I
mean, of course, if you will go with me this
evening — or any future evening."

Pauline put forth her hand, and laid it for an
instant on his full-moulded arm.

"I will go with you this evening," she said.

V.

KINDELON found Pauline in a very light-some and animated state of mind when he called at her house that evening. She had a touch of positive excitement in her way of referring to the proposed visit. He thought he had never seen her look more attractive than when she received him, already wrapped in a fleecy white over-garment and drawing on her gloves, while a piquant smile played at the corners of her mouth and a vivacious glitter filled her gray eyes.

"You are here before the carriage," she said to him, "though we shan't have to wait long for that. — Hark — there is the bell, now; my men would not presume to be a minute late this evening. The footman must have detected in my manner a great seriousness when I gave him my order; I felt very serious, I can assure you, as I did so. It meant the first step in a totally new career."

"Upon my word, you look fluttered," said Kindelon, in his mellow, jocose voice.

"Naturally I do!" exclaimed Pauline, as she nodded to the servant who now announced that the carriage was in readiness. "I am going to have a fresh, genuine sensation. I am going to emancipate myself — to break my tether, as it were. I've been a prisoner for life; I don't know how the sunshine looks, or how it feels to take a gulp of good, free air."

He watched her puzzledly until the outer darkness obscured her face, and they entered the carriage together. She mystified him while she talked on, buoyant enough, yet always in the same key. He was not sure whether or no her sparkling manner had a certain sincere trepidation behind it. Now and then it seemed to him as if her voluble professions of anxiety rang false — as if she were making sport of herself, of him, or of the projected diversion.

"Do you really take the whole matter so much to heart," he presently said, while the vehicle rolled them along the wintry, lamplit streets, "or is this only some bit of dainty and graceful masquerading?"

"Masquerading?" she echoed, with a shocked accent.

"Oh, well, you are accustomed to meeting all sorts of people. You can't think that any human classes are so sharply divided that to cross a new threshold means to enter a new world."

She was silent, and he could see her face only vaguely for some little time; but when a passing light cast an evanescent gleam upon it he thought that he detected something like a look of delicate mischief there. Her next words, rather promptly spoken, bore with them an explanatory bluntness.

"I am convinced that if everybody else disappoints me Miss Dares will not."

"Miss Dares?" he almost faltered, in the tone of one thrown off his guard.

"Miss Cora Dares," Pauline continued, with a self-correcting precision. "The younger of the two daughters, the one who paints. Oh, you see," she continued, after a little laugh that was merry, though faint, "I have forgotten nothing. I 've a great curiosity to see this young artist. You had not half so much to tell me about her as about her mother, and yet you have somehow contrived to make her quite as interesting."

"Why?" Kindelon asked, with a soft abruptness to which the fact of his almost invisible face lent a greater force. "Is it because you think that I like Cora Dares? I should like to

think that was your reason for being interested
in her."

Another brief silence on Pauline's part followed
his words, and then she suddenly responded, with
the most non-committal innocence of tone:

"Why, what other reason could I possibly
have? Of course I suppose that you like her.
And of course that is why I am anxious to meet
her."

There was a repelling pleasautry in these
three short sentences. If Kindelon had been
inclined to slip any further into the realm of sentiment, the very reverse of encouragement had
now met him. Pauline's matter-of-course com-
placency had a distinct chill under its superficial
warmth. "Don't misunderstand me, please," she
went on, with so altered a voice that her listener
felt as if she had indeed been masquerading
through some caprice best known to herself, and
now chose once and for all to drop masque and
cloak. "I really expect a most novel and entertaining experience to-night. You say that I have
met all sorts of people. I have by no means done
so. It strikes me that our acquaintance is not
so young that I should tell you this. It is true
that I made a few pleasant and even valuable
friendships in Europe; but these have been ex-

ceptional in my life, and I now return to my native city to disapprove everybody whom I once approved."

"And you expect to approve all the people whom you shall meet to-night?"

"You ask that in a tone of positive alarm."

"I can't help betraying some nervous fear. Your expectations are so exorbitant."

Pauline tossed her head in the dimness. "Oh, you will find me more easily suited than you suppose."

Kindelon gave a kind of dubious laugh. "I 'm not so sure that you will be easily suited," he said. "You are very pessimistic in your judgments of the fashionable throng. It strikes me that you are a rigid critic of nearly everybody. How can I tell that you will not denounce me, in an hour or so, as the worst of impostors, for having presumed to introduce you among a lot of objectionable bores?"

"I think you will admit," said Pauline, in offended reply, "that most of Mrs. Dares's friends have brains."

"Brains? Oh, yes, all sorts of brains."

"That is just what I want to meet," she rapidly exclaimed — "all sorts of brains. I am accustomed, at present, to only two or three sorts. —

Oh, you need not be afraid that I shall become bored. No, indeed! On the contrary, I expect to be exhilarated. I shall fraternize with most of them — I shall be one of them almost immediately. Wait until you see!"

"I shan't see that," said Kindelon, with an amused *brusquerie*.

"What do you mean?" she questioned, once more offendedly.

He began to speak, with his old glib fleetness. "Why, my dear lady, because you are *not* one of them, and never can be. You are a patrician, reared differently, and you will carry your stamp with you wherever you go. Your very voice will betray you in ten seconds. You may show them that you want to be their good friend, but you can't convince them that you and they are of the same stock. Some of them will envy you, others may secretly presume to despise you, and still others may very cordially like you. I don't think it has ever dawned upon me until lately how different you are from these persons whom you wish to make your allies and supporters. That night, when I went into your aunt's opera-box, I had a very slight understanding of the matter. I've always scoffed at the idea of a New York aristocracy. It seemed so absurd, so self-contradictory.

And if it existed at all, I 've always told myself, it must be the merest nonsensical sham. But now I begin to recognize it as an undeniable fact. There 's a sort of irony, too, in my finding it out so late — after I have knocked about as a journalist in a city which I believed to be democratic if it was anything. However, you 've made the whole matter plain to me. You did n't intend to open my plebeian eyes, but you have done so. It is really wonderful how you have set me thinking. I 've often told myself that America was a political failure as a republic, but I never realized that it was a social one."

Just then the carriage stopped. "I am sorry," said Pauline, "to have unconsciously made you think ill of the literary society of New York." She paused for a moment, and there was a rebuking solemnity in her voice as she added: "I believe — I insist upon believing till I see otherwise — that it does not deserve to be condemned."

VI

THE footman was now heard, as he sprang from the box. "Good gracious!" exclaimed Kindelon; "I have n't condemned it! It condemns itself."

Pauline gave a laugh full of accusative satire. "Oh!" she burst forth. "I should like to hear you speak against it before Mrs. Dares — and your friend Miss Cora, too — as you have just done before me!"

The footman had by this time opened the carriage door. He kept one white-gloved hand on the knob, standing, with his cockaded hat and his long-skirted coat, motionless and respectful in the outer gloom.

Kindelon threw up both hands, and waved them in a burlesque of despair. "There is *no* literary society in New York," he murmured, as if the admission had been wrung from him. "Don't go inside there with any idea of meeting it, for it is not to be found! Mrs. Dares herself will tell you so!"

Pauline shook her head vigorously. "I'm sure you can't mean that," she exclaimed, in grieved reproach.

Kindelon gave one of his laughs, and jumped out of the carriage. Pauline took the hand which he offered her, while the displaced footman decorously receded.

"I do mean it," he said, as they went up a high, narrow stoop together, and saw two slim, lit windows loom before them.

"I hope I am not responsible for this last change of faith in you," she answered, while Kindelon was ringing the bell.

"Well," he at once said, "I believe you are. There is no kind of real society here except one. Mind you, I don't say this in any but the most dispassionate and critical way. And I'm not glad to say it, either; I'm sorry, in fact. But it is true" — And then, after a second of silence, he repeated — "no kind of society except one."

Pauline smiled as she watched him, but there was both exasperation and challenge in the smile.

"What kind is that?" she queried.

"Ask your aunt, Mrs. Poughkeepsie," he replied.

Pauline gave an irritated sigh. As she did so the door of Mrs. Dares's house was opened by a spruce-looking young negress, and they both passed into the little limited hall beyond. Tapestries of tasteful design were looped back from the small doors which gave upon the hall. Their blended stuffs of different colors produced a novel effect, wholly disproportioned to the real worth of the fabrics themselves. The deft skill of Mrs. Dares's younger daughter was responsible, not alone for these, but for other equally happy embellishments throughout this delightful miniature dwelling. In every chamber there was to be found some pretty decorative stratagem whereby a maximum of graceful and even brilliant ornamentation had been won from a minimum of pecuniary expense. Pauline's eye had swept too many costly objects of upholstery not to recognize that a slender purse had here gone with a keen artistic sense. The true instinct of beauty seemed never to err, and its constant accompaniment of simplicity in the way of actual material lent it a new charm. Screen, rug, panelling, mantel-cover, tidy, and chair-cushion took for her a quick value because of their being wrought through no luxurious means. It was so easy to buy all these things in velvet, in silk, in choice woods; it was so hard, so rare, to be able to plan them all from less pretentious resources. Before she had been five minutes in Mrs. Dares's abode, Pauline found herself affected by the mingled attractiveness and modesty of its details, as we are allured by the tints, contours, and even perfumes of certain wildflowers which glow only the more sweetly because of their contrast with cultured blooms.

Mrs. Dares herself had a look not unlike that of some timid little wildflower. She was short of stature and very fragile; Kindelon's past accounts of her incessant accomplishments took the hue of fable as Pauline gazed upon her. She was extremely pale, with large, warm, dark eyes set in a face of cameo-like delicacy. Her dress hung in folds about her slight person, as if there had been some pitying motive in the looseness of its fit. But she wore it with an air of her own. It was a timid air, and yet it was one of ease and repose. The intelligence and earnestness of her clear-cut face gave her an undeniable dignity; you soon became sure that she was wholly unassuming, but you as soon realized that this trait of diffidence had no weakness in mind or character for its cause. It seemed, in truth, to correspond with her bodily frailty, and to make her individualism more complete while none the less emphatic. The personality that pushes itself upon our heed does not always make us notice it the quickest. Mrs. Dares never pushed herself upon anybody's heed, yet she was seldom unnoticed. Her voice rarely passed beyond a musical semitone, and yet you rarely failed to catch each word it uttered. Pauline not only caught each word, as her new hostess now stood and addressed her, leaving for the time all other guests who were crowding the rather meagre apartments, but she tacitly decided, as well, that there was an elegance and purity in the expressions used by this notable little lady which some of the grander-mannered dames whom she had intimately known might have copied with profit. One peculiarity about Mrs. Dares, however, was not slow to strike her: the pale, delicate face never smiled. Not that it was melancholy or even uncheerful, but simply serious. Mrs. Dares had no sense of humor. She could sometimes say a witty thing that bit hard and sharp, but she was without any power to wear that lazier mental fatigue-dress from which some of the most vigorous minds have been unable, before hers, to win the least relaxation. This was probably the true reason why her small drawing-room often contained guests whose eccentricity of garb or deportment would otherwise have excluded them from her civilities. She could not enjoy the foibles of her fellow-creatures ; she was too perpetually busy in taking a grave view of their sterner and more rational traits. She found something in nearly everybody that interested her, and it always interested her because it was human, solemn, important — a part, so to speak, of the great struggle, the great development, the great problem. This may, after all, be no real explanation of why she never smiled ; for a smile, as we know, can hold the sadness of tears in its gleam, just as a drop of morning dew will hold the moisture of the autumn rainfall. But the absence of all mirthful trace on her gentle lips accorded, nevertheless, with the inherent sobriety of her nature, and they who got to know her well would unconsciously assign for both a common origin.

"My dear Mrs. Varick," she said to Pauline, " I am very glad that you chose to seek my poor hospitality this evening. Mr. Kindelon has already prophesied that we shall be good friends, and as I look at you I find myself beginning to form a most presumptuous certainty that he will not prove a false prophet. He tells me that you are weary of the fashionable world ; I have seen nothing of that, myself, though I fancy I know what it is like. — A great Castle of Indolence, I mean, where there are many beautiful chambers, but where the carpets yield too luxuriously under foot, and the couches have too inviting a breadth. Now, in this little drawing-room of mine you will meet few people who have not some daily task to perform — however ill many of us may accomplish it. In that way the change will have an accent for you — the air will be fresher and more tonic, though shifting from warm to chilly in the most irregular manner. I want to warn you, my dear. lady, that you will miss that evenness of temperature which makes such easy breathing elsewhere. Be prepared for a decided atmospheric shock, now and then : but you will find it rather stimulating when it arrives, and by no means unwholesome."

Pauline could scarcely repress her astonishment at this very original speech of welcome. She and Mrs. Dares were separated from all other occupants of the room while it was being delivered; Kindelon had moved away after making his two friends known to each other, and doubtless with the intention of letting his hostess stand or fall on her own conversational merits, as far as concerned the first impression which Pauline should receive from her. But this impression was one in which admiration and approval played quite as strong a part as surprise. Pauline had wanted just such a spur and impetus as her faculties were now receiving; she kept silent for a few brief seconds, in silent enjoyment of the complex emotions which Mrs. Dares had wakened. Then she said, with a low laugh that had not the least suspicion of frivolity, —

"If it is a social temperature with those barometric tricks and freaks, Mrs. Dares, I promise you that I shan't catch cold in it. But I fear Mr. Kindelon has wasted too many premonitory words upon me. He should have politely allowed me to betray myself, as a specimen of harmless and humble commonplace. I am sure to do it sooner or later."

"Oh, he has told me of your aim, your purpose," said Mrs. Dares.

Pauline colored, and laid one hand on the lady's slender arm. "Then we are rivals, I suppose?" she murmured, with an arch smile.

Mrs. Dares turned and looked at her guest before answering; there was a mild, dreamy comprehensiveness in the way she seemed to survey their many shapes, letting her large, soft, dusky eyes dwell upon no special one of them. A little later she regarded Pauline again. She now shook her head negatively before replying.

"Oh, no, no," she said. "What you see here is

not in any sense a representative assemblage. I have often wished that some one would establish a stricter and more definite standard than mine. We need it sadly. There are no entertainments given in New York where the mentally alert people — those who read, and think, and write — can meet with an assurance that their company has been desired for reasons of an exceptional personal valuation. The guest without the wedding-garment is always certain to be there. I fear that I have paid too little heed to the wedding-garment; my daughters — and especially my eldest daughter, Martha — are always telling me that, in various ways. — Oh, no, Mrs. Varick, we shall not be rivals. You will have the leisure to sift, to weigh, to admit or exclude, to label, to indorse, to classify — to make order, in short, out of chaos. This *I* have never had the leisure to do." She looked at Pauline with an almost pensive gravity. Then she slowly repeated the word, "Never."

"I fancy you have never had the cruelty," said Pauline.

"There would be considerable solid mercy in it," was the firm answer.

"Yes. To those who were both called and chosen. But how about the repulsed candidates for admission?"

"They would deserve their defeat," said Mrs. Dares, with thoughtful deliberation. "Morals and manners properly combined would be their sole passport."

"And ability," amended Pauline.

"Ability? Oh, they all have ability who care to mingle night after night where that qualification is the dominating necessity for mutual enjoyment. Remember, an organized literary and intellectual society would not demand what that other society, of which you have seen so much, imperatively demands. I mean wealth, position, modishness, *ton*. All these would go for nothing with an aristocracy of talent, of high and true culture, of progress, of fine and wise achievement in all domains where human thought held rule. There, gross egotism, priggishness, raw eccentricity, false assumption of leadership, facile jealousy, dogmatic intolerance—these, and a hundred other faults, would justly exert a debarring influence."

Pauline did not know how her cheeks were glowing and her eyes were sparkling as she now quickly said, after having swept her gaze along the groups of guests not far away.

"And this is what you call making order out of chaos? Ah, yes, I understand. It is very delightful to contemplate. It quite stirs one with ambition. It is like having the merciless and senseless snobbery of mere fashionable life given a reasonable, animating motive. I should like to take upon myself such a task." Here she suddenly frowned in a moderate but rather distressed way. "Not long ago," she went on, "Mr. Kindelon told me that I would find no literary society in New York. But I contested this point. I'm inclined to contest it still, though you have shaken my faith, I admit."

"The word 'literary' is very specializing," said Mrs. Dares. She had drooped her large, musing eyes.

"Do you mean that for an evasion?" asked Pauline with a tart pungency that she at once regretted as almost discourteous. "Allow," she went on, promptly softening her tone, "that the word does cover a multitude of definitions as I use it — that it is used *faute de mieux*, and that no society has ever existed anywhere which one could call strictly literary. Come, then, my dear Mrs. Dares, allowing all this, do you consider that Mr. Kindelon was right? Is it all chaos to-day in New York? Is there no gleam of order?" And here Pauline broke into a furtive tremor of laughter. "Must I begin my good work at the very

earliest possible beginning if I am to commence
at all ? "

Mrs. Dares's dark eyes seemed to smile now, if
her lips did not. "Yes," she said. "Mr. Kindelon was right. You are to begin at the very
beginning. — In London it is so different," she
went on, lapsing into the meditative seriousness
from which nothing could permanently distract her.
"I spent a happy and memorable month there not
many years ago. It was a delicious holiday, taken
because of overwork here at home, and a blessed
medicine I found it. I had brought with me a
few lucky letters. They opened doors to me,
and beyond those doors I met faces and voices
full of a precious welcome. You would know the
names of not a few of those who were gracious to
me; they are names that are household words.
And there, in London, I saw, strongly established, a
dignified, important and influential society. Rarely, once in a while, I met some man or woman
with a title, but he or she had always either done
something to win the title, or something — if it
was inherited — to outshine it. I did not stay long
enough to pick flaws, to cavil; I enjoyed and
appreciated — and I have never forgotten ! "

Just at this point, and somewhat to Pauline's
secret annoyance, Kindelon returned with a lady

at his side. Pauline was soon told the lady's name, and as she heard it her annoyance was swiftly dissipated by a new curiosity. She at once concluded that Miss Cora Dares bore very slight resemblance to her mother. She was taller, and her figure was of a full if not generous moulding. Her rippled chestnut hair grew low over the forehead; almost too low for beauty, though her calm, straight-featured face, lit by a pair of singularly luminous blue eyes, and ending in a deep-dimpled chin of exquisite symmetry, needed but a glance to make good its attractive claim. Miss Cora Dares was quite profuse in her smiles; she gave Pauline, while taking the latter's hand, a very bright and charming one, which made her look still less like her mother.

"We saw you and mamma talking very earnestly together, Mrs. Varick," she said, with a brief side-glance toward Kindelon, "and so we concluded that it would be safe to leave you undisturbed for at least a little while. But mamma is curiously unsafe as an entertainer." This was said with an extremely sweet and amiable look in Mrs. Dares's direction. "She sometimes loses herself in gentle rhapsodies. My sister Martha and I have to keep watch upon her by turns, out of pity for the unliberated victims."

"I need not tell you how I scorn the injustice of that charge, my dear Mrs. Dares!" here cried Kindelon. "It would be late in the day to inform you of my devoted admiration!"

"I fear it is early in the day for me to speak of mine," said Pauline; but the laugh that went with her words (or was it the words themselves?) rang sincerely, and took from what she said the levity of mere idle compliment.

"But you will surely care to meet some of our friends, Mrs. Varick," now said Cora Dares.

"Oh, by all means, yes!" exclaimed Pauline. The girl's limpid, steadfast eyes fascinated her, and she gazed into their lucent depths longer than she was perhaps aware. It was almost like an abrupt awakening to find that she and Mrs. Dares's youngest daughter were standing alone together, Kindelon and the elder lady having gone. "I want very much to meet many of your friends," Pauline proceeded. She put her head a little on one side, while her lips broke into a smile that her companion appeared to understand perfectly and to answer with mute, gay intelligence. "I suppose you have heard all about me and my grand project, just as your charming mother has heard, Miss Dares?"

"Oh, yes," returned Cora.

"And you think it practicable?"

"I think it praiseworthy."

"Which means that I shall fail."

Cora looked humorously troubled. "If you do, it will not be your fault. I am not doubtful on that point."

"Your mother has by no means encouraged me. She says that I must be careful in my selections, but she gives me very little hope of finding many worthy subjects to select. She seems to think that when the wheat has been taken from the tares, as it were, there will be very little wheat left."

"Yes, I know mamma's opinions. I don't quite share them. My sister Martha does, however, thoroughly.—Ah, here is Martha now. Let me make you acquainted."

Martha Dares proved to be still more unlike her mother than Cora, save as regarded her stature, which was very short. She had a plump person, and a face which was prepossessing solely from its expression of honest good-nature. It was a face whose fat cheeks, merry little black eyes and shapeless nose were all a stout defiance of the classic type. Pauline at once decided that Martha was shrewd, energetic and cheerful, and that she might reveal, under due provocation, a temper of hot flash and acute sting.

"And now you know the whole family, Mrs. Varick," said Cora, when her sister had been presented.

"Yes, I complete the group," said Miss Dares, with a jocund trip of the tongue about her speech, that suggested a person who did all her thinking in the same fleet and impetuous way. "I hope you find it an interesting group, Mrs. Varick?"

"Very," said Pauline. "Its members have so much individuality. They are all three so different."

"True enough," hurried Martha. "We react upon each other, for this reason, in a very salutary way. You 've no idea what a corrective agent my practical turn is for this poetic sister of mine, who would be up in the clouds nearly all the time, trying to paint the unpaintable, but for an occasional downward jerk from me, you know, such as a boy will give to a refractory kite. But I 'll grant you that Cora has more than partially convinced me that life is n't entirely made up of spelling, arithmetic, geography and the use of the globes — for I 'm a school-teacher, please understand, though in a rather humble way. And there 's poor dear mamma. Goodness knows what would become of *her* if it were not for both of us. She has n't an idea how to economize her wonderful powers of work. Cora and I have established a kind of military despotism; we have to say 'halt' and 'shoulder your pen,' just as if she were a sort of soldier. But it will never do for me to rattle on like this. I'm as bad, after my own fashion, as our mutual friend, Mr. Kindelon, when I once really get started, By the way, you know Mr. Kindelon very well indeed, don't you?"

"Very well, though I have not known him very long," answered Pauline.

She somehow felt that Martha's question concealed more interest than its framer wished to betray. The little black eyes had taken a new keenness, but the genial face had sobered as well. And for some reason just at this point both Martha and Pauline turned their looks upon Cora.

She had slightly flushed; the change, however, was scarcely noticeable. She at once spoke, as though being thus observed had made her speak.

"He always has something pleasant to say of you," softly declared Cora. Here she turned to her sister. "Will you bring up some people to Mrs. Varick," she asked, "or shall I?"

"Oh, just as you choose," answered Martha. She had fixed her eyes on Pauline again. The next moment Cora had glided off.

"What my sister says is quite true," affirmed Martha.

"You mean —?" Pauline questioned, with a faint start which she could scarcely have explained.

"That Mr. Kindelon admires you very much."

"I am glad to hear it," returned Pauline, thinking how commonplace the sentence sounded, and at the same time feeling her color rise and deepen under the persistent scrutiny of those sharp dark eyes.

"Don't you think him intensely able?" said Martha, much more slowly than usual. "We do."

Pauline bowed assent. "Brilliantly able," she answered. "Tell me, Miss Dares, with which of you is he the more intimate, your sister or yourself?"

Martha gave a laugh that was crisp and curt. She looked away from Pauline as she answered. "Oh, he's more intimate with me than with Cora," she said. "We are stanch friends. He tells me nearly everything. I think he would tell me if he were to fall in love."

"Really?" laughed Pauline. Her face was wreathed in smiles of apparent amusement. She looked, just then, as she had often looked in the fashionable world, when everything around her seemed so artificial that she took the tints of her environment and became as artificial herself.

But it pleased her swiftly to change the subject. "I am quite excited this evening," she went on. "I am beginning a new career; you understand, of course. Tell me, Miss Dares, how do *you* think I shall succeed in it?"

Martha was watching her fixedly. And Martha's reply had a short, odd sound. "I think you are almost clever enough not to fail," she said.

VII

BEFORE Pauline had been an hour longer in the Dares's drawing-room she had become acquainted with many new people. She could not count them all when she afterward tried to do so; the introductions had been very rapid for some little time; one, so to speak, had trodden upon the heel of another. Her meditated project had transpired, and not a few of her recent acquaintances eyed her with a critical estimate of her capability to become their future leader.

She soon found herself an object of such general scrutiny that she was in danger of growing embarrassed to the verge of actual bewilderment. She was now the centre of a little group, and every member of it regarded her with more or less marked attentiveness.

"I've a tragic soul in a comic body, Mrs. Varick," said a fat little spinster, with a round moon of a face and a high color, whose name was Miss Upton. "That is the way I announce myself to all strangers. I should have gone on the stage and played *Juliet* if it had n't been for my unpoetic person. But imagine a bouncing, obese Juliet! No; I realized that it would never do. I shall have to die with all my music in me, as it were."

"A great many poets have done that," said a pale young gentleman with very black hair and eyes, and an expression of ironical fatigue which seldom varied. He was Mr. Leander Prawle, and he was known to have written verses for which he himself had unbounded admiration. "Indeed," the young poet continued, lifting one thin, white hand to where his moustache was not yet, "it is hard to sing a pure and noble song with the discords of daily life about one."

"Not if you can make the world stop its discords and listen to you, Mr. Prawle," said Pauline.

"Oh, Prawle can never do that," said a broad-shouldered young blond, with a face full of drowsy reverie and hair rolled back from it in a sort of yellow mane. "He 's always writing transcendental verses about Man with a capital M and the grand amelioration of Humanity with a capital H. Prawle has no color. He hates an adjective as if it were a viper. He should have lived with me in the *Quartier Latin;* he should have read, studied and loved the divine Théophile Gautier — most perfect of all French poets!"

The speaker fixed his sleepy blue eyes upon Leander Prawle while he thus spoke. A slight smile touched his lips, leaving a faint dimple in either smooth oval cheek. He was certainly very handsome, in an unconventional, audacious way. His collar gave a lower glimpse of his firm yet soft throat than usage ordinarily sanctions; the backward wave of his hair was certainly against any conceded form. He had been made known to Pauline as Mr. Arthur Trevor, and she had felt surprised at his name being so English; she had expected to find it French; Mr. Trevor had appeared to her extremely French.

"When you speak of Paris and of Gautier," she now said to him, "you really relieve me, Mr. Trevor. I was so prepared, on first meeting you, to find that you were not an American."

"Oh, Trevor is very French," said Leander Prawle coldly.

Trevor laughed, lifting one hand, on the middle finger of which was the tawny tell-tale mark of the confirmed cigarette-smoker.

"And my friend, Prawle," he said, "is enormously English."

"Not English — American," slowly corrected Leander Prawle.

"It is the same thing!" cried Arthur Trevor. "He is cold-blooded, Mrs. Varick," the young gentleman continued, with emphasis and a certain excitement. "We are always fighting, Prawle and I. I tell Prawle that in his own beloved literature, he should have but one model outside of Shakespeare. That is Keats — the sweet, sensuous, adorable Keats."

"I loathe Keats," said Leander Prawle, as if he were repeating some fragment of a litany. "I think him a word-monger."

"Aha," laughed Arthur Trevor, showing his white, sound teeth, "Keats was an immense genius. He knew the art of expression."

"And he expressed nothing," said Leander Prawle.

"He expressed beauty," declared Trevor. "Poetry is that. There is nothing else. Even the great master, Hugo, would tell you so."

"Hugo is a mere rhapsodist," said Leander Prawle.

Trevor laughed again. He gave a comic, exaggerated shudder while he did so. He now exclusively addressed Pauline. "My dear Mrs. Varick," he said, "are you not horrified?"

Before Pauline could answer, the fat little Miss Upton spoke. "Oh, Mr. Trevor," she said, "you know that though you and Mr. Prawle are always quarrelling about poetry, and belong to two different schools, still, each of you, in his way, is admirable. You are the North and South poles."

"No," said Arthur Trevor, "for the North and South poles never come together, while Prawle and I are continually clashing."

"It looks very much as if chaos were the result," said Pauline.

Arthur Trevor gazed at her reproachfully. "I hope you don't mean that," he said. He put his arm while he spoke, about the neck of a short and fleshy man, with a bald, pink scalp and a pair of dull, uneasy eyes. "Here is our friend, Rufus Corson," he continued. "Rufus has not spoken a word to you since he was presented, Mrs. Varick. But he's a tremendously important fellow. He doesn't look it, but he is the poet of death, decay, and horror."

"Good Heavens!" murmured Pauline playfully.

"It is true," pursued Arthur Trevor. "Rufus, here, is a wonderful fellow, and he has written some verses that will one day make him famous as the American Baudelaire."

"I have not read Baudelaire," said Pauline.

Mr. Corson at once answered her. He spoke in a forced, loitering way. He wore the dress of a man who scorns all edicts of mode, and yet he was very commonplace in appearance.

"The literature of the present age is in a state of decadence," he said. Mr. Corson, himself, looked to be in a state of plump prosperity; even his rosy baldness had a vivid suggestion of youth and of the enjoyments which youth bestows. "I write hopelessly," he continued, "because I live in a hopeless time. My 'Sonnet to a Skull' has been praised, because " —

"It has *not* been praised," said Leander Prawle firmly and severely.

Mr. Corson regarded Prawle with an amused pity. "It has been praised by people whom you don't know," he said, "and who don't want to know you."

"It is horrible," enunciated Leander Prawle, while he appealingly rolled toward Pauline his dark eyes, which the confirmed pallor of his face made still darker. "Mrs. Varick," he went on, "I am sure that you will agree with me in asserting that skulls and skeletons and disease are not fit subjects for poetical treatment."

"Yes," answered Pauline, "I think that they are

not beautiful — and for this reason I should condemn them."

"Then you will make a great mistake, Mrs. Varick," now quickly interposed Arthur Trevor. He passed one hand backward along the yellow mane of his hair while he thus spoke. But he still kept an arm about the neck of his friend, Corson. "I maintain," he continued, "that Corson has a perfect right to sing of autumnal things. A corpse is as legitimate a subject as a sunset. They are both morbid; they both mean what is moribund."

"Oh, but they are so different!" exclaimed the fat Miss Upton. "One is the work of Gawd, to delight man, and the other is — oh, dear! the other is — well, it's only a mere dead body! None of the great poets have ever written in that dreadful style, Mr. Trevor. Of course, I know that Mr. Corson has done some *powerful* work, but is it right to give people the shudders and horrors, as he does? Why not have sunshine in poetry, instead of gloom and misery?"

"Sunshine is commonplace," said Arthur Trevor.

"Very," said Mr. Corson.

"Sunshine means hope," declared Leander

Prawle. "It means evolution, development, progress."

"Art is art!" cried Trevor. "Sing of what you please, so long as your *technique* is good, so long as you have the right *chic*, the right *façon*, the right way of putting things!"

"True," said Corson. "I write of skulls and corpses because you can get new effects out of them. They have n't been done to death, like faith, and philanthropy, and freedom. Optimism is so tiresome, nowadays. All the Greeks are dead. Nôtre Dame stands intact, but the Parthenon is a ruin."

Leander Prawle shivered. "You can make clever rhymes about charnel-houses," he said, "but that is not poetry. You can deplore the allurements of women with green eyes and stony hearts, but you degrade womanhood while you do so. You " —

" Are you not bored? " whispered Kindelon, in his mellow Irish brogue to Pauline, as he just then stole to her side. " If so, let us walk away together."

Pauline slipped her hand into his proffered arm. "I was not bored," she said, as they moved off, "but I was just beginning to be. Are there nothing but belligerent poets here to-night?"

"Oh, you will find other sorts of people."

"But, who are these three wranglers, Mr. Trevor, Mr. Prawle, and Mr. Corson?"

Kindelon laughed. "They are fanatics," he said. "Each one believes himself a Milton in ability."

"Are they successful?"

"They send poems (with stamps inclosed) to the magazines, and have them rejected. They make believe to despise the magazines, but secretly they would give worlds to see their names in print. Heaven knows, the magazines print rubbish enough. But they are sensible in rejecting Arthur Trevor's poems, which are something in this style — I quote from memory: —

> "'The hot, fierce tiger-lily madly yearns
> To kill with passionate poison the wild moth
> That reels in drunken ecstasy above
> Its gorgeous bosom. . . .'

"Or in rejecting that bald-pated posing Corson's trash, which runs like this: —

> "'Death is far better than the loathsome lot
> Of kissing lips that soon must pale and rot,
> Of clasping forms that soon must cease their breath
> Within the black embrace of haughty death!'

"Or in declining to publish Mr. Leander Prawle's

buncombe, which sounds somewhat after this fashion :

> " ' Man shall one day develop to a god,
>   Though now he walks unwinged, unaureoled . . .
>   To-day we moil and mope — to-morrow's dawn
>   Shall bring us pinions to outsoar the stars.'

" That 's the sort of the thing this brave trio does. All poets are partially mad, of course. But then *they* are mad without being poets; it 's this that makes their lunacy so tiresome."

" And are they always quarrelling when they meet ? "

" Oh, they do it for effect. They are privately very good friends. They are all equally obscure; they 've no cause, yet, to hate one another. If one of them should get a book published before either of the other two, they would probably both abominate him in good earnest."

Just then a tall, sallow gentleman, with small, gray eyes and a nose like the beak of a carnivorous bird, laid his hand on Kindelon's sleeve.

" Powers has just asked me to write the Fenimore Cooper article for his new American Cyclopædia," declared this gentleman, whose name was Barrowe, and whom Pauline had already met.

"Well, you 're precisely the man," replied Kindelon. "Nobody can do it better."

"Precisely the man!" exclaimed Mr. Barrowe. "Perhaps I would be if I were not so overwhelmed with other duties — so unmercifully handicapped." He turned to Pauline. "I am devoted to literature, madam," he went on, "but I am forced into commerce for the purpose of keeping starvation away from my family and myself. There is the plain, unvarnished truth. And now, as it is, I return home after hours of hard, uncongenial work, to snatch a short interval between dinner-time and bed-time for whatever I can accomplish with my poor tired pen. My case is a peculiar and pathetic one — and this Powers ought to understand it. But, no; he comes to me in the coolest manner, and makes my doing that article for him a question of actual good-nature and friendly support. So, of course, I consent. But it shows a great want of delicacy in Powers. He knows well enough that I am obliged to neglect many social duties — that I should not even be here at this moment — that besides my daily business I am besieged with countless applications from literary people for all sorts of favors. Why, this very week, I have received no less than fourteen requests for my autograph. How are my wife and little ones to live if I am perpetually to oblige inconsiderate and thoughtless friends?"

"Your complaints would indicate," said Kindelon, rather dryly, "that Powers has not offered you the requisite cheque for proposed services."

Mr. Barrowe gave an irritated groan. "Kindelon!" he exclaimed, "do you know you can be a very rude man when you want?"

"You've told me that several times before, Barrowe," said Kindelon, quite jovially, moving on with Pauline.

He did this briskly enough to prevent the indignant Mr. Barrowe from making any further reply.

"I'm afraid you'll have trouble with that man," he said to Pauline, presently, "if you admit him into your *salon*."

"I have read some of his essays," she answered. "They are published abroad, you know. I thought them very clever."

"So they are — amazingly. But Barrowe himself is a sort of monomaniac. He believes that he is the most maltreated of authors. He is forever boring his friends with these egotistic lamentations. Now, the truth of the matter is that he has more to solidly congratulate himself upon than almost any author whom I know. He was sensible enough, years ago, to embark in commercial affairs. I forget just what he does; I think he is a wholesale druggist, or grocer. He writes brilliantly and with extraordinary speed. His neglect of social duties, as he calls them, is the purest nonsense. He goes wherever he is asked, and finds plenty of time for work besides. This request from Powers secretly pleases him. The new Cyclopædia is going to be a splendid series of volumes. But Barrowe must have his little elegiac moan over his blighted life."

"And the applications from fellow-authors?" asked Pauline. "The requests for autographs?"

"Pshaw! those are a figment of his fancy, I suspect. He imagines that he is of vast importance in the literary world. His sensitiveness is something ridiculous. He's a far worse monologuist than I am, which is surely saying a great deal; but if you answer him he considers it an interruption, and if you disagree with him he ranks it as impertinence. I think he rather likes me because I persistently, fearlessly, and relentlessly do both. But with all his faults, Barrowe has a large, warm heart. Still, it's astonishing how a fine and true character can often enshroud itself with repellent mannerisms, just as a firm breadth of sea-rock will become overcrusted with brittle barnacles. . . . Ah, Whitcomb, good evening."

A corpulent man, with silver-gray hair and a somewhat pensive expression, was the recipient of Kindelon's last cordial sentence of salutation. After he had made the needful introduction, Kindelon said, addressing Pauline while he regarded Mr. Whitcomb, —

" This is the author of no less than five standard histories."

" Kindelon is very good to call them standard, Mrs. Varick," said Mr. Whitcomb, in a voice quite as pensive as his face. "I wish that a few thousands more would only share his opinion."

" Oh, but they are gradually getting to do it, my dear Whitcomb!" declared Kindelon. "Don't make any mistake on that point. A few days ago I chanced to meet your publisher, Sours. Now, an author must stand pretty sure of success when his publisher pays him a round compliment."

" What did Sours say?" asked Mr. Whitcomb, with an almost boyish eagerness.

" He said," exclaimed Kindelon, "that Whitcomb was our coming American historian. There, my dear sir, what do you think of that?"

Mr. Whitcomb sadly shook his silver-gray head.

"I've been coming," he murmured, "ever since I was twenty-eight, and I shall be fifty-seven next May. I can't say that I think Sours's compliment meant much. It's got to be a sort of set phrase about me, that I'm coming. It never occurs to anybody to say that I've come, and I suppose it will not if I live to be eighty and totter round with white hair. No, I shall always be coming, coming. . . ."

As the gentleman repeated this final word he smiled with a kind of weary amiability, still shaking his gray head; and a moment later he had passed from sight.

"Mrs. Varick," now said a cold, rasping voice to Pauline, "have you managed to enjoy yourself, thus far? If you recollect, we were introduced a little while ago . . . Miss Cragge, you know."

"Oh, yes, I remember, Miss Cragge," said Pauline. "And I find it very pleasant here, I assure you."

Miss Cragge had given Kindelon a short nod, which he returned somewhat faintly. She was a lady of masculine height, with a square-jawed face, a rather mottled complexion, and a pair of slaty-blue eyes that looked at you very directly indeed from beneath a broad, flat forehead. She was dressed in a habit of some shabby gray stuff, and wore at her throat a large antique cameo pin, which might have been unearthed from an ancestral chest near the lavendered laces and faded love-letters of a long-dead grandmother. She was by no means an agreeable-looking lady; she was so ungentle in her quick, snapping speech and so unfeminine in her gaunt, bony, and almost towering figure, that she promptly impressed you with an idea of Nature having maliciously blended the harsher traits of both sexes in one austere personality, and at the same time leaving the result sarcastically feminine. She seldom addressed you without appearing to be bent on something which she thought you might have to tell her, or which she would like you very much to reveal. Her affirmations often had the sound of interrogatories. She had none of the tact, the grace, the *finesse* of the ordinary "interviewer;" she went to her task rough-handed and undexterous.

"I 'm glad you like it," she at once said to Pauline. "I know you've moved a good deal in fashionable society, and I should be gratified to learn how this change affects you."

"Quite refreshingly," returned Pauline.

"You don't feel like a fish out of water, then?" said Miss Cragge, with a sombre little laugh. "Or like a cat in a strange garret? . . . I saw you at the opera the other evening. You were with Mrs. Poughkeepsie and her daughter; I was down stairs in the orchestra. I go a good deal to places of amusement — in a professional way, you know; I 'm a dead-head, as the managers call it — I help to paper the house."

"You are rather too idiomatic, I fear," now said Kindelon, with a chilly ring in his tones, "for Mrs. Varick to understand you."

"Idiomatic is very good — excellent, in fact," replied Miss Cragge, with a pleasantry that barely missed being morose. "I suppose you mean that I am slangy. You 're always trying to snub me, Kindelon, but I don't mind you. You can't snub me — nobody can. I 'm too thick-skinned." Here the strangely self-poised lady laughed again, if the grim little sound that left her mirthless lips could really be called a laugh. "I know the Pough-keepsies by sight," she continued, re-addressing Pauline, "because it 's my business as a newspaper correspondent to get all the fashionable items that I can collect, and whenever I 'm at any public place of amusement where there 's a chance of meeting those upper-ten people, I always keep my eyes and ears open as wide as possible. I 'm cor-respondent for eight weekly papers outside of New York, besides doing work for two of the city dailies. I never saw anything like the craze for society gossip nowadays. One good story from high life, with a moderate spice of scandal in it, will pay me six times as well as anything else. They say I'm always hunting about for material, and no wonder that I am. The thing is bread and butter to me — and not much butter, either. You see, the rich classes here are getting to represent so large a body; so many people are trying to push themselves into society. And when they can't elbow their way into the swell balls and parties, why, the next best thing is to read about who were there, and what they had on, and who led the German, and what they ate and drank, and how the house was decorated. It seemed a queer enough business for me, at first; I started with grand ideas, but I've had to come down a good many pegs; I've had to pull in my horns. And now I don't mind it a bit; I suppose Kindelon would say that I enjoyed it ... eh, Kindelon? Why, Mrs. Varick, I used to write book-reviews for the New York 'Daily Criterion,' and my pay kept growing less and less. One day I wrote a very careful review of a book that I admired greatly — it was George Eliot's 'Middlemarch,' in fact. The editor-in-chief sent for me. He named the article, and then said, 'I hear that you wrote it. It's a very fine piece of work.' 'Thank you, sir,' I replied, with a tingle of gratification. 'Yes, a very fine piece of work, indeed,' continued the editor; 'I read it with much pleasure. But don't do that sort of thing again, Miss Cragge — we've no use for it on the 'Criterion.' After that I became less ambitious and more mercenary. There's no use pounding against stone walls. The reading public will have what it wants, and if I don't give it to them, somebody else will be only too glad to take my place. . . . By the way, Mrs. Varick, do you think that Miss Poughkeepsie is going to marry that Scotch earl — Lord Glen-artney?"

"I can't tell you, really," said Pauline. She had made up her mind to dislike Miss Cragge very much indeed. At the same time she felt a certain pity for her.

Kindelon began to press quietly forward, and Pauline, who still had his arm, by no means resisted this measure.

"I've been very candid," called Miss Cragge, while the two were slipping away from her. She spoke with even more than her usual blunt, curt manner. "It was because I knew Kindelon would be apt to say hard things of me, and I wanted to spike a few of his guns. But I hope I have n't shocked you, Mrs. Varick."

"Oh, not at all," said Pauline, as blandly as her feelings would permit. . . .

"You were a good deal disgusted, no doubt," said Kindelon, when they were beyond Miss Cragge's hearing.

"She is n't the most charming person I have ever met," replied Pauline. "I will grant you that."

"How amiably you denounce her! But I forget," he added. "Such a little time ago you were prepared to be exhilarated and . . . what was the other word? . . to fraternize with most of the company here." .

She chose not to heed the last stroke of light irony.

"Are you and Miss Cragge enemies?" she asked.

"Well, I abominate her, and she knows it. I rarely abominate anybody, and I think she knows that also. To my mind she is a conscienceless, hybrid creature. She is a result of a terrible modern license — the license of the Press. There is a frank confession, for a newspaper man like myself. But, between ourselves, I don't know where modern journalism, in some of its ferocious phases, is going to stop, unless it stops at a legislative veto. Miss Cragge would sacrifice her best friend (if she had any friends — which she has n't) to the requirements of what she calls 'an item.' She thinks no more of assailing a reputation, in her quest for so-termed 'material,' than a rat would think of carrying off a lump of cheese. She knows very well that I will never forgive her for having printed a lot of libellous folly about a certain friend of mine. He had written a rather harmless and weak novel of New York society, New York manners. Miss Cragge had some old grudge against him; I think it was on account of an adverse criticism which she believed him to have written regarding some dreary, amateurish poems for whose author she had conceived a liking. This was quite enough for Miss Cragge. She filled a column of the Rochester "Rocket," or the Topeka "Trumpet," or some such sheet, with irate fictions about poor Charley Erskine. He had no redress, poor fellow; she declared that he had slandered a pure, high-minded lady in society here by caricaturing her in his novel. She parodied some of poor Charley's rather fragile verses; she accused him of habitually talking fatuous stuff at a certain Bohemian sort of beer-garden which he had visited scarcely five times within that same year. Oh, well, the whole thing was so atrocious that I offered my friend the New York "Asteroid" in which to hurl back any epistolary thunder-bolt he should care to manufacture. But Charley would n't; he might have written a bad novel and worse poems, but he had sense enough to know that his best scorn lay in severe silence. Still, apart from all this, I have excellent reasons for shunning Miss Cragge, and I have told you some of them. She is the most aggravated form of the American newspaper correspondent, prowling about and seeking whom she may devour. I consider her a dangerous person, and I advise you not to allow her within your *salon*."

"Oh, I shan't," quickly answered Pauline. "You need not have counselled me on that point. It was quite unnecessary. I intend to pick and choose." She gave a long, worried sigh, now, which Kindelon just heard above the conversational hum surrounding them. "I am afraid it all comes to picking and choosing, everywhere," she went on. "Aunt Cynthia Poughkeepsie is perpetually doing it in *her* world, and I begin to think that there is none other where it must not be done."

Kindelon leaned his handsome crisp-curled head nearer to her own; he fixed his light-blue eyes, in which lay so warm and liquid a sparkle, intently upon the lifted gaze of Pauline.

"You are right," he said. "You will learn that, among other lessons, before you are much older. There is no such thing as not picking and choosing. Whatever the grade of life, it is always done by those who have any sort of social impulse. I believe it is done in Eighth Avenue and Avenue A, when they give parties in little rooms of tenement houses and hire a fiddler to speed the dance. There is always some Michael or Fritz who has been ostracized. The O'Haras and the Schneiders follow the universal law. Wherever three are gathered together, the third is pretty sure to be of questionable welcome. This is n't an ideal planet, my dear lady, and 'liberty' and 'fraternity' are good enough watchwords, but 'equality' never yet was one;—if I did n't remember my Buckle, my Spencer, my Huxley, and my dear old Whig Macaulay, I should add that it never *would* be one."

Just at this point Kindelon and Pauline found themselves face to face with two gentlemen who were both in a seemingly excited frame of mind. Pauline remembered that they had both been presented to her not long ago. She recollected their names, too; her memory had been nerved to meet all retentive exigencies. The large, florid man, with the bush of sorrel beard, was Mr. Bedlowe, and the smaller, smooth-shaven man, with the consumptive stoop and the professorial blue spectacles, was Mr. Howe.

Mr. Howe and Mr. Bedlowe were two novelists of very opposite repute. Kindelon had already caught a few words from the latter, querulously spoken.

"Ah, so you think modern novel-writing a sham, my dear Howe?" he said, pausing with his companion, while either gentleman bowed recognition to Pauline. "Isn't that rank heresy from the author of a book that has just been storming the town?"

"My book didn't storm the town, Kindelon," retorted Mr. Howe, lifting a hand of scholarly slimness and pallor toward his opaque goggles. "I wish it had," he proceeded, somewhat wearily. "No; Bedlowe and I were having one of our old quarrels. I say that we novelists of the Anglo-Saxon tongue are altogether too limited. That is what I mean by declaring that modern novel-writing is a sham."

"He means a great deal more, I'm sorry to say," here cried Mr. Bedlowe, who had a habit of grasping his sorrel beard in one hand and thrusting its end toward his hirsute lips as though they were about to be allured by some edible mouthful.

"He means, Kindelon, that because we have n't the shocking immoral latitude of the French race, we can't properly express ourselves in fiction. And he goes still further — Howe is always going still further every fresh time that I meet him. He says that if the modern novelist dared to express himself on religious subjects, he would be an agnostic."

"Precisely!" cried Mr. Howe, with the pale hand wavering downward from the eerie glasses. "But he does n't dare! If he did, his publisher would n't publish him!"

"My publisher publishes *me!*" frowned Mr. Bedlowe.

"Oh, you 're a pietist," was the excited answer. "At least, you go in for that when you write your novels. It pays, and you do it. I don't say that you do it *because* it pays, but" . . .

"You infer it," grumbled Mr. Bedlowe, "and that's almost the same as saying it." He visibly bristled here. "I 've got a wholesome faith," he proceeded, with hostility. "That 's why I wrote 'The Christian Knight in Armor' and 'The Doubtful Soul Satisfied.' Each of them sold seventy thousand copies apiece. There 's a proof that the public wanted them — that they filled a need."

"So does the 'Weekly Wake-Me-Up,'" said Mr. Howe, with mild disdain. "My dear Bedlowe, you have two qualities as a modern novel-writer which are simply atrocious — I mean, plot and piety. The natural result of these is popularity. But your popularity means nothing. You utterly neglect analysis "—

"I despise analysis!"

"You entirely ignore style "—

"I express my thoughts without affectation."

"Your characters are wholly devoid of subtlety "—

"I abhor subtlety!"

"You preach sermons "—

"Which thousands listen to!"

"You fail completely to represent your time "—

"My readers, who represent my time, don't agree with you."

"You end your books with marriages and christenings in the most absurdly old-fashioned way "—

"I end a story as every story *should* end. Sensible people have a sensible curiosity to know what becomes of hero and heroine."

"Curiosity is the vice of the vulgar novel-reader. Psychological interest is the one sole interest that should concern the more cultured mind.

And though you may sell your seventy thousand copies, I beg to assure you that " . . .

"Had we not heard quite enough of that hot squabble?" said Kindelon to Pauline, after he had pressed with her into other conversational regions, beyond the assault and defence of these two inimical novelists.

"I rather enjoyed it," said Pauline.

"They would have presently dragged us into their argument," returned Kindelon. "It was just as well that we retired without committing ourselves by an opinion. I should have sided with Howe, though I think him an extremist."

"I know some of Mr. Bedlowe's novels," said Pauline. "They are very popular in England. I thought them simply dire."

"And Howe is a real artist. He has a sort of cult here, though not a large one. What he says is true enough, in the main. The modern novelist dares not express his religious views, unless they be of the most conventional and tame sort. And how few fine minds are there to-day which are not rationalistic, unorthodox? A man like Bedlowe coins money from his milk-and-water platitudes, while Howe must content himself with the recognition of a small though devout circle . . . Did you meet the great American dramatist, by the way? I mean Mr. Osgood Paiseley. He is standing over yonder near the mantel . . . that slender little man with the abnormally massive head."

"Yes, I met him," returned Pauline. "He is coming this way."

"Have you any new dramatic work in preparation, Paiseley?" asked Kindelon, as the gentleman who had just been mentioned now drew near himself and Pauline.

"Yes," was Mr. Paiseley's reply. He spoke with a nasal tone and without much grammatical punctilio. "I've got a piece on hand that I'm doing for Mattie Molloy. Do you know her at all? She does the song-and-dance business with comedy variations. I think the piece'll be a go; it'll just suit her, I guess."

"Your last melodrama, 'The Brand of Cain,' was very successful, was it not?" pursued Kindelon.

"Well," said Mr. Paiseley, as he threw back an errant lock or two from his great width of swollen-looking forehead, "I'm afraid it isn't going to catch on so very well, after all. The piece is all right, but the company can't play it. Cooke guys his part because he don't like it, and does n't get a hand on some of the strongest lines that have been put into any actor's mouth for the past twenty years—fact! as sure as you're born! Moore makes up horribly, and Kitty Vane is so over-weighted that Miss Cowes, in a straight little part of only a few lengths, gets away with her for two scenes; and Sanders is awfully preachy. If I could have had my own say about casting the piece, we'd have turned away money for six weeks and made it a sure thing for the road. I mean for the big towns, not the one-night places; it's got too many utility-people to make it pay there. But I shan't offer anything more to the stock-theatres; after this, I'm going to fit stars."

Pauline turned a covertly puzzled look upon her companion. She seemed to be hearing a new language. And yet, although the words were all familiar enough, their collocation mystified her.

"You think there is more profit, then, in fitting stars," said Kindelon, "if there *is* less fame?"

Mr. Paiseley laughed, with not a little bitterness. "Oh, fame," he said, "is the infirmity of the young American dramatist. I've outgrown it. I used to have it. But what's the use of fighting against France and England in the stock-theatres? Give me a fair show there, and I can draw bigger money than Dennery or Sardou— don't you make any mistake! But those foreign fellows are always crowding us natives out of New

York. The managers hem and smirk over our
pieces, and say they're good enough, but they've
got something that's running well at the Porte
Sang Martang or the Odeun in Paris. The best
we can do is to have our plays done by a scratch
company at some second-rate house, or, if it's a
first-class house, they give us bad time. No, I
fit travelling stars at so much cash down, and so
much royalty afterward — that is, when I can't get
a percentage on the gross. I don't work any more
for fame; I want my dinner." . . .

"Your friend takes a rather commercial view of
the American stage," said Pauline to Kindelon,
after they had again moved onward.

"I am sorry to say that it is almost the only
view taken by any of our dramatists. Paiseley
is thoroughly representative of his class. They
would all like to write a fine play, but they nearly
all make the getting of money their primary object. Now, I do not believe that the lust of gain
has ever been a foremost incentive in the produc-
tion of any great mental achievement. Our novels
and poems are to-day better than our plays, I
think, because they are written with a more artistic and a less monetary stimulus. The rewards of
the successful playwright may mean a fortune to
him; he always remembers that when he begins,

and he usually begins for the reason that he does remember it." . . .

Pauline had glimpses of not a few more individualities, that evening, before she at length took her leave.

"Well, how have you enjoyed it?" asked Kindelon, as they were being driven home together.

"I have not entirely enjoyed it," was the slow answer.

"You have been disappointed?"

"Yes."

"But your purpose of the *salon* still remains good?"

"Indeed it does!" she exclaimed with eagerness. "I shall begin my work — I shall issue my invitations in a few days. Mrs. Dares will no doubt supply me with a full list of names and addresses."

"And you will invite everybody?"

"Oh, by no means. I shall pick and choose."

"Beware of calamity!" said Kindelon. And his voice was so odd a blending of the jocose and serious that she could ill guess whether he were in earnest or not.

VIII.

PAULINE now began in excellent earnest the preparations for embarking upon her somewhat quaint enterprise. During the next three or four days she saw a good deal of Kindelon. They visited together the little editorial sanctum in Spruce Street, where Mrs. Dares sat dictating some of her inexhaustible "copy" to a pale and rather jaded-looking female amanuensis. The lady received her visitors with a most courteous hospitality. Pauline had a sense of shocking idleness as she looked at the great cumbrous writing-desk covered with ink-stains, files or clippings of newspapers, and long ribbon-like rolls of "proof." Her own fine garments seemed to crackle ostentatiously beside the noiseless folds of Mrs. Dares's work-day cashmere.

"We shall not take up much of your valuable time," she said to the large-eyed, serious little lady. "We have called principally to ask a favor of you, and I hope you will not think it a presumptuous request."

"I hope it is presumptuous," said Mrs. Dares,

"for that, provided I can grant it at all, will make it so much pleasanter to grant."

"You may be sure," cried Kindelon gayly to Pauline, "that you have made a complete conquest of Mrs. Dares. She is usually quite miserly with her compliments. She puts me on the wretched allowance of one a year."

"Perhaps you don't deserve a more liberal income," said Pauline. Then she re-addressed Mrs. Dares. "I want to ask you," she proceeded, with a shy kind of venture in her tone, "if you will kindly loan me your visiting-book for a little while."

"My visiting-book?" murmured Mrs. Dares. Then she slowly shook her head, while the pale girl at the desk knitted her brows perplexedly, as though she had encountered some tantalizing foreign word. "I would gladly lend it if I had one," Mrs. Dares went on; "but I possess no such article."

"Good gracious!" exclaimed Pauline, with an involuntary surprise that instantly afterward she regretted as uncivil. "You *have* none!"

But Mrs. Dares did not seem to detect the least incivility in Pauline's amazement.

"No, my dear Mrs. Varick, I have no need of a visiting-book, for I have no time to visit."

"But you surely have some sort of list, have you not?" now inquired Kindelon.

Mrs. Dares lightly touched her forehead. "Only here in my memory," she said, "and that is decidedly an imperfect list. My guests understand that to be invited to one of my evenings is to be invited to all. I suppose that in the fashionable world," she proceeded, fixing her great dark eyes on Pauline, "it is wholly different. There, matters of this sort are managed with much ceremony, no doubt."

"With much trivial ceremony," said Pauline. "A little scrap of pasteboard there represents an individuality — and in just as efficient manner as if it were truly the person represented. To be in society, as it is called, is to receive a perpetual shower of cards. I strongly doubt if many people ever care to meet in a truly social way those whose company they pretend to solicit. There are few more perfect mockeries in that most false and mocking life, than the ordinary visit of etiquette." Pauline here gave a little meaning smile as she briefly paused. "But I suppose you will understand, Mrs. Dares," she continued, "that I regret your having no regular list. I wanted to borrow it — and with what purpose I am sure you can readily imagine."

"Yes," was the reply. "My daughter Cora shall prepare you one, however. She has an admirable memory. If she fails in the matter of addresses, there is the directory as a help, you know. And so your idea about the *salon* is unchanged?"

"It is unalterable," said Pauline, with a laugh. "But I hate so to trouble your daughter."

"She will not think it any trouble," said Kindelon quickly.

Pauline looked at him with a slight elevation of the brows. "You speak confidently for Miss Cora," she said.

Kindelon lifted one hand, and waved it a trifle embarrassedly. "Oh, I have always found her so accommodating," he answered.

"Yes, Cora is always glad to please those whom she likes," said Mrs. Dares. . . .

A little later Pauline and Kindelon took leave of their hostess. They had been driven to Spruce Street in the carriage of the former, and as they quitted the huge building in which Mrs. Dares's tiny sanctum was situated, Kindelon said to his companion: "You shall return home at once?"

Pauline gave a careless laugh. She looked about her at all the commercial hurry and bustle of the placarded, vehicle-thronged street. "I have nowhere else to go just at present," she said. "Not that I should not like to stay down town, as you call it, a little longer. The noise and activity please me. . . . Oh, by the way," she added, "did you not say that you must repair to your office?"

"The 'Asteroid' imperatively claims me," said Kindelon, taking out his watch. "Only twelve o'clock," he proceeded; "I thought it later. Well, I have at least an hour at your service still. Have you any commands?"

"Where on earth could we pass your hour of leisure?" said Pauline. "It would probably not be proper if I accompanied you into the office of the 'Asteroid.'"

"It would be sadly dull."

"Then I will drive up town after I have left you there."

"Why not remain *down* town, since the change pleases you?"

"Driving aimlessly about for a whole hour?"

"By no means. I have an idea of what we might do. I think you might not find the idea at all disagreeable. If you will permit, I will give your footman an order, and plan for you a little surprise."

"Do so, by all means," said Pauline lightsomely,

entering the carriage. "I throw myself upon your mercy and your protection."

Kindelon soon afterward seated himself at her side, and the carriage was immediately borne into the clamorous region of what we term lower Broadway.

"I hope I shall like your surprise," said Pauline, as she leaned back against the cushions, not knowing how pretty she looked in her patrician elegance of garb and person. "But we will not talk of it; I might guess what it is if we did, and that would spoil all. My faith in you shall be blind and unquestioning, and I shall expect a proportionately rich reward. . . . What gulfs of difference lie between that interesting little Mrs. Dares and most of the women whom I have met! People tell us that we must travel to see life. I begin to think that one great city like New York can give us the most majestic experience, if only we know how to receive it. Take my Aunt Cynthia Poughkeepsie, for example, and compare her with Mrs. Dares! A whole continent seems to lie between them, and yet they are continually living at scarcely a stone's-throw apart."

Kindelon gave a brisk, acquiescent nod.

"True enough," he said. "Travel shows us only the outsides of men and women. We go abroad to discover better what profits of observation lie at home " . . .

The carriage at length stopped.

"Is my surprise all ready to burst upon me?" asked Pauline, at this point.

"Yes. Its explosion is now imminent," said Kindelon, with dry solemnity of accent.

Pauline, after she had alighted, surveyed her surroundings for a moment, and then said, —

"I knew we were approaching the Battery, but I did not suppose you meant to stop there. And why *have* you stopped, pray?"

Kindelon pointed toward a distant flash of water glimpsed between the nude black boughs of many high trees. "You can't think what a delightful stroll we could take over yonder," he said, "along the esplanade. The carriage could wait here for us, you know."

"Certainly," acceded Pauline.

They soon entered the noble park lying on their right. It was a day of unusual warmth for that wintry season, but the air freshened and sharpened as they drew further seaward. There are many New Yorkers to whom our beautiful Battery is but a name, and Pauline was one of them. As she neared the rotund wooden building of Castle Garden, a wholly novel and unexpected sight awaited her.   Not long ago one of the great ocean-steamers had discharged here many German immigrants, and some of these had come forth from the big sea-fronting structure beyond, to meet the stares of that dingy, unkempt rabble which always collects, on such occasions, about its doorways. Pauline and Kindelon paused to watch the poor dazed-looking creatures, with their pinched, vacuous faces, their timid miens, their coarse, dirty bundles. The women mostly had blond braids of hair matted in close coils against the backs of their heads; they wore no bonnets, and one or two of them led a bewildered, dull-eyed child by the hand, while one or two more clasped infants to their breasts, wrapped in soiled shawls. The men had a spare, haggard, slavish demeanor; the liberal air and sun, the very amplitude and brilliancy of sky and water, seemed to cow and depress them; they slunk instead of walking; there was something in their visages of an animal suggestion; they did not appear entirely human, and made you recall the mythic combinations of man and beast.

"They are Germans, I suppose," said Kindelon to Pauline; "or perhaps they hail from some of the Austrian provinces. Many of my own country people, the Irish, are not much less shocking to behold when they first land here."

"These do not shock me," said Pauline; "they sadden me. They look as if they had not wit enough to understand whither they had come, but quite enough to feel alarmed and distrustful of their present environment."

"This drama of immigration is constantly unfolding itself here, day after day," answered Kindelon. "It surely has its mournful side, but you, as an American, ought by all means to discern its bright one. These poor souls are the social refuse of Europe; they are the pathetic fugitives from vile and time-honored abuses; they are the dreary consequences of kingdoms and empires. Their state is almost brutish, as you see; they don't think themselves half as far above the brute as you think them, depend upon it. They have had manhood and womanhood crushed into the dust for generations. It is as much their hereditary instinct to fawn and crawl as it is for a dog to bark or a cat to lap milk. They represent the enlightened and thrifty peasantry over-sea. Bah! how it sickens a man to consider that because a few insolent kings must have their hands kissed and their pride of rule glutted, millions of their people are degraded into such doltish satires upon humanity!   But I mentioned the bright side of this question, from the American standpoint."

"Yes," said Pauline quickly, lifting her face to his.   "I hope it is really a bright side."

"It is — very.   America receives these pitiful wretches, and after a few short months they are regenerated, transformed.   There has never, in the history of the world, been a nation of the same magnificent hospitality as this.   Before such droves of deplorable beings any other nation would shut her ports or arm her barriers, in strong affright.   But America (which I have always thought a much more terse and expressive name than the United States) does nothing of the sort.   With a superb kindness, which has behind it a sense of unexampled power, she bids them all welcome.   And in a little while they breathe her vitalizing air with a new and splendid result. They forget the soldiers who kicked them, the tyrants who made them shoulder muskets in defence of thrones, the taxes wrung from their scant wages that princes might dance and feast.   They forget all this gross despotism; they begin to live; their very frames and features change; their miserable past is like a broken fetter flung gladly away.   And America does all this for them — this, which no other country has done or can do!"

He spoke with a fine heat, an impressive enthusiasm. Pauline, standing beside him, had earnestly fixed her look upon his handsome, virile face, noting the spark that pierced his light-blue eyes, between the black gloss of their lashes, and the little sensitive tremor that disturbed his nostril. She had never felt more swayed by his force of personality than now. She had never felt more keenly than now that his manful countenance and shape were both fit accompaniments of an important and robust nature.

"And what does America really do with these poor, maltreated creatures, after having greeted and domesticated them?" came her next words, filled with an appealing sincerity of utterance.

Something appeared suddenly to have changed Kindelon's mood. He laughed shortly and half turned away.

"Oh," he said, in wholly altered voice, "if they are Irish she sometimes makes Tammany politicians of them, and if they are Germans she sometimes turns them into howling socialists."

"Do you mean what you say?" exclaimed Pauline almost indignantly.

He bent his head and looked at her intently, for a moment, with a covert play of mirth under the crisp, dark flow of his mustache.

"I am afraid that I do," he replied, with another laugh.

"Then you think this grand American hospitality of which you have just spoken to be a failure — a sham?"

"No, no — far from that," he said rapidly, and with recurring seriousness. "I was only going back to the dark side of the question — that is all. You know, I told you it had both its dark and its bright side. . . . Come, let us leave this rabble. You have not really seen the Battery yet. Its true splendors lie just beyond." . . .

They were presently strolling along the stone-paved esplanade, with its granite posts connected by loops of one continuous iron chainwork. To the south they had a partial view of Brooklyn, that city which is a sort of reflective and imitative New York, with masts bristling from her distant wharves and more than a single remote church-spire telling of the large religious impulse which has given her a quaint ecclesiastical fame. But westward your eye could traverse the spacious bay until it met the dull-red semicircle of Fort Columbus, planted low and stout upon the shore of Governor's Island, and the soft, swelling, purplish hills of Staten Island, where they loomed still further beyond. Boats of all shapes and kinds were passing over the luminous waters, from the squat, ugly tug, with its hoarse whistle, to the huge black bulk of an Atlantic steamer, bound for transpontine shores and soon to move majestically ocean-ward through the fair sea-gate of the Narrows. A few loiterers leaned against the stone posts, and a few more lounged upon the seats ranged further inland along this salubrious marine promenade. Back among the turfy levels that stretched broadly between the flagged pathways, you saw the timorous green of hardy grass, where an occasional pale wreath of unmelted snow yet lingered. People were passing to and fro, with steps that rang hollow on the hard pavement. If you listened intently you could catch a kind of dreamy hum from the vast city, which might almost be said to begin its busy, tumultuous life here in this very spot, thence pushing through many a life-crowded street and avenue, sheer on to the rocky fields and goat-haunted gutters of dreary Harlem.

"What a glorious bay it is!" exclaimed Kindelon, while he and Pauline stood on the breezy esplanade. "There never was a city with more royal approaches than New York."

"That fort yonder," said Pauline, "will perhaps thunder broadsides, one day, at the fleet of an invading enemy. This is still such a young city compared with those of other lands. . . . I suppose these waters, centuries later, will see grand sights, as civilization augments."

"Perhaps they may see very mournful ones," objected Kindelon.

"But you are an evolutionist," declared Pauline, with a priggish little pursing of the lips that he found secretly very amusing. "You believe that everything is working toward nobler conditions, though you laughed at Leander Prawle, the optimistic poet, the other evening, for his roseate prophecies about the human race."

"Oh, I 'm an evolutionist," answered Kindelon. "I believe it will all come right by-and-by, like the gigantic unravelling of a gigantic skein . . . But such views don't prevent me from feeling the probability of New York being reduced to ashes more than once in the coming centuries."

"Oh, yes, I remember," said Pauline. "There are often the apparent retrogressions — rhythmic variations of movement which temporarily retard all progress in societies."

Kindelon burst into one of his mellowest and heartiest laughs. "You are delicious," he said, "when you try to recollect your Herbert Spencer.

You make me think of a flower that has been dropped among the leaves of an Algebra."

"I am not at all sure that I like your simile," said Pauline, tossing her head somewhat. "It is pleasant to be likened to a flower, but in this case it is rather belittling. And if it comes to recollecting my Herbert Spencer, perhaps the process is not one of very violent *effort*, either."

"Oh," said Kindelon ruefully, "I have offended you."

A sunny smile broke from her lips the next moment. "I can't be offended," she replied, "when I think how you rebuked my absurd outburst of pedantry. Ah! truly a little knowledge *is* a dangerous thing, and I am afraid I have very little. . . . How lovely it all is, here," she proceeded, changing the subject, as they now began to move onward, while they still kept close to the edge of the smooth-paven terrace. "And what a pity that our dwelling-houses should all be away from the water! My grandparents — or my great-grandparents, I forget which — once lived close to the Battery. I recollect poor mamma telling me that I had an ancestress whom they used to call the belle of Bowling Green."

"That was certainly in the days before commerce had seized every yard of these unrivalled water-fronts," laughed Kindelon. "Babylon on its Euphrates, or Nineveh on its Tigris, could not eclipse New York in stately beauty if mansions were built along its North and East rivers. But trade is a tyrant, as you see. She concedes to you Fifth Avenue, but she denies you anything more poetic."

"I wonder who is the belle of Bowling Green now?" said Pauline, looking up at her companion with a serio-comic smile.

He shook his head. "I am afraid your favored progenitress was the last of the dynasty."

"Oh, no," dissented Pauline, appearing to muse a trifle. "I fancy there is still a belle. Perhaps she has a German or an Irish name."

"It may be Kindelon," he suggested.

"No — it is something more usual than that. If she is not a Schmitt I suspect that she is an O'Brien. I picture her as pretty, but somewhat delicate; she works in some dreadful factory, you know, not far away, all through the week. But on Sunday she emerges from her narrow little room in a tenement-house, brave and smart as you please. The beaux fight for her smiles as they join her, and she knows just how to distribute them; she is a most astute little coquette, in her way."

"And the beaux? Are they worthy of her coquetries?"

"Oh, well, she thinks them so. I fear that most of them have soiled finger-nails, and that their Sunday coats fit them very ill . . . But now let me pursue my little romance. The poor creature is terribly fond of one of them. There is always one, you know, dearer than the rest."

"Is there?" said Kindelon oddly. "You're quite elucidating. I did n't know that."

"Don't be sarcastic," reproved Pauline with mock grimness. "Sarcasm is always the death of romance. I have an idea that the secretly-adored one is more of a convert than all his fellows to the beautifying influences of soap. His Sunday face is bright and fresh; it looks conscientiously washed."

"And his finger-nails? Does your imagination also include those, or do they transcend its limits?"

"I have a vague perception of their relative superiority . . . Pray let me continue without your prosaic interruptions. Poor little Mary . . . Did 1 not say that her first name was Mary, by-the-by?"

"I have been under the impression for several seconds that you called her Bridget."

"Very well. I will call her so, if you insist. Poor little Bridget, who steals forth, *endimanchée* and expectant, fails for an hour or two to catch a glimpse of her beloved. She is beginning to be sadly bored by the society of her present three, four, or five admirers, when suddenly she sees the Beloved approaching. Then she brightens and becomes quite sparklingly animated. And when her Ideal draws near, twirling a licorice cane — I insist upon having her Ideal twirl a licorice cane — she receives him with an air of the most unconcerned indifference. It is exquisite to observe the calm, careless way in which she asks him " . . .

"Pardon me," interrupted Kindelon, with a short and almost brusque tone, "but is not this gentleman coming toward us your cousin?"

"My cousin?" faltered Pauline.

"Yes — Mr. Courtlandt Beekman."

Pauline did not answer, for she had already caught sight of Courtlandt, advancing in her own direction from that of the South Ferry, which she and Kindelon were now rather near. She stopped abruptly in her walk, and perceptibly colored.

A moment afterward Courtlandt saw both herself and her escort. He showed great surprise, and then quickly conquered it. As he came forward, Pauline gave a shrill, nervous laugh. "I suppose you feel like asking me what on earth I am doing here," she said, in by no means her natural voice, and with a good deal of fluttered insecurity about her demeanor.

"I should n't think that necessary," replied Courtlandt. His sallow face had not quite its usual hue, but nothing could be steadier than the cool light of his eye. "It 's very evident that you are taking a stroll with Mr. Kindelon." He then extended his hand, cased in a yellow dogskin glove, to Kindelon. "How are you?" he said to the man whom he entirely disliked, in a tone of neutral civility.

"Very well, this pleasant day," returned Kindelon, jovially imperturbable. "And you, Mr. Beekman?"

"Quite well, thanks." He spoke as if he were stating a series of brief commercial facts. "I had some business with a man over in Brooklyn, and took this way back to my office, which is only a street or two beyond." He turned toward the brilliant expanse of the bay, lifting a big silver-knobbed stick which he carried, waving it right and left. "Very nice down here, is n't it?" he went on. His look now dwelt in the most casual way upon Pauline. "Well, I must be off," he continued. "I've a lot of business to-day."

He had passed them, when Pauline, turning, said composedly but sharply:

"Can't I take you to your office, Court?"

"Thanks, no. I won't trouble you. It's just a step from here." He lifted his hat — an act which he had already performed a second or so previously — and walked onward. He had not betrayed the least sign of annoyance all through this transient and peculiarly awkward interview. He had been precisely the same serene, quiescent, demure Courtlandt as of old.

Pauline stood for some little time watching him as he gradually disappeared. When the curve near Castle Garden hid him, she gave an impatient, irritated sigh.

"You seem vexed," said Kindelon, who had been intently though furtively regarding her.

"I am vexed," she murmured. Her increased color was still a deep rose.

"Is there anything very horrible in walking for a little while on the Battery?" he questioned.

She gave a broken laugh. "Yes," she answered. "I'm afraid there is."

Kindelon shrugged his shoulders. "But surely you are your own mistress?"

"Rather too much so," she said, with lowered eyes. "At least that is what people will say, I suppose."

"I thought you were above idle and aimless comments."

"Let us go back to the carriage."

"By all means, if you prefer it."

They reversed their course, and moved along for some time in silence. "I think you must understand," Pauline suddenly said, lifting her eyes to Kindelon's face.

"I understand," he replied, with hurt seriousness, "that I was having one of the pleasantest hours I have ever spent, until that man accosted us like a grim fate."

"You must not call my cousin Courtlandt 'that man.' I don't like it."

"I am sorry," he said curtly, and a little doggedly. "I might have spoken more ill of him, but I didn't."

Pauline was biting her lips. "You have no right to speak ill of him," she retorted. "He is my cousin."

"That is just the reason why I held my tongue."

"You don't like him, then?"

"I do not."

"I can readily comprehend it."

Kindelon's light-blue eyes fired a little under their black lashes. " You say that in a way I do not understand," he answered.

" You and Courtlandt are of a different world."

" I am not a combination of a fop and a parson, if you mean that."

Pauline felt herself grow pale with anger as she shot a look up into her companion's face.

" You would not dare say that to my cousin himself," she exclaimed defiantly, " though you dare say it to me ! "

Kindelon had grown quite pale. His voice trembled as he replied. " I dare do anything that needs the courage of a man," he said. " I thought you knew me well enough to be sure of this."

" Our acquaintance is a recent one," responded Pauline. She felt nearly certain that she had shot a wounding shaft in those few words, but she chose to keep her eyes averted and not see whether wrath or pain had followed its delivery.

A long silence followed. They had nearly reached her carriage when Kindelon spoke.

" You are in love with your cousin," he said.

She threw back her head, laughing ironically. " What a seer you are ! " she exclaimed. " How did you guess that ? "

"Ah," he answered her, with a melancholy gravity, "you will not deny it!"

She repeated her laugh, though it rang less bitterly than before. She had expected him to meet her irony in a much more rebellious spirit.

"I don't like to have my blood-relations abused in my hearing," she said. "I am in love with all of them, that way, if that is the way you mean."

"That is not the way I mean."

They were now but a few yards from the waiting carriage. The footman, seeing them, descended from his box, and stood beside the opened door.

"I shall not return with you," continued Kindelon, "since I perceive you do not wish my company longer. But I offer you my apologies for having spoken disparagingly of your cousin. I was wrong, and I beg your pardon."

With the last words he extended his hand. Pauline took it.

"I have not said that I did not wish your company," she answered, "but if you choose to infer so, it is your own affair."

"I do infer so, and I infer more. . . . It is best that I — I should not see you often, like this. There is a great difference between you and me. That cousin of yours hated me at sight. Your aunt, Mrs. Poughkeepsie, hated me at sight as well. Perhaps their worldly wisdom was by no means to blame, either. . . . Oh, I understand more than you imagine ! "

There was not only real grief in Kindelon's voice, but an under-throb of real passion.

"Understand?" Pauline murmured. "What do you understand?"

"That you are as stanch and loyal as ever to your old traditions. That this idea of change, of amelioration, of casting aside your so-called patrician bondage, has only the meaning of a dainty gentlewoman's dainty caprice . . . that "—

His voice broke. It almost seemed to her as if his large frame was shaken by some visible tremor. She had no thought of being angry at him now.

She pitied him, and yet with an irresistible impulse her thought flew to Cora Dares, the sweet-faced young painter, and what she herself had of late grown to surmise, to suspect. A sort of involuntary triumph blent itself with her pity, on this account.

She spoke in a kind voice, but also in a firm one. She slightly waved her hand toward the adjacent carriage. "Will you accompany me, then?" she asked.

He looked at her fixedly for an instant. Then he shook his head. "No," he answered. "Good-by." He lifted his hat, and walked swiftly away.

She had seen his eyes just before he went. Their look haunted her. She entered the carriage, and was driven up town. She told herself that he had behaved very badly to her. But she did not really think this. She was inwardly thrilled by a strange, new pleasure, and she had shed many tears before reaching home.

IX

THE excitement of Pauline had by no means passed when she regained her home. Kindelon's last words still rang in her ears.

She declared to herself that it was something horrible to have been called a dainty gentlewoman. At the same time, she remembered the impetuosity of his address, and instinctively forgave even while she condemned. Still, there remained with her a certain severe resentful sense. "What right," she asked herself, "has this man to undervalue and contemn my purpose? Is it not based upon a proper and worthy impulse? Is egotism at its root? Is not a wholesome disgust there, instead? Have I not seen, with a radical survey, the aimless folly of the life led by men and women who presume to call themselves social leaders and social grandees? Has Kindelon any shred of excuse for telling me to my face that I am a mere politic trimmer?"

She had scarcely been home an hour before she

received a note from Cora Dares. The note was brief, but very accurate in meaning. It informed Pauline that Mrs. Dares had just sent a message to her daughter's studio, and that Cora would be glad to receive Mrs. Varick on that or any succeeding afternoon, with the view of a consultation regarding the proposed list of guests.

Pauline promptly resolved to visit Cora that same day. She ordered her carriage, and then countermanded the order. Not solely because of the pleasant weather, and not solely because she was in a mood for walking, did she thus alter her first design. She reflected that there might be a touch of apparent ostentation in the use of a carriage to call upon this young self-supporting artist. She even made a change of toilet, and robed herself in a street costume much plainer than that which she had previously worn.

Cora Dares's studio was on Fourth Avenue, and one of many others in a large building which artists principally peopled. It was in the top floor of this structure, and was reached, like her mother's sanctum, by that most simplifying of modern conveniences, the elevator. Pauline's knock at a certain rather shadowy door in an obscure passage was at once answered by Cora herself.

The studio was extremely pretty; you saw this

at a glance. Its one ample window let in a flood of unrestricted sunlight. Its space was small, and doubtless for this reason a few brilliant draperies and effective though uncostly embellishments had made its interior bloom and glow picturesquely enough. But it contained no ornament of a more alluring pattern than Cora herself, as Pauline soon decided.

"Pray don't let me disturb you in your painting," said the latter, after an exchange of greetings had occurred. "I see that you were busily engaged at your easel. I hope you can talk and paint at the same time."

"Oh, yes," said Cora, with her bright, winsome smile. She was dressed in some dark, soft stuff, whose sombre hue brought into lovely relief the chestnut ripples of her hair and the placid refinement of her clear-chiselled face. "But if I am to give you a list of names," she went on, "that will be quite another matter."

"Oh, never mind the list of names," replied Pauline, who had just seated herself. "I mean, not for the present. It will be more convenient for you, no doubt, to send me this list to-morrow or next day. Meanwhile I shall be willing to wait very patiently. I am in no great hurry, Miss Dares. It was exceedingly kind of you to communicate with me in this expeditious way. And now, if you will only extend your benevolence a little further and give an hour or two of future leisure toward the development of my little plan, I shall feel myself still more in your debt."

Cora nodded amiably. "Perhaps that *would* be the better arrangement," she said. Her profile was now turned toward Pauline, as she stood in front of her canvas and began to make little touches upon it with her long, slim brush. "I think, Mrs. Varick, that I can easily send you the list to-morrow. I will make it out to-night; I shall not forget anybody; at least I am nearly sure that I shall not."

"You are more than kind," said Pauline. She paused for a slight while, and then added: "You spend all day here, Miss Dares?"

"All day," was Cora's answer; and the face momentarily turned in Pauline's direction, with its glimpse of charming, dimpled chin, with the transitory light from its sweet, blue, lustrous eyes, affected her as a rarity of feminine beauty. "But I often have my hours of stupidity," Cora continued. "It is not so with me to-day. I have somehow seized my idea and mastered it, such as it is. You can see nothing on the canvas as yet. It is all obscure and sketchy."

"It is still very vague," said Pauline. "But have you no finished pictures?"

"Oh, yes, five or six. They are some yonder, if you choose to look at them."

"I do choose," Pauline replied, rising. She went toward the wall which Cora had indicated by a slight wave of her brush.

The pictures were four in number. They were without frames. Pauline examined each attentively. She knew nothing of Art in a technical and professional way; but she had seen scores of good pictures abroad; she knew what she liked without being able to tell why she liked it, and not seldom it befell that she liked what was intrinsically and solidly good.

"You paint figures as if you had studied in foreign schools," she said, quite suddenly, turning toward her hostess.

"I studied in Paris for a year," Cora replied. "That was all mamma could afford for me." And she gave a sad though by no means despondent little laugh.

"You surely studied to advantage," declared Pauline. "Your color makes me think of Henner ... and your flesh-tints, too. And as for these two landscapes, they remind me of Daubigny. It is a proof of your remarkable talent that you should paint both landscapes and figure-pieces with so much positive success."

Cora's face was glowing, now. "You have just named two artists," she exclaimed, "whose work I have always specially admired and loved. If I resemble either of them in the least, I am only too happy and thankful!"

Pauline was silent for several minutes. She was watching Cora with great intentness. "Ah! how I envy you!" she at length murmured, and as she thus spoke her voice betrayed excessive feeling.

"I thought *you* envied nobody," answered Cora, somewhat wonderingly.

Pauline gave a little soft cry. "You mean because I am rich, no doubt!" she said, a kind of melancholy sarcasm tinging her words.

"Riches mean a great deal," said Cora.

"But if you have no special endowment that separates you from the rest of the world, you are still a woman."

"I am not sorry to be a woman."

"No! because you are a living protest against the inferiority of our sex. You can do something; you need not forever have men doing something for you, like the great majority of us!" Pauline's gray eyes had kindled, and her lips were slightly tremulous as they began to shape her next sentence. "Most of us *are* sorry to be women," she went on, "but I think a great many of us are sorry to be the sort of women fate or circumstance makes us. There is the galling trouble. If we have no gift, like yours, that can compel men's recognition and respect, we must content ourselves with being merged into the big commonplace multitude. And to be merged into the big commonplace multitude is to be more or less despised. This may sound like the worst kind of cynicism, but I assure you, Miss Dares, that it is by no means as flippant as that. I have seen more of life than you . . . why not? You perhaps have heard a fact or two about my past. I have *had* a past — and not a pleasant one, either. And experience (which is the name we give our disappointments, very often) has taught me that if we could see down to the innermost depth of any good man's liking for any good woman, we would find there an undercurrent of real contempt."

"Contempt!" echoed Cora. She had slightly thrown back her head, either in dismay or denial.

"Yes — contempt," asseverated Pauline. "I believe, in all honesty, at this hour, that if the charm which our sex exerts over the other — the physical fascination, and the fascination of sentiment, tenderness, idealization — had never existed, we would have been literally crushed out of being long ago. Men have permitted us to live thus far through the centuries, not because we are weaker than they, but because some extraordinary and undiscoverable law has made them bow to our weakness instead of destroying it outright. They always destroy every other thing weaker than themselves, except woman. They have no compunction, no hesitation. History will show you this, if you accept its annals in an unbiassed spirit. They either eat the lower animals, or else put them into usages of the most severe labor. They leave woman unharmed because Nature has so commanded them. But here they are the slaves of an edict which they obey more blindly, more instinctively, than even the best of them know."

"I can't believe that these are your actual views!" now exclaimed Cora. "I can't believe that you rate the sacred emotion of love as something to be discussed like a mere scientific problem!"

Pauline went up to the speaker and stood close beside her while she responded, —

"Ah! my dear Miss Dares, the love between man and woman is entitled to no more respect than the law of gravitation. Both belong to the great unknown scheme. We may shake our heads in transcendental disapprobation, but it is quite useless. The loftiest affection of the human heart is no more important and no more mysterious than the question of why Newton's apple fell from the tree or why a plant buds in spring. All causes are unknown, and to seek their solution is to idly grope."

Cora was regarding Pauline, as the latter finished, with a look full of sad interest. "You speak like . . . like some one whom we both know," she said hesitatingly. "You speak as if you did not believe in God."

"I do not disbelieve in God," quickly answered Pauline. "The carelessly-applied term of 'atheist' is to my thinking a name fit only for some pitiable braggart. He who denies the existence of a God is of no account among people of sense; but he who says, 'I am ignorant of all that concerns the conceivability of a God' has full right to express such ignorance."

Cora slowly inclined her head. "That is the way I have heard *him* talk," she said, almost musingly. Then she gave a quick glance straight into Pauline's watchful eyes. "I — I mean," she added, confusedly, as if she had betrayed herself into avowing some secret reflection, "that Mr.

Kindelon has more than once spoken in a similar way."

"Mr. Kindelon?" replied Pauline, with a gentle, peculiar, interrogative emphasis. "And did you agree with him?"

"No," swiftly answered Cora. "I have a faith that he cannot shake — that no one can shake! But he has not tried to do so; I must render him that justice."

Pauline turned away, with a faint laugh. "The wise men, who have thought and therefore doubted," she returned, "are often fond of orthodoxy in the women whom they like. They think it picturesque."

She laughed again, and Cora's eyes followed her as she moved toward the pictures which she had previously been examining. "Let us change the subject," she went on, with a note of cold composure in her voice. "I see that you don't like rationalism . . . Well, you are a poet, as your pictures tell me, and few poets like to do more than feel first and think afterward. . . . Are these pictures for sale, Miss Dares?"

Cora's answer came a trifle tardily. "Three of them," she said.

"Which three?" Pauline asked, somewhat carelessly, as it seemed.

"All but that study of a head.   As you see, it is scarcely finished."

"It is the one I should like to purchase.   You say it is not for sale?"

"No, Mrs. Varick."

"It is very clever," commented Pauline, almost as though she addressed her own thoughts.   She turned her face toward Cora's; it wore an indefinite flickering sort of smile.   "Has it any name?"

"Oh, no; it is a mere study."

"I like it extremely . . . By the way, is it a portrait?"

Cora did not reply for several seconds.   She had begun to put little touches upon her canvas again — or to seem as if she were so putting them.

"It's not good enough to be called anything," she presently replied.

"I want it," said Pauline.   She was looking straight at the picture — a small square of rather recklessly rich color.   "I want it very much indeed.   I . . I will give you a considerable sum for it."

She named the sum that she was willing to give, and in an admirably cool, loitering voice. It was something that surpassed any price ever proposed to Cora Dares for one of her paintings, by several hundreds of dollars.

Cora kept silent. She was touching her canvas. Pauline waited. Suddenly she turned and regarded her companion.

"Well?" she said.

Cora flung aside her brush. The two women faced each other.

"I think you are cruel!" cried Cora. It was evident that she was nearly in straits for speech, and her very lovely blue eyes seemed to sparkle through unshed tears. "I — I told you that I did not wish to sell the picture," she hurried on. "I — I don't call it a picture at all, as I also told you. It — it is far from being worth the price that you have offered me. It . . it . ." And here Cora paused. Her last words had a choked sound.

Pauline was looking at her fixedly but quite courteously.

"It is Ralph Kindelon's portrait," she said.

Cora started. "Well! and if it is!" she exclaimed.

Instantly, after that, Pauline went over to her and took one of her hands.

"My dear Miss Dares," she said, with that singular sweetness which she could always throw into her voice, "I beg you to forgive me. If you really wish to retain that picture — and I see that you do — why, then I would not take it from you even as a voluntary gift. Let us speak no more on the subject."

Cora gave a pained, difficult smile, now. She looked full into Pauline's steady eyes for a brief space, and then withdrew her own.

"Very well," she almost faltered, "let us speak no more on the subject." . . .

"I have been horribly merciless," Pauline told herself, when she had quitted Cora Dares's studio about ten minutes later. "I have made that poor girl confess to me that she loves Ralph Kindelon. And how suited they are to each other! She has actual genius — he is brimming with intellectual power. I have made a sad failure in my visit to Cora Dares. . . . I hope all my vain exploits among these people, who are so different from the people with whom my surroundings of fortune and destiny have thus far brought me into natural contact, will not result so disastrously."

Her thoughts returned to Kindelon, as she walked homeward, and to the hostile terms on which they had parted but a few hours ago.

"My project begins badly," she again mused. "Everything about it seems to promise ill. But it is too late to draw back. Besides, I am very far from wishing to draw back. I am like an enthusiastic explorer; I want to face new discoveries in the very teeth of disaster."

On reaching home she had scarcely time to take off her bonnet before the name of her cousin Court-landt was brought to her by a servant. She went down into the little reception-room to meet him, with rather lively anticipations of being forced to put herself on the defensive. Her sensations had not been unlike those with which we regard the lowering of the mercury in a thermometer, while ordering extra fuel so as to be on guard against a sudden chill.

Courtlandt was standing before the silver-grated hearth-place; he watched the black, tumbled blocks of coal with eyes bent down upon their snapping and crackling flames as Pauline appeared. He did not immediately raise his eyes as her entering step sounded. But when he did raise them, she saw that he was clad in his old impregnable calm.

She sank into a chair, not far from the fire. "Well," she said, with an amused smile playing about her lips, "I suppose you have come to scold me dreadfully."

"What makes you suppose so?" he asked.

"You darted away, there at the Battery, as if you were fearfully shocked."

"I don't think I darted away.

"Oh, well, we won't split hairs. You would n't stay, and you might easily have stayed. You pleaded stress of business, and you had n't any, or this appearance up-town at so early an hour could n't have taken place."

"It is remarkable," said Courtlandt, with his gravest serenity, "how you pierce through people's pitiful disguises. You make me feel conscience-stricken by a realization of my own deceit."

"That is fortunate," said Pauline, with a slight, curt laugh. "For then you will, perhaps, express your disapprobation less impudently."

"I might speak pretty plainly to you and yet not be at all impudent."

Pauline threw back her head with a defiant stolidity. "Oh, speak as plainly as you please," she said. "I shall have my own views of just how impudent you are. I generally have."

"You did something that was a good deal off color for a woman who wants herself always regarded as careful of the proprieties. I found you doing it, and I was shocked, as you say."

Pauline straightened herself in her chair. "I don't know what you mean," she replied, a little crisply, "by 'off color.' I suppose it is slang, and I choose, with a good reason, to believe that it conveys an unjustly contemptuous estimate of my very harmless act. I took a stroll along that beautiful Battery with a friend."

"With an adventuring newspaper fellow, you mean," said Courtlandt, cool as always, but a little more sombre.

Pauline rose. "I will stand a certain amount of rudeness toward myself," she declared, "but I will not stand sneers at Mr. Kindelon. No doubt if you had met me walking with some empty-headed fop, like Fyshkille, or Van Arsdale, you would have thought my conduct perfectly proper."

"I 'd have thought it devilish odd," said Courtlandt, "and rather bad form. I 've no more respect for those fellows than you have. But if you got engaged to one of them I should n't call it a horrible disaster."

Pauline smiled, with a threat of rising ire in the smile. "Who thought of my becoming 'engaged' to anybody?" she asked. And her accentuation of the word which Courtlandt had just employed produced the effect of its being scornfully quoted.

He was toying with the links of his watch-chain, and he kept his eyes lowered while he said: "Are you in love with this Kindelon chap?"

She flushed to the roots of her hair. "I — I

shall leave the room," she said unsteadily, " if you presume to talk any further in this strain."

" You are a very rich woman," pursued Courtlandt. What he said had somehow the effect of a man exploding something with a hand of admirable firmness.

Pauline bit her lips excitedly. She made a movement as if about to quit the chamber. Then some new decision seemed to actuate her. " Oh, Court! " she exclaimed reproachfully, " how can you treat me in this unhandsome way?"

He had lifted his eyes, now. "I am trying to save you from making a ridiculous marriage," he said. " I tried once before — a good while ago — to save you from making a frightful one. My attempt was useless then. I suppose it will be equally useless now."

Pauline gave an agitated moan, and covered her face with both hands. . . . Hideous memories had been evoked by the words to which she had just listened. But immediately afterward a knock sounded at the partly closed door which led into the hall. She started, uncovered her face, and moved toward this door. Courtlandt watched her while she exchanged certain low words with a servant. Then, a little later, she approached him, and he saw that her agitation had vanished, and that it appeared to have so vanished because of a strong controlling effort.

"Mr. Kindelon is here," she said, in abrupt undertone. "If you do not wish to meet him you can go back into the dining-room." She made a gesture toward a *portière* not far away. "That leads to the dining-room," she went on. "Act just as you choose, but be civil, be courteous, or do not remain."

"I will not remain," said Courtlandt.

He had passed from the room some little time before Kindelon entered it.

"You did not expect to see me," said the latter, facing Pauline. His big frame had a certain droop that suggested humility and even contrition. He held his soft hat crushed in one hand, and he made no sign of greeting with the other.

"No," said Pauline softly, "I did not expect to see you." She was waiting for the sound of the hall-door outside; she soon heard it, and knew that it meant the exit of Courtlandt. Then she went on: "but since you are here, will you not be seated?"

"Not until you have forgiven me!" Kindelon murmured. Between the rich, fervent, emotional voice which now addressed her and the even regularity of the tones she had just heard, what a world of difference lay!

"You were certainly rude," she said, thinking how chivalrously his repentance became him, and how strong a creature he looked in this weaker submissive phase. "You know that I had only the most friendly feelings toward you. You accused me of actual hypocrisy. But I will choose to believe that you did not mean to lose your temper in that positively wild way. Yes, I forgive you, and, in token of my forgiveness there is my hand."

She extended her hand, and as she did so he literally sprang forward, seizing it. The next instant he had stooped and kissed it. After that he sank into a near chair.

"If you had not forgiven me," he said, "I should have been a very miserable man. Your pardon makes me happy. Now I am ready to turn over a new page of — of friendship — yes, friendship, of course. I shall never say those absurd, accusatory things again. What right have I to say them? What right have I to anything more than the honor of your notice, as long as you choose to bestow it? I have thought everything over; I've realized that the fact of your being willing to know me at all is an immense extended privilege!"

Pauline still remained standing. She had half turned from him while he thus impetuously spoke; she was staring down into the ruddy turmoil of the fire.

"Don't say anything more with regard to the little disagreement," she answered. "It is all ended. Now let us talk of other things."

He did not answer, and she let quite a long pause ensue while she still kept her eyes upon the snapping coal-blocks. At length she continued, —

"I shall have the full list of Mrs. Dares's guests quite soon. It has been promised me."

"Yes?" she heard him say, a little absently.

"I shall, no doubt, have it by to-morrow morning," she went on. "Then I shall begin my arrangements. I shall issue invitations to those whom I wish for my guests. And I shall expect you to help me. You promised to help me, as you know. There will be people on the list whom I have not yet met — a good many of them. You shall tell me all about these, or, if you prefer, you shall simply draw your pen through their names — Why don't you ask me how I shall obtain this boasted list?"

"You mean that Mrs. Dares will send it?" she heard him ask.

"No, I mean that I shall secure it from her daughter."

"Her daughter?"

"Yes—Cora. I have been to see Cora. I visited her studio— By the way, what a good portrait she has there of you. It is really an excellent likeness."

She slowly turned and let a furtive look sweep his face. It struck her that he was confused and discomfited in a wholly new way.

"I think it a fair likeness," he returned. "But I did not sit for it," he added quickly. "She painted it from memory. It—it is for sale like her other things."

"Oh, no, it is not for sale," said Pauline. She saw his color alter a little as her gaze again found stealthy means of scrutinizing it. "Miss Cora told me that very decidedly. She wants to keep it—no doubt as a precious memento. I thought the wish very flattering— I—I wondered why you did not ask Cora Dares to marry you."

She perceived that he had grown pale, now, as he rose and said,—

"I think I shall never ask any woman to marry me." He walked slowly toward the door, pausing at a little distance from its threshold. "When you want me," he now proceeded, " will you send for me?   Then I will most gladly come."

" You mean — about the *salon?* " she questioned.

" Yes — about the *salon*.   In that and all other ways I am yours to command —"

When he had gone she sat musing before the fire for nearly an hour.   That night, at a little after nine o'clock, she was surprised to receive a copious list of names from Cora Dares, accompanied by a brief note.

She sent for Kindelon on the following day, and they spent the next evening together from eight until eleven.   He was his old, easy, gay, brilliant self again.   What had occurred between them seemed to have been absolutely erased from his memory.   It almost piqued her to see how perfectly he played what she knew to be a part.

Soon afterward her invitations were sent out for the following Thursday.   Each one was a simple " At Home."   She awaited Thursday with much interest and suspense.

X.

BY nine o'clock on Thursday evening all her guests had arrived. They comfortably filled her two smart and brilliant drawing-rooms, but quite failed to produce the crowded effect notice-able in Mrs. Dares's less ample quarters.

Pauline saw with pleasure that the fine pictures, bronzes, and bric-à-brac which she had brought from Europe were most admiringly noticed. Small groups were constantly being formed be-fore this canvas or that cabinet, table, and pedes-tal. She had kept for some time quite close to Mrs. Dares, having a practical sense of the little lady's valuable social assistance on an occasion like the present, apart from all personal feelings of liking.

"You make it much easier for me," she said at length, after the assemblage appeared complete and no new arrivals had occurred for at least ten minutes. "It was so kind of you to come, when I know that you make a rule of not going any-where."

"This was a very exceptional invitation, my dear," answered Mrs. Dares. "It was something wholly out of the common, you know."

"I understand," said Pauline, with her sweetest laugh. "You wanted to see your mantle descend, after a manner, upon my younger shoulders. You wanted to observe whether I should wear it gracefully or not."

"I had few doubts on that point," was the slow, soft reply.

"So you really think me a worthy pupil?" continued Pauline, glancing about her with an air of pretty and very pardonable pride.

"You have a most lovely home," said Mrs. Dares, "and one exquisitely designed for the species of entertainment which you are generous enough to have resolved upon."

"Ah, don't say 'generous,'" broke in Pauline. "You give me a twinge of conscience. I am afraid my motive has been quite a selfishly ambitious one. At least, I sometimes fancy so. How many human motives *are* thoroughly disinterested? But if I succeed with my *salon* — which before long I hope to make as fixed and inevitable a matter as the day of the week on which it is held — the result must surely be a most salutary and even reformatory one. In securing my guerdon for work accomplished I shall have done society a solid benefit; and when I wear my little crown I shall feel, unlike most royal personages, that it is blessed by friends and not stained by the blood of enemies."

Her tone was one of airy jest, but a voice at her side instantly said, as she finished, —

"Do not be too sure of that. Very few crowns are ever won without some sort of bloodshed."

She turned and saw Kindelon, who had overheard nearly all her last speech to Mrs. Dares. Something in his manner lessened the full smile on Pauline's lips without actually putting it to flight.

"You speak as if you bore gloomy tidings," she said.

Kindelon's eyes twinkled, though his mouth preserved perfect sobriety. "You have done precisely what I expected you would do," he said, "in undertaking an arbitrary selection of certain guests and an arbitrary exclusion of certain others. You have raised a growl."

"A growl!" murmured Mrs. Dares, with a slight dismayed gesture.

Pauline's face grew serious. "Who, pray, are the growlers?" she asked.

"Well, the chief one is that incorrigible and

irrepressible Barrowe. He has his revolutionary opinions, of course. He is always having revolutionary opinions. He makes me think of the Frenchman who declared that if he ever found himself in Heaven his first impulse would be to throw up barricades."

Pauline bit her lip. "Barricades are usually thrown up in streets," she said, with a faint, ired ring of the voice. "Mr. Barrowe probably forgets that fact."

"Do you mean that you would like to show him the street now?" asked Kindelon.

"I have not heard of what his alleged growl consists."

"I warned you against him, but you thought it best that he should be invited. Since you had decided upon weeding, there was no one whom you could more profitably weed."

"Mr. Barrowe has a very kind heart," here asserted Mrs. Dares, with tone and mien at their gentlest and sweetest. "He is clad with bristles, if you please, but the longer you know him the more clearly you recognize that his savage irritability is external and superficial."

"I think it very appropriate to say that he is clad with bristles," retorted Kindelon. "It makes me wish that I had reported him as grunting instead

of growling.   In that case the simile would be perfect."

Mrs. Dares shook her head remonstratingly.
"Don't try to misrepresent your own good heart
by sarcasm," she replied.   She spoke with her
unchangeable gravity; she had no lightsome mo-
ments, and the perpetually serious views which
she took of everything made you sometimes wonder how and why it was that she managed to make
her smileless repose miss the austere note and
sound the winsome one.

"I am certain of not losing your esteem," exclaimed Kindelon, with all his most characteristic
warmth.   "Your own heart is so large and kind
that everybody who has got to know it can feel
secure in drawing recklessly upon its charity."

Mrs. Dares made him no answer, for just then a
gentleman who had approached claimed her attention.   And Pauline, now feeling that she and
Kindelon were virtually alone together, said with
abrupt speed, —

"You told me that this Mr. Barrowe had a kind
heart, in spite of his gruff, unreasonable manners.
You admitted as much, and so, remembering how
clever his writings are, I decided to retain him on
the list.   But please tell me just what he has been
saying."

"Oh, he's tempestuous on the subject of your having done any weeding at all. He thinks it arrogant and patronizing of you. He thinks that I am at the bottom of it; he always delights in blaming me for something. He positively revels, I suppose, in his present opportunity."

"But if he is indignant and condemnatory," said Pauline, "why does he not remain away? He has the right of discountenancing my conduct by his absence."

"Ah, you don't know him! He never neglects a chance for being turbulent. I heard him assert, just now, that Miss Cragge had received a most cruel insult from you."

"Miss Cragge!" exclaimed Pauline, with a flash of her gray eyes. "I would not have such a creature as that in my drawing-rooms for a very great deal! Upon my word," she went on, with a sudden laugh that had considerable cold bitterness, "this irascible personage needs a piece of my mind. I don't say that I intend giving it to him, for I am at home, and the requirements of the hostess mark imperative limits. But I have ways left me of showing distinct disfavor, for all that. Are there any other acts of mine which Mr. Barrowe does me the honor to disapprove?"

"Oh, yes. I hear that he considers you have

acted most unfairly toward the triad of poets, Leander Prawle, Arthur Trevor, and Rufus Corson."

Pauline gave a smile that was really but a curl of the lip. "Indeed!" she murmured. "I was rather amused by Mr. Prawle's poetic prophecy of a divine future race; it may be bad poetry, as he puts it, but I thought it rather good evolution. Then the *Quartier Latin* floridity of Mr. Trevor amused me as well: I have always liked fervor of expression in verse, and I am not prepared to say that Mr. Trevor has always written ludicrous exaggeration — especially since he reveres Théophile Gautier, who is an enchanting singer. But when it comes to treating with that morbid *poseur*, Mr. Corson, who affects to see beauty in decay and corruption, and who makes a silly attempt to deify indecency, I draw my line, and shut my doors."

"Of course you do," said Kindelon. "No doubt if you had opened them to Mr. Corson, Barrowe would have been scandalized at your doing so. As it is, he chooses to championize Mr. Corson and Miss Cragge. He is a natural grumbler, a constitutional fighter. By the way, he is coming in our direction. Do you see him approaching?"

"Oh, yes, I see him," said Pauline resolutely, "and I am quite prepared for him."

Mr. Barrowe presented himself at her side in another minute or two. His tall frame accomplished a very awkward bow, while his little eyes twinkled above his beak-like nose, with a suggestion of restrained belligerence.

"Your entertainment is very successful, Mrs. Varick," he began, ignoring Kindelon, who had already receded a step or two.

"Have you found it so?" returned Pauline coolly. "I had fancied otherwise."

Mr. Barrowe shrugged his frail shoulders. "Your rooms are beautiful," he said, "and of course you must know that I like the assemblage; it contains so many of my good friends."

"I hope you miss nobody," said Pauline, after a slight pause.

Mr. Barrowe gave a thin, acid cough. "Yes," he declared, "I miss more than one. I miss them, and I hear that you have not invited them. I am very sorry that you have not. It is going to cause ill-feeling. Everybody knows that you took Mrs. Dares's list — my dear, worthy friend's list. It is too bad, Mrs. Varick; I assure you that it is too bad."

"I do not think that it is too bad," said Pauline freezingly, with the edges of her lips. "I do not think that it is bad at all. I have invited those whom I wished to invite."

"Precisely!" cried Mr. Barrowe, with a shrill, snapping sound in the utterance of the word. "You have been wrongly advised, however — horribly advised. I don't pretend to state *who* has advised you, but if you had consulted me — well, handicapped as I am by a hundred other duties, bored to death as I am by people applying for all sorts of favors, I would nevertheless, in so good a cause, have willingly spared you some of my valuable time. I would have told you by no means to exclude so excellent a person as poor, hard-working Miss Cragge. To slight her like that was a very unkind cut. You must excuse my speaking plainly."

"I must either excuse it or resent it," said Pauline, meeting the glitter of Mr. Barrowe's small eyes with the very calm and direct gaze of her own. "But suppose I do the latter? It has usually been my custom, thus far through life, to resent interference of any sort."

"Interference!" echoed Mr. Barrowe, with querulous asperity. "Ah, madam, I think I recognize just who *has* been advising you, now; you make my suspicion a certainty." He glanced irately enough toward Kindelon as he spoke the last words.

Kindelon took a step or two forward, reaching

Pauline's side and pausing there. His manner, as
he began to speak, showed no anger, but rather
that blending of decision and carelessness roused
by an adversary from whom we have slight fear
of defeat.

"Come, Barrowe," he said, "if you mean me
you had better state so plainly. As it happens,
Mrs. Varick was advised, in the matter of not
sending Miss Cragge an invitation, solely by herself. But if she had asked my counsel it would
entirely have agreed with her present course."

"No doubt," almost snarled Mr. Barrowe. "The
ill turn comes to the same thing. We need not
split hairs. I made no personal reference to you,
Kindelon; but if the cap fits you can wear it."

"I should like to hand it back to you with a
bunch of bells on it," said Kindelon.

"Is that what you call Irish wit?" replied Mr.
Barrowe, while his lips grew pale. "If so, you
should save it for the columns of the 'Asteroid,'
which sadly needs a little."

"The 'Asteroid' never prints personalities,"
returned Kindelon, with nonchalant mockery.
"It leaves that kind of journalism to your friend
Miss Cragge."

"Miss Cragge, sir," muttered Barrowe, "is a
lady."

"I did not say she was a gentleman," retorted Kindelon, "though her general deportment has more than once cast a doubt upon her sex."

Mr. Barrowe gave a faint shiver. "I'm glad I have n't it on my conscience," he declared, "that I injured an honest girl to gratify a mere spite." He at once turned to Pauline, now. "Madam," he pursued, "I must warn you that your project will prove a dire failure if you attempt to develop it on a system of despotic preferences. We were all glad to come to you, in a liberal, democratic, intellectual spirit. But the very moment you undertake the establishment of a society formed on a basis of capricious likes and dislikes, I assure you that you are building on sand and that your structure will fall."

"In that case, Mr. Barrowe," said Pauline, stung by his unwarranted officiousness into the employment of biting irony, "you can have no excuse if you allow yourself to be buried in my ruins."

She passed rapidly away, while Kindelon accompanied her. "You were quite right," came his speedy encouragement, as they moved onward together. "You showed that insufferable egotist the door in the politest and firmest manner possible."

" I was in my own house, though," said Pauline, with an intonation that betokened the dawn of repentance. " He was very exasperating, truly, but—I was in my own house, you know."

"Of course you were," exclaimed Kindelon, "and he treated you as if it belonged to somebody else. We are all apt to assert a proprietary right when a fellow-citizen ventures to relieve us of our purse, and I think a similar claim holds good with regard to our self-respect."

Pauline presently came to a standstill. She looked troubled, and her gaze remained downcast for a little while. But soon she lifted it and met Kindelon's eyes steadily watching her.

"You don't think I was unjustifiably rude?" she asked.

"No; indeed I do not. I don't think you were rude at all."

She was silent for a brief interval. Then she said, without taking her eyes in the least from her companion's face,—

"Do you believe that most women would have acted the same?"

"No," he said, with a quick, slight laugh, "because most women have neither your brains nor your independence."

"And you like both in a woman?"

"I like both in you," he said, lowering his handsome head a little as he uttered the words.

"Do you think Cora Dares would have acted as I have done?" Pauline asked.

He made an impatient gesture; he appeared for a moment distressed and embarrassed.

"You and Cora Dares are — are not the same," he said, almost stammeringly.

"Oh, I know that very well," answered Pauline. "I have had very good reason to know that we are not the same. We are extremely different. By the way, she is not here to-night."

"Not here?" he repeated interrogatively, but with a suggestion of drolly helpless duplicity.

Pauline raised one finger, shaking it at him for an instant and no more. The gesture, transient as it was, seemed to convey a world of significance. No doubt Kindelon tacitly admitted this, though his face preserved both its ordinary color and composure.

"You are well aware that she is not here," Pauline said.

"Why do you say that?" he asked.

"I think so."

"But perhaps you may be mistaken. Perhaps you have merely fancied that I have noticed Miss Cora's non-appearance."

"Perhaps," Pauline repeated. She seemed to be saying the word to her own thoughts. But suddenly her manner became far less absent. "Mrs. Dares told me that Miss Cora had a headache to-night," she said, with brisk activity. "We can all have headaches, you know," she went on, "when we choose."

Kindelon nodded slowly. "I have heard that it is an accommodating malady," he said, in tones that were singularly lifeless and neutral.

Pauline put forth her hand, and let it rest on his broad, strong arm for a second or two.

"Did Miss Cora have a headache?" she asked.

He threw back his head, and shook it with a sudden sound of his breath which resembled a sigh of irritation, and yet was not quite that.

"Upon my word, I don't know!" he cried softly.

Just then Pauline found herself confronted by Mr. Howe, the novelist. His stoop was very apparent; it seemed even more consumptive than usual; his slim hand was incessantly touching and retouching his blue spectacles, which gleamed opaque and with a goblin suggestion from the smooth-shaven, scholarly pallor of his visage.

"Excuse me, Mrs. Varick," he began, "but I— I wish to speak a word with you."

Pauline smiled and assumed an affable demeanor. It cost her an effort to do so, for certain acute reasons; but she nevertheless achieved good results.

"A great many words, Mr. Howe," she answered, "if you wish."

Mr. Howe gave a sickly smile. "Oh, I don't ask a great many," he faltered; and it at once became evident that he was for some reason ill at ease, disconsolate, abysmally depressed.

"You are annoyed," said Pauline, chiefly because she found nothing else, as a would-be courteous hostess, to say.

"Annoyed?" came the hesitant reply, while Mr. Howe rearranged his blue spectacles with a hand that seemed to assume a new momentary decisiveness. "I am grieved, Mrs. Varick. I am grieved because a friend of mine has received a slight from you, and I hope that it is an unintentional slight. I—I want to ask you whether it cannot be corrected. I allude to Mr. Bedlowe."

"Mr. Bedlowe!" repeated Pauline amazedly. She turned to Kindelon as she spoke.

"Oh, yes," came Kindelon's ready answer; "you remember Bedlowe, of course."

"I remember Mr. Bedlowe," said Pauline, sedately.

"Ah! you seem to have forgotten him!" exclaimed Mr. Howe, with a great deal of gentlemanly distress. He had discontinued all manual connection with his blue glasses; he had even pressed both hands together, in a rotatory, nervous way, while he went on speaking. "I hope you did not mean to leave poor Bedlowe out," he proceeded, with quite a funereal pathos. "The poor fellow feels it dreadfully. I promised him I would say nothing about the matter, and yet (as you see) I have broken my promise."

"I think Mrs. Varick is sorry to see that you have broken your promise," said Kindelon, shortly and tepidly.

Mr. Howe glanced at Kindelon through his glasses. He was obliged to raise his head as he did so, on account of their differing statures.

"Kindelon!" he cried, in reproach, "I thought you were one of my friends."

"So I am," came Kindelon's reply, "and that is why I don't like the pietistic novelist, Bedlowe, who wrote 'The Christian Knight in Armor' and the 'Doubtful Soul Satisfied.'"

If there could be the ghost of a cough, Mr. Howe gave it. He again lifted his wan, lank hand toward his spectacles.

"Oh, Kindelon," he remonstrated, "you must

not be as uncharitable as that. Bedlowe does the best he can — and really, between ourselves, his best is remarkably good. Think of his great popularity. Think of the way he appeals to the large masses. Think "—

But here Pauline broke in, with the merriest laugh that had left her lips that night.

" My dear Mr. Howe ! " she exclaimed, "you forget that I heard a bitter wrangle between you and Mr. Bedlowe only a few days ago. You had a great many hard things to say of him then. I hope you have not so easily altered your convictions."

" I — I have n't altered my convictions at all," stammered Mr. Howe, quite miserably. " But between Bedlowe as a literary man, and — and Bedlowe as a social companion — I draw a very marked line."

Kindelon here put his big hand on Mr. Howe's slight shoulder, jovially and amicably, while he said, —

" Come, now, my dear Howe, you mean that the analytical and agnostic novelist wants the romantic and pietistic novelist, only for the purpose of breaking a lance with him. You want him for that reason and no other."

Mr. Howe removed his spectacles, and while he

performed this act it was evident that he was extremely agitated. The removal of his spectacles revealed two very red-rimmed eyes, whose color escaped all note because of their smallness.

"I — I want Mr. Bedlowe for no such reason," he asserted. "But I — I do not want to attend a — so-called *salon* at which mere fashionable fancy takes the place of solid hospitality."

"You forget," said Pauline, with rapid coolness, "that you are speaking in the presence of your hostess."

"He remembers only," came the fleet words of Kindelon, "that he speaks at the prompting of Barrowe."

Pauline tossed her head; she was angry again. "I don't care anything about Mr. Barrowe," she asserted, with a very positive glance at the unspectacled Mr. Howe. "I should prefer to believe that Mr. Howe expresses his own opinions. Even if they are very rude ones, I should prefer having them original."

"They are original," said Mr. Howe feebly, but somehow with the manner of a man who possesses a reserve of strength which he is unable to readily command. "I do not borrow my opinions. I — I think nearly all people must know this."

"I know it," said Pauline very tranquilly, and

with an accent suave yet sincere. "I have read your novels, Mr. Howe, and I have liked them very much. I don't say that this is the reason why I have asked you here to-night, and I don't say that my dislike of Mr. Bedlowe's novels is the reason why I have not asked Mr. Bedlowe here to-night.   But I hope you will let my admiration of your talent cover all delinquencies, and permit me to be the judge of whom I shall choose and whom I shall not choose for my guests."

Mr. Howe put on his spectacles.   While he was putting them on, he said in a voice that had a choked and also mournfully reproachful sound, —

"I have no social gifts, Mrs. Varick.   I can't measure swords with you.   I can only measure pens.   That is the trouble with so many of us writers.   We can only write; we can't talk.   I— I think it grows worse with us, in these days when one has to write with the most careful selection of words, so as to escape what is now called commonplace diction.   We get into the habit of striving after novelty of expression — we have to use our 'Thesaurus,' and search for synonyms — we have to smoke excessively (a good many of us) in order to keep our nerves at the proper literary pitch — we have to take stimulants (a good many of us — though I don't understand that, for I never touch wine) in order to drag up the words and ideas from an underlying stagnancy. Frankly, for myself, I talk quite ill. But I don't want to have you think that I am talking in another voice than my own. I don't want, in spite of my failure as a man of words, that you should suppose " —

"I suppose nothing, Mr. Howe," broke in Pauline, while she caught the speaker's hand in hers, gloved modishly up to the elbow with soft, tawny kid. "I insist upon supposing nothing except that you are glad to come here and will be glad to come again. I know three or four of your novels very well, and I know them so well that I love them, and have read them twice or thrice, which is a great deal to say of a novel, as even you, a novelist, will admit. But I don't like Mr. Bedlowe's novels any more than you do; and if Mr. Barrowe has tried to set you on fire with his incendiary feelings, I shall be excessively sorry. You have written lovely and brilliant things; you know the human soul, and you have shown that you know it. You may not have sold seventy thousand copies, as the commercial phrase goes, but I don't care whether you have sold seventy thousand or only a plain seventy; you are a true artist, all the same. . . And now I am going to leave you, for my other guests claim me. But I hope you will not care for anything severe and bitter which that dyspeptic Mr. Barrowe may say; for, depend upon it, he only wins your adherence because he is a clever man on paper, and not because he is even tolerable in the stern operations of real life. Frankly, between ourselves, I am sure that he makes a very bad husband, though he is always talking of being handicapped by autograph-bores and interviewers who keep him away from Mrs. Barrowe. I suspect that Mrs. Barrowe must be a very unhappy lady. And I'm sure, on the other hand, that Mrs. Howe is very happy — for I know there *is* a Mrs. Howe, or you could n't describe the American women as ably as you do. . ." Pauline passed onward as she ended her final sentence. Kindelon, still at her side, soon said to her, —

"What a clever farewell you made: you have won Howe. You flattered him very adroitly. It's an open secret that his wife helps him in those exquisite novels of his. She is his one type of woman. I think that is why Howe will never be great; he will always be exquisite instead. He adores his wife, who hates society and always stays at home. If Howe had once committed a genuine fault it might have served posterity as a crystallized masterpiece."

Pauline shook her head with negative emphasis. "I like him just as he is," she murmured. She was silent for a moment, and then added, almost plaintively: "My entertainment looks pleasant enough, but I fear that it is all a disastrous failure."

"A failure?" echoed Kindelon, with no sympathy in the interrogation.

"Yes, everybody is grumbling. I distinctly feel it. It is not only that Barrowe has infected everybody; it is that everybody has a latent hostility towards anything like harmonious reunion."

"Isn't there a bit of pure imagination in your verdict?" Kindelon asked.

"Premonition," answered Pauline, "if you choose to call it by that name." She stood, while she thus spoke, under an effulgent chandelier, whose jets, wrought in the semblance of candles, dispersed from ornate metallic sconces a truly splendid glow.

"We have a new arrival," he said. He was glancing toward a near doorway while he spoke. Pauline's eyes had followed his own.

"My aunt!" she exclaimed. "And Sallie — and Courtlandt, too!"

"Yes, Courtlandt, too — my friend, Courtlandt," said Kindelon oddly.

"I told Aunt Cynthia she had best not come," murmured Pauline.

"And your cousin, Courtlandt?" said Kindelon. "Did you tell *him* not to come?"

"I am sorry that they came — I somehow can't help but be sorry!" exclaimed Pauline, while she moved towards the door by which she had seen her kindred enter.

"Sorry? So am I," said Kindelon. He spoke below his breath, but Pauline heard him.

XI

I AM very glad to see you," Pauline was telling her aunt, a little later. She felt, while she spoke them, that her words were the merest polite falsehood. " I did not suppose you would care to honor me this evening — I mean all three of you," she added, with a rather mechanical smile in the direction of Miss Sallie and Courtlandt.

Mrs. Poughkeepsie promptly spoke. She was looking about her through a pair of gold-rimmed glasses while she did so. Her portliness was not without a modish majesty; folds of a black, close-clinging, lace-like fabric fell about her large person with much grace of effect; her severe nose appeared to describe an even more definite arc than usual.

" Sallie and I had nothing for to-night," said Mrs. Poughkeepsie. " Lent began to-day, you know, and there was n't even a dinner to go to."

" I am pleased to afford you a refuge in your social distress," returned Pauline. It flashed

through her mind that circumstance was drawing upon her, to-night, for a good deal of bitter
feeling.   What subtle thunder was in the air,
ready to sour the milk of human kindness to its
last drop?

"My dear," murmured her aunt, temporarily
discontinuing her stares, and speaking more in
reproach than conciliation, "you must not be so
very quick to take offence when none is intended."

Pauline gave a laugh which she tried to make
amiable.   "It pleases me to think that no offence
was intended," she declared.

"Your little party was by no means a *pis-aller*
with *me*, dear Pauline," here stated Sallie, "whatever it may have been in mamma's case.   I really
wanted so much, don't you know, to see these —
a — persons."   The peculiar pause which Sallie
managed to make before she pronounced the word
"persons," and the gentle yet assertive accent
which she managed to place upon the word itself,
were both, in their way, beyond description.   Not
that either was of the import which would render
description requisite, except from the point of
view which considers all weightless trifles valuable.

Pauline bit her lip.   She had long ago thought
Sallie disqualified for contest by her native silli-

ness. The girl had not a tithe of her mother's brains;. she possessed all the servitude of an echo and all the imitativeness of a reflection. But like most weak things she had the power to wound, though her little sting was no doubt quite unintentional at present.

Courtlandt here spoke. He was perfectly his ordinary sober self as he said, —

" I happened to drop in upon Aunt Cynthia to-night, and she brought me here. I believe that I come without an invitation. Don't I? I 've forgotten."

" You have n't forgotten," contradicted Pauline, though not at all unpleasantly. " You know I did n't invite you, because I did n't think you would care to come. You gave me every reason to think so."

" That was very rude," commented Sallie, with a rebuking look at Courtlandt. She had a great idea of manners, but her reverence was quite theoretical, as more than one ineligible and undesirable young gentleman knew, when she had chosen to freeze him at parties with the blank, indifferent regard of a sphinx. " It is so odd, really, Pauline," she went on, with her supercilious drawl, which produced a more irritating effect upon her cousin because apparently so spontaneous and unaffected — "it is so odd to meet people whom one does not know. I have always been accustomed to go to places where I knew everybody, and bowed, and had them come up and speak."

Pauline busied herself for an instant in smoothing the creases of her long gloves between wrist and elbow. "Don't you find it rather pleasant, Sallie," she said, "to procure an occasional change?"

"It ought to be refreshing," struck in Courtlandt, neutrally.

"You can have people to talk to you this evening, if you wish," pursued Pauline, while a certain sense that she was being persecuted by her relatives waged war with a decorous recognition of who and where she was.

Before Sallie could answer, Mrs. Poughkeepsie, who had ceased her determined survey, said in her naturally high, cool, suave tones, —

"Oh, of course we want you to present some of them to us, Pauline, dear. We came for that, Sallie and I. We want to see what has made you so fond of them. They are all immensely clever, of course. But one can listen and be instructed, if one does not talk. Do they expect you to talk, by the way? Will they not be quite willing to do all the talking themselves? I have heard—I don't just remember when or how—that they usually *are* willing."

"My dear Aunt Cynthia," said Pauline, in a low but not wholly composed voice, "you speak of my guests as if they were the inmates of a menagerie."

Mrs. Poughkeepsie threw back her head a very little. The motion made a jewel of great price and fine lustre shoot sparks of pale fire from the black lace shrouding her ample bosom. She laughed at the same moment, and by no means ill-naturedly. "I am sure they would n't like to have you suggest anything so dreadful," she said, "you, their protectress and patroness."

"I am neither," affirmed Pauline stoutly.

Mrs. Poughkeepsie lifted her brow in surprise. She almost lifted her august shoulders as well. "Then pray what are you, my dear?" she asked.

"Their hostess—and their equal," asserted Pauline. She spoke with momentary seriousness, but immediately afterward she chose to assume an air of careless raillery.

"Ah, Aunt Cynthia," she went on, "you don't know how you make me envy you!"

"Envy me, Pauline?"

"Oh, yes; you have settled matters so abso-

lutely. You have no misgivings, no distrusts.
You are so magnificently secure."

"I don't understand," politely faltered Mrs.
Poughkeepsie. She looked inquiringly at Courtlandt.

"It is metaphysics," Courtlandt at once said.
"They are a branch of study in which Pauline
has made great progress." His face remained so
completely placid and controlled that he might
have been giving the number of a residence or
recording the last quotation in stocks.

Sallie had become absorbed in staring here and
there, just as her mother had been a brief while
ago; Mrs. Poughkeepsie was at a little distance
from her niece; Courtlandt stood close at Pauline's side, so that the latter could ask him, in an
undertone full of curt, covert imperiousness, —

"Did you come here to say and do rude things?"

"I never say nor do rude things if I can help
it," he answered, with a leaden stolidity in his
own undertone.

"Why did *they* come?" continued Pauline,
lowering her voice still more.

"You invited them, I believe. That is, at least,
my impression."

"I mentioned the affair. I never imagined they
would wish to come."

"You see that you were mistaken. If I had been you I wouldn't have given them the awful opportunity."

"What awful opportunity?" queried Pauline, furtively bristling.

"Of coming," said Courtlandt.

"My dear Pauline," here broke in Mrs. Poughkeepsie, "shall you not present anybody to us?"

"Anyone whom you please to meet, Aunt," responded Pauline.

"But, my *dear*, we please to meet *anyone*. We have no preferences. How *can* we have?"

"This is torment," thought poor Pauline. She glanced toward Courtlandt, but she might as well have appealed to one of her chairs. "What shall I do?" her thoughts sped fleetly on. "This woman and this girl would shock and repel whomever I should bring to them. It would be like introducing the North Pole and the South."

But her face revealed no sign of her perplexity. She quietly put her hand within Courtlandt's arm. "Come, Court," she said, with a very creditable counterfeit of gay sociality, "let us find a few devotees for Aunt Cynthia and Sallie."

"We shall find a good many," said Courtlandt, as they moved away. "Have no fear of that."

"I am by no means sure that we shall find

any," protested Pauline, both with dismay and antagonism.

"Pshaw," retorted Courtlandt. "Mention the name. It will work like magic."

"The name? What name?"

"Poughkeepsie. Do you suppose these haphazard Bohemians would n't like to better themselves if they could?"

Pauline took her hand from his arm, though he made a slight muscular movement of detention.

"They are not haphazard Bohemians," she said. "You know, too, that they are not. They are mostly people of intellect, of culture, of high and large views. I don't know what you mean by saying that they would 'like to better themselves.' Where have they ever heard of Aunt Cynthia? Her name would be simply a dead letter to them."

Courtlandt gave a low laugh, that was almost gruff, and was certainly harsh. "Where have they ever heard of Aunt Cynthia?" he repeated. "Why, she never dines out that the society column of half-a-dozen newspapers does not record it, and her name would be very far from a dead letter. It would be a decidedly living letter."

"But you don't understand," insisted Pauline,

exasperatedly. "These people have no aims to know the so-called higher classes."

"Excuse me," said Courtlandt, with superb calm. "Everybody has aims to know the so-called higher classes — if he or she possibly can. Especially 'she'," he added in his colorless monotone.

Just then Pauline found herself confronted by Miss Upton. The moon-like face of this diminutive lady wore a flushed eagerness as she began to speak.

"Oh, Mrs. Varick," she said, "I 've a great, *great* favor to ask of you! I want you to introduce me to your aunt, Mrs. Poughkeepsie."

"With pleasure," answered Pauline, feeling as if the request had been a sort of jeer. "You know my aunt by sight, then, Miss Upton?"

"Oh, yes, I 've known her for some time by sight, Mrs. Varick. Miss Cragge pointed her out to me one night at Wallack's. She had a box, with her daughter and several other people. One of them was an English lord — or so Miss Cragge said . . . But excuse my mentioning my friend's name, as you don't like her."

"Who told you that I did not like Miss Cragge?" asked Pauline, with abrupt crispness.

"Oh, nobody, nobody," hurried Miss Upton.

"But you have n't invited her here to-night — you left her out, you know. That was all. And I thought . . ."

"Are you a friend of Miss Cragge's?" asked Pauline.

"Oh, yes . . . that is, I know her quite well. She writes dramatic criticisms, you know, and she has seen me in amateur theatricals. She's kind enough to tell me that she *does n't* think that I have a tragic soul in a comic body." Here Miss Upton gave a formidably resonant laugh. "But I'm convinced that I have, and so I've never gone on the stage. But if I could get a few of the *very* aristocratic people, Mrs. Varick, — like yourself, and your aunt, Mrs. Poughkeepsie — to hear me give a private reading or two, from 'Romeo and Juliet' or 'The Hunchback' or 'Parthenia', why, I should be prepared to receive a *new opinion,* don't you understand, with regard to my abilities. There is nothing like being endorsed at the start by people who belong to the real upper circles of society."

"Of course there is n't," said Courtlandt, speaking too low for Miss Upton to catch his words, and almost in the ear of Pauline. "Introduce me," he went swiftly on. "I will save you the bore of further introductions. You will soon see

how they will all flock about the great nabob,
though she may be ignorant of æsthetics, philosophy, Emerson, Herbert Spencer, Carlyle, and
anybody you please."

Pauline turned and looked at him. There was
the shadow of a sparkle in the familiar brown
eyes — the eyes that she never regarded closely
without being reminded of her girlhood, even of
her childhood as well.

" It is a challenge then ? " she asked softly.

For a second he seemed not to understand her.
Then he nodded his head. " Yes — a challenge,"
he answered.

She gave an inward sigh. . . . A little later she
had made the desired introduction. . . . Presently,
as Miss Upton moved away on Courtlandt's arm
in the direction of her aunt and Sallie, she burst
into a laugh, of whose loudness and acerbity she
was equally unconscious.

Martha Dares, appearing at her side, arrested
the laugh. Pauline grew promptly serious as she
looked into Martha's homely face, with its little
black eyes beaming above the fat cheeks and the
unclassic nose, but not beaming by any means so
merrily as when she had last given all its features
her full heed.

" You don't laugh a bit as if you were pleased,"

said Martha, in her short, alert way. "I hope nothing has gone wrong."

"It seems to me as if everything were going wrong," returned Pauline, with a momentary burst of frankness which she at once regretted.

"Good gracious!" said Martha. "I 'm astonished to hear you tell me so."

"Forget that I have told you so," said Pauline, throwing a little delicate repulsion into voice and mien. "By the way, your sister is not here to-night, Miss Dares."

Martha's plump figure receded a step or two.

"No," she replied, in the tone of one somewhat puzzled for a reply. "I came with my mother."

"And your sister had a headache."

"A headache," repeated Martha, showing what strongly resembled involuntary surprise.

"Yes. So your mother told me."

"Well, it 's true," said Martha. Pauline was watching her more closely than she perhaps detected. "Cora's been working very hard, of late. She works altogether too hard. I often tell her so — Here comes Mr. Kindelon," Martha pursued, very abruptly changing the subject, while her gaze seemed to fix itself on some point behind her companion. "He wants to speak with you, I suppose. I 'll move along — you see, I go about

just as I choose. What's the use of my waiting
for an escort? I'm not accustomed to attentions
from the other sex, so I just behave as if it did n't
exist. That's the wisest plan."

"But you surely need not be afraid of Mr. Kindelon," said Pauline.

"Oh, we're not the best of friends just now,"
returned Martha. . . . She had passed quite fleetly
away in another instant. And while Pauline was
wondering at the oddity of her departure, Kindelon presented himself.

"You and Martha Dares are not good friends?"
she quickly asked. She did not stop to consider
whether or no her curiosity was unwarrantable,
but she felt it to be a very distinct and cogent
curiosity.

Kindelon frowned. "I don't want to talk of
Martha Dares," he said, "and I hope that you do
not, either. She is a very unattractive topic."

"Is n't that a rather recent discovery?"

"Oh, no — Shall we speak of something else?
Your aunt's arrival, for instance. I see that she
is quite surrounded."

"Surrounded?" replied Pauline falteringly.
Her eyes turned in the direction of Mrs. Poughkeepsie and Sallie.

It was true. Seven or eight ladies and gentlemen were gathered about the stately lady and her daughter. Both appeared to be holding a little separate and exclusive reception of their own.

"Courtlandt was right!" exclaimed Pauline ruefully, and with a stab of mortification. She turned to meet the inquiring look of Kindelon. "I thought Aunt Cynthia would be unpopular here," she continued. "I supposed that no one in my rooms to-night would care to seek her acquaintance."

"This is a grandee," said Kindelon, "and so they are glad enough to know her. If your cousin, Mr. Beekman, prophesied anything of that sort, he was indeed perfectly right."

Pauline shook her head musingly. "Good heavens!" she murmured, "are there any people in the world who can stand tests? I begin to think not." Her speech grew more animated, her eyes began to brighten indignantly and with an almost tearful light. "Here am I," she went on, "determined to encourage certain individuals in what I believed was their contempt of social frivolity and the void delusion which has been misnamed position and birth. With a sort of polite irony Aunt Cynthia appears and shows me that I am egregiously wrong — that she can hold her court here as well as at the most giddily fashionable assemblage . . . Look; my cousin has just presented Mr. Whitcomb, the 'coming historian' with the pensive face, and Mr. Paiseley, the great American dramatist with the abnormal head. How pleased they both seem! They appear to tingle with deference. Aunt Cynthia is patronizing them, I am sure, as she now addresses them. She thinks them entirely her inferiors; she considers them out of her world, which is the correct world to be in, and there's an end of it. You can lay the Atlantic cable, you can build the Brooklyn Bridge, but you can't budge the granitic prejudices of Aunt Cynthia . . . Yet why do they consent to be patronized by her? Do they not know and feel that she represents a mere sham? Do they value her for what she is, or misvalue her for something that she is not?"

Kindelon laughed a little gravely as he answered: "I am afraid they do the former. And in being what she is, she is a great deal."

"Surely not in the estimate of those who are at all serious on the subject of living — those whom superficialities in all conduct or thought weary and even disgust."

"But these," said Kindelon, with one of his hand-sweeps, "are not that sort of people."

"I supposed a great many of them were."

" You supposed wrongly."

Pauline gave a momentary frown, whose gloom meant pain. And before her face had re-brightened she had begun to speak. " But they cannot care to do as Aunt Cynthia does — to trifle, to idle."

" I fancy that a good many of them would trifle and idle if they had your ·aunt's facilities for that employment — or lack of it."

" But they paint, they read, they write, they think; they make poems, novels, dramas. They are people with an occupation, an ideal. How can they be interested in a fellow-creature who does nothing with her time except waste it?"

" She wastes it very picturesquely," replied Kindelon. " She is Mrs. Poughkeepsie; she represents great prosperity, aristocratic ease, lofty security above need. They read about her; they should not do so, but that they do is more the fault of modern journalism than theirs. Theoretically they may consider that she deserves their hardest feelings; but this has no concern whatever with their curiosity, their interest, their hope of advancement."

" Their hope of advancement!" echoed Pauline, forlornly, almost aghast. " What possible hope of advancement could *they* have from such a source?"

Her querulous question had scarcely ended
when she perceived that Arthur Trevor had presented himself at her side. The young poet was
exceedingly smart to-night. His tawny hair was
rolled off his wide brow with a sort of precise
negligence; it looked as if a deliberative brush
and not a careless hand had so rolled it. He fixed
his dreamy blue eyes with steadfastness upon Pauline's face before speaking.

"I am so sorry, Mrs. Varick," he began, giving
a distinct sigh and slowly shaking his head from
side to side. "I wonder if you know what I am
sorry about."

"Oh, yes," returned Pauline, with a nervous
trill of laughter. "You have come to me with a
complaint on the subject of Mr. Rufus Corson.
You see, Mr. Trevor, rumor has forestalled you.
I heard that you were furious because I omitted to
ask your intimate enemy."

Arthur Trevor gave an exaggerated start; it
was a very French start; he lifted his blond eye-
brows as much as his shoulders. And he looked
at Kindelon while he responded:

"Ah! I see! Kindelon has been telling you
horrid things. Kindelon hates us poets. These
men of the newspapers always do. But there is a
wide gulf between the poetry of to-day and the
newspapers of to-day."

" Of course there is," quickly struck in Kindelon. " That is why the modern newspaper is read so much and the modern poetry so little."

Arthur Trevor chose to ignore this barbed rejoinder. His dreamy eyes and general air of placid reverie made such an attitude singularly easy of assumption.

" Poor Rufus feels your slight," he said, addressing Pauline solely. " Why do you call him my intimate enemy? We are the dearest of friends. He adores decay, and sings of it. I do not sing of it, but I adore it for its color. There is always color in decay."

" Discolor," said Kindelon, with better wit than grammar.

" Decay," pursued Arthur Trevor, " is the untried realm of the future poet. Scarcely anything else is left him. He is driven to find a beauty in ugliness, and there is an immense beauty in ugliness, if one can only perceive it. The province of the future poet shall be to make one perceive it."

" That is like saying," declared Kindelon, " that the province of the future gentleman shall be to make one perceive the courtesy in discourtesy or the refinement in vulgarity."

Again Mr. Trevor ignored Kindelon. " Poor Rufus was so much less to blame than Leander

Prawle," he continued. " And yet you invited Leander Prawle. Prawle is so absurdly optimistic. Prawle has absolutely no color. Prawle is irretrievably statuesque and sculpturesque. It is so nonsensical to be that in poetry. Sculpture is the only art that gives an imperious *rien ne va plus* to the imagination. Prawle should have been a sculptor. He would have made a very bad one, because his ideas are too cold even for marble. But his poetry would not have been such an icy failure if it had been carved instead of written."

" You need not put up with this kind of thing any longer than you want," whispered Kindelon to Pauline. " Hostship, like Mr. Prawle's poetry, remember, has its limitations."

Pauline pretended not to hear this audacious aside. " Mr. Trevor," she said, making her voice very even and collected, " I regret that I could not quite bring myself to ask your friend. The Egyptians, you recollect, used to have a death's-head at their banquets. But that was a good many years ago, and New York is n't Thebes . . . Please pardon me if I tell you that I must leave you for a little while."

As Pauline was passing him, Trevor lifted his eyes toward the ceiling. He did so without a hint of rhapsody, but in a sort of solemn exaltation.

"New York is surely not Thebes!" he exclaimed. "Ah, if it only were! To have lived in Thebes for one day, to have got its real and actual color, would be worth ten years of dull existence here!"

"How I wish fate had treated him more to his taste!" said Kindelon, when Pauline and himself were a little distance off. "He meant to make an appeal for that mortuary Corson. He might better have tried to perpetuate his own welcome at your next *salon*."

"My next *salon!*" echoed Pauline, with a laugh full of fatigue and derision.

"What do you mean?" he asked shortly.

"I mean that I had best give no other *salon*," she replied. "I mean that this is a failure and a mockery."

She looked full up into his eyes as she spoke. They both paused. "So soon?" questioned Kindelon, as if in soft amazement.

"Yes — so soon," she answered, with a quiver in her voice and a slight upward movement of both hands. "What is it all amounting to?"

"What did I tell you?" he said.

"Oh, confirm your prophecy?" she broke forth, somewhat excitedly. "I know you warned me against disappointment. Enjoy your satisfaction — Look at Aunt Cynthia now. She is holding a perfect court. How they *do* flock round Sallie and herself, just as Courtlandt said that they would! I feel that this is the beginning and the end. I have misjudged, miscalculated, misinterpreted. And I am miserably dejected!"

Just then Martha Dares approached Pauline. " Will you please introduce me to your aunt?" said Martha.

· " With the greatest pleasure, Miss Dares," returned Pauline.

" *Et tu Brute?* " said Kindelon, under his breath. Pauline heard him, but Martha did not. . . .

A little later Courtlandt had joined her, and Kindelon had glided away.

" Are you convinced?" said Courtlandt.

" Convinced of what?" she retorted, with an almost fierce defiance.

" Oh, of nothing, since you take it so ferociously." She saw that his calm brown eyes were coolly watching her face.

" When is your next *salon?* " he asked. " Is it to be a week from to-night?"

" It is never to be again," she answered.

She meant the words, precisely as she spoke them. She longed for the entertainment to end, and when it had ended she felt relieved, as if from a painful tension and strain. Musing a little later in her bed-chamber, before retiring, she began to feel a slight change of mood. Had she not, after all, expected, demanded, exacted, too much? Was she justified in giving way to this depression and disappointment? Was she not more blamable in deceiving herself than these people were in surprising her? She had been warned by Kindelon; she had, in a certain way, been warned by Mrs. Dares. But these were not her desired band of plain livers and high thinkers. They were very far below any such elevated standard. They had seemed to make a sort of selfish rush into her drawing-rooms for the purpose of getting there, and afterward boasting that they had got there. She was by no means sure if the very quality and liberality of her refreshments had not made for them the prospect of another Thursday evening offer increased allurements. Many of them were full of the most distressing trivialities. The conduct of Mr. Barrowe had seemed to her atrociously unpleasant. His action with regard to the excluded Miss Cragge struck her as a superlative bit of impudence. If she went on giving more receptions she would doubtless only accumulate more annoyances of a similar sort.

No; the intellectual life of the country was young, like the country itself. It was not only young; it was raw and crude. To continue in her task would be to fail hopelessly. She had best not continue in it. She might be wrong in abandoning it so soon; there might be hope yet. But, after all, she was undertaking no holy crusade; conscience made no demands upon her for the perpetuation and triumph of her project. Let it pass into the limbo of abortive efforts. Let it go to make another stone in that infernal pathway proverbially paved by good intentions. . . .

She slept ill that night, and breakfasted later than usual. And she had scarcely finished breakfasting when a card was handed her, which it heightened her color a little to peruse.

The card bore Miss Cragge's name, and one portion of its rather imposing square was filled with the names of many Eastern and Western journals besides, of which the owner evidently desired to record that she was a special correspondent. It seemed to Pauline, while she gazed at the scrap of pasteboard, that this was exactly the sort of card which a person like Miss Cragge would be apt to use for presentation. She was at a loss to understand why Miss Cragge could have visited her at all, and perhaps the acquiescing answer which she presently gave her servant was given because curiosity surpassed and conquered repulsion.

But after the servant had departed, Pauline regretted that she had agreed to see Miss Cragge. "What can the woman want of me?" she now reflected, "except to abuse and possibly insult me?"

Still, the word had been sent. She must hold to it.

Pauline gave Miss Cragge a cool yet perfectly courteous bow, as they met a little later.

"You are Miss Cragge, I believe," she said, very quietly and amiably.

"Oh, I did n't suppose you 'd forgotten me so soon!" came the reproachful and rather unsteady answer. Miss Cragge had risen some time before Pauline entered the room, and her gaunt shape, clad in scant gear, looked notably awkward. Her street costume was untidy, shabby, and even bedraggled. She held a bundle of newspapers, which she shifted nervously from hand to hand.

"You wish to speak with me, then?" said Pauline, still courteously.

"Yes," returned Miss Cragge. It was evident that she underwent a certain distinct agitation. "I have called upon you, Mrs. Varick, because I felt that I ought to do so."

"It is, then, a matter of duty, Miss Cragge?"

"Yes—a matter of duty. A matter of duty

toward myself. Toward myself as a woman, you know — I think that I have been wronged — greatly wronged."

"Not wronged by me, I hope."

"Through you, by someone else."

"I do not understand you."

"I — I shall try to make myself plain."

"I trust you will succeed."

"Oh, I shall succeed," declared Miss Cragge, gasping a little for breath as she now continued. "I have an enemy, Mrs. Varick, and that enemy is your friend. Yes, I mean Mr. Kindelon, of course. He has set you against me. He has made you shut your doors upon me. Oh, you need not deny that this is true. I am perfectly certain of its truth. I am always received by Hagar Williamson Dares. She is a noble, true woman, and she lets me come to her house because she knows I have my battle to fight, just as she has always had her own, and that I deserve her sympathy and her friendship. I don't maintain that I've been always blameless. A newspaper woman can't always be that. She gives wounds, just as she gets wounds. But I never did Ralph Kindelon any harm in my life. He hates me, but he has no business to hate me. I never cared much about his hatred till now. But now he has shown

me that he is an active and dangerous enemy.
I mean, of course, about this affair of yours. I
wanted to be invited to your house last evening;
I expected to be invited. I was on the Dareses'
list. I 'm going to be perfectly candid. It would
have been a feather in my cap to have come here.
I know exactly what your position in society is,
and I appreciate the value of your acquaintance.
If you had snubbed me of your own accord, I
would have pocketed the snub without a murmur.
I 'm used to snubbings ; I have to be, for I get a
good many. Nobody can go abroad picking up
society-items as I do, and not receive the cold
shoulder. But in this case it was no spontaneous
rebuff on your part; it was the malicious interference of a third party; it was Kindelon's mean-
spirited persuasion used against me behind my
back. And it has been an injury to me. It 's
going to hurt me more than you think. It has
been found out and talked over that I was dropped
by you . . . Now, I don't want to be dropped. I
want to claim my rights — to ask if you will not
do me justice — if you will not waive any personal
concern with a private quarrel and allow me to
have the same chance that you have given so
many others. To put it plainly and frankly, Mrs.
Varick, I have come here this morning for the

purpose of asking you if you will not give me an invitation to your next entertainment."

All the time she had thus spoken, Miss Cragge had remained standing. Pauline, who also stood, had shown no desire that her visitor should sit. She was biting her lip as Miss Cragge ended, and her tones were full of a haughty repulsion as she now said, —

"Really, I am unprepared to give you any answer whatever. But you seem to demand an answer, and therefore I shall give you one. You are very straightforward with me, and so I do not see why I should not be equally straightforward with you."

Miss Cragge gave a bitter, crisp little laugh. "I see what is coming," she said. "You think me abominable, and you are going to tell me so."

"I should not tell you if I thought it," replied Pauline. "But I must tell you that I think you unwarrantably bold."

"And you refuse me any other explanation?" now almost panted Miss Cragge. "You will not give me even the satisfaction of knowing why you have dropped me?"

Pauline shook her head. "I do not recognize your right to question me on that point," she returned. " You assume to know my reason for not having asked you here. I object to the form and the quality of your question. I deny that I have dropped you, as you choose to term it. I think your present course a presumptuous one, and I am ignorant of having violated any rights of your own by not having sent you a card to my reception. There are a great many other people in New York besides yourself to whom I did not send a card. Any quarrel between you and Mr. Kindelon is a matter of no concern to me. And as for my having dealt you an injury, that assertion is quite preposterous. I do not for an instant admit it, and since your attitude toward me is painfully unpleasant, I beg that this conversation may be terminated at once."

" Oh, you show me the door, do you?" exclaimed Miss Cragge. She looked very angry as she now spoke, and her anger was almost repulsively unbecoming. Her next words had the effect of a harsh snarl. " I might have expected just this sort of treatment," she proceeded, with both her dingy-gloved hands manipulating the bundle of newspapers at still brisker speed. " But I 'm a very good hater, Mrs. Varick, and I 'm not stamped on quite so easily as you may suppose. I usually die pretty hard in such cases, and perhaps you'll find that your outrageous behavior will get the punishment it merits. Oh, you need n't throw back your proud head like that, as if I were the dirt under your feet! I guess you'll be sorry before very long. I intend to make you so if I can!"

Pauline felt herself turn pale. "You are insolent," she said, "and I desire you to leave my house immediately."

Miss Cragge walked to the door, but paused as she reached its threshold, looking back across one of her square shoulders with a most malevolent scowl.

"You've got no more heart than a block of wood," she broke forth. "You never had any. I know all about you. You married an old man for his money a few years ago. He was old enough to be your grandfather, and a wretched libertine at that. You knew it, too, when you married him. So now that you've got his money you're going to play the literary patron with it. And like the cold-blooded coquette that you are, you've made Ralph Kindelon leave poor Cora Dares, who's madly in love with him, and dance attendance on yourself. I suppose you think Kindelon really cares for you. Well, you're mightily mistaken if you do think so, and if he ever marries you I guess it won't be long before he makes you find it out!"

Miss Cragge disappeared after the delivery of this tirade, and as she closed the outer hall-door with a loud slam Pauline had sank into a chair. She sat thus for a longer time than she knew, with hands knotted in her lap, and with breast and lips quivering.

The vulgarity, the brutality of those parting words had literally stunned her. It is no exaggeration to state that Miss Cragge's reference to her marriage had inflicted a positive agony of shame. But the allusion to Cora Dares's love for Kindelon, and to Kindelon's merely mercenary regard for herself, had also stabbed with depth and suffering. Was it then true that this man's feelings toward her were only the hypocritical sham of an aim at worldly advancement? "How shall I act to him when we again meet?" Pauline asked herself. "If I really thought this charge true, I should treat him with entire contempt. And have I the right to believe it true? This Cragge creature has a viperish nature. Should I credit such information from such a source?"

That was a day of days with poor Pauline. She seemed to look upon Ralph Kindelon in a totally new light. She realized that the man's brilliant personality had made his society very dear to her. She told herself that she cared for him as she had cared for none other in her life. But the thought that personal ambition was solely at the root of his devotion affected her with something not far from horror.

By degrees the memory of Miss Cragge's final outburst stung her less and less. The whole speech had been so despicable, the intention to wantonly insult had been so evident. After a few hours had passed, Pauline found that she had regained nearly all her customary composure. She felt that if Kindelon should come that evening she could discuss with him calmly and rationally the almost hideous occurrence of the morning.

He did come, and she told him a great deal, but she did not tell him all. No mention of Cora Dares left her lips, nor of the acrid slur at his own relations toward herself. He listened to the recital with a face that wrath paled, while it lit a keener spark in his eyes. But he at length answered in tones thoroughly controlled, if a little husky and roughened:

"I can scarcely express to you my disgust for that woman's conduct. I did not think her capable of it. She represents one of the most baleful forces of modern times—the nearly unbridled license of the newspaper. She has dipped her pen for years into poisonous ink; she is one of our American monstrosities and abominations. Her threat of punishment to you would be ridiculous if it were not so serious."

"You think that she will carry it out?" asked Pauline.

"I should not be at all surprised if she did so."

"Do you mean that she may write some slanderous article about me?"

"It is quite possible."

Pauline gave a plaintive sigh. "Oh, have I no means of preventing her?" she exclaimed.

Kindelon shook his head negatively. "She attacks from an ambuscade, nearly always," he answered. "There is no such thing as spiking her guns, for they are kept so hidden. Still, let us hope for the best."

Pauline burst into tears. "What a wretched failure I have made of it all!" she cried. "Ah, if I had only known sooner that my project would bring such disaster upon me!"

"It has brought no disaster as yet," said Kindelon, with a voice full of the most earnest sympathy.

"It has brought distress, regret, torment!"

asseverated Pauline, still struggling with her tears.

" Have you told me all ? " he suddenly asked, with an acute, anxious look.

" All ? " murmured Pauline.

" Yes.   Did that woman say anything more ? "

" Yes," Pauline answered, after a little silence, with lowered eyes.

" Ah ! " sounded Kindelon's exasperated sigh. " I can almost guess what it was," he went on. " She was not content, then, with saying atrocious things of your marriage ; she must couple our names together — yours and mine."

" She mentioned another name still," said Pauline, who continued to gaze at the floor.   " It was the name of Cora Dares."   Pauline lifted her eyes, now ; they wore a determined, glittering look. " She said that Cora Dares was madly in love with you.   ' Madly ' struck me as an odd enough word to apply to that gentle, dignified girl."

" It might well do so ! " burst from Kindelon, in a smothered voice.   He rose and began to pace the floor.   She had never seen him show such an excited manner ; all his past volatility was as nothing to it.   And yet he was plainly endeavoring to repress his excitement.   " However," he proceeded, in a swift undertone, " this absurd slander need not concern you."

"You call it slander, as if you did not really think it so," she said.

He paused, facing her. "Are you going to let the venomous spite of an inferior win your respectful credence?" he questioned.

"We can't help believing certain things," said Pauline, measuredly, "no matter who utters them. I believed that Cora Dares was in love with you before I heard Miss Cragge say it. Or, at least, I seriously suspected as much. But of course this could not be a matter of the least concern to myself, until"— And here she paused very suddenly.

"Well?" he queried. "Until?"—

She appeared to reflect, for an instant, on the advisability of saying more. Then she lifted both hands, with a tossing, reckless motion. "Oh," she declared, "not until that woman had the audacity to accuse me of heartlessly standing in the path of Cora Dares's happiness — of alienating your regard from her — of using, moreover, a hatefully treacherous means toward this end — a means which I should despise myself if I ever dreamed of using!" . . . Pauline's voice had begun to tremble while she pronounced the latter word.

"I understand," he said. His own voice was unsteady, though the anger had in great measure left it. To her surprise, he drew quite near her, and then seated himself close at her side. "If you did truly care for me," came his next sentence, "how little I should care what false witness that woman bore against the attachment! But since that day down at the Battery, when I wore my heart on my sleeve so daringly, I have made a resolve. It will be your fault, too, if I fail to keep it. And if I do fail, I shall fail most wretchedly. I—I shall make a sort of desperate leap at the barrier which now separates you and me."

"You say it will be my fault," was Pauline's response. The color had stolen into her cheeks before she framed her next sentence, and with a most clear glow. "How will it be my fault?"

"You must have given me encouragement," he said, "or at least something that I shall take for encouragement."

A silence followed. She was looking straight at the opposite wall; her cheeks were almost roseate now; a tearful light shone in her eyes as his sidelong look watched them. "Perhaps," she faltered, "you might take for encouragement what I did not mean as such."

"Ah, that is cruel!" he retorted.

She turned quickly; she put one hand on his

arm. "I did not wish to be cruel!" she affirmed, gently and very feelingly.

It seemed to her, then, that the strong arm on which her hand rested underwent a faint tremor.

"It is easy for you to be cruel, where I am concerned."

"Easy!" she repeated, rapidly withdrawing her hand, and using a hurt intonation.

He leaned closer to her, then. "Yes," he said. "And you know why. I have told you of the difference between us. I have told you, because I am incessantly feeling it."

"There is a great difference," she answered, with a brisk little nod, as though of relief and gratification. "You have more intellect than I — far more. You are exceptional, capable, important. I am simply usual, strenuous, and quite of the general herd. That is the only difference which I will admit, although you have reproached me for practising a certain kind of masquerade — for secretly respecting the shadow and vanity called caste, birth, place. Yes," she went on, with a soft fervor that partook of exultation, while she turned her eyes upon his face and thought how extraordinary a face it was in its look of power and manliness, "I will accede to no other difference than this. You are above me, and I will not let you place yourself on my level!"

She felt his breath touch her cheek, then, as he replied: "You are so fine and high and pure that I think you could love only one whom you set above yourself — however mistakenly."

"My love must go with respect — always," she said.

"I am not worthy of your respect."

"Do you want me to credit Miss Cragge?"

"Did *she* say that I was unworthy of it?"

"I — I cannot tell you what she said on that point. I would not tell you, though you begged me to do so."

She saw a bitter smile cross his face, but it lingered there merely an instant. "I can guess," he avowed, "that she tried to make you believe I do not really love you! It is so like her to do that."

"I — I will say nothing," stammered Pauline, once more averting her eyes.

Immediately afterward he had taken her hand in his own. She resisted neither its clasp nor its pressure.

"You know that I love you," she now heard him say, though the leap of her heart made his words sound far off, confused, unreal. "You must have known it days ago! There—my resolve is broken! But what can I do? You have stooped downward from your high state by telling me that I am better than you. I am not better than you, Pauline! I am below you—all the world would say so except yourself. But you don't care for the world. Well, then I will despise it, too, because you bid me. I never respected what you represent until you made me respect it by making me love you. Now I respect and love it, both, because you are a part of it. This is what your project, your ambition, has come to. Ah! how pitiful a failure! you're disgusted with your *salon*—you have been ill-treated, rebuffed, deceived! The little comedy is played to the end—and what remains? Only a poor newspaper-fellow, a sort of Irish adventuring journalist, who offers you his worthless heart to do what you choose with it! What *will* you choose to do with it? I don't presume to advise, to demand—not even to ask! If you said you would marry Ralph Kindelon you would be making a horrible match! Don't let us forget that. Don't let us forget how Mrs. Poughkeepsie would storm and scold!"

He had both her hands in both his own, now. She looked at him with eyes that sparkled and swam in tears. But though she did not withdraw her hands, she receded from him while brokenly saying:

"I — I don't care anything about Aunt Cynthia Poughkeepsie. But there — there is something else that I do care about. It — it seems to steal almost like a ghost between us — I can't tell why — I have no real reason to be troubled as I am — it is like a last and most severe distress wrought by this failure of mine with all those new people. . . It is the thought that you have made Cora Dares believe that you meant to marry her."

Pauline's voice died away wretchedly, and she drooped her head as the final faint word was spoken. But she still let Kindelon hold her hands. And his grasp tightened about them as she heard him answer:

"I suppose Cora Dares *may* have believed that . . But, good God! am I so much to blame? I had never met *you*, Pauline. It was before I went to Ireland the last time — I never asked her to marry me — It was what they call a flirtation. Am I to be held to account for it? Hundreds of men have been foolish in this way before myself — Have you raised me so high only to dash me down? — Won't you speak? Won't you tell me that you forgive a dead fancy for the sake of a living love? Are you so cruel? — so exacting?"

"I am not cruel," she denied, lifting her eyes. . .

It was a good many minutes later that she said to him, with the tears standing on her flushed cheeks, and her fluttered voice in truly sad case,

"I — I am going to accept the Irish adventuring journalist (as — as he calls himself) for my husband, though he — he has never really asked me yet."

"He could not ask you," affirmed Kindelon, with by no means his first kiss. "Like every subject who wishes to marry a princess, he was forced to recognize a new matrimonial code!"

XII.

PAULINE was surprised, during the several ensuing days, to find how greatly her indignation toward Miss Cragge had diminished. The new happiness which had come to her looked in a way resultant, as she reflected upon it, from that most trying and oppressive interview.

"I could almost find it in my heart to forgive her completely," she told Kindelon, with a beaming look.

"I wish that my forgiveness were to be secured as easily," replied Kindelon.

"Your forgiveness from whom?" asked Pauline, with a pretty start of amazement.

"Oh, you know. From your aunt, the vastly conservative Mrs. Poughkeepsie, and her equally conservative daughter."

Pauline gave a laugh of mock irritation. She could not be really irritated; she was too drenched with the wholesome sunshine of good spirits. "It is so ridiculous, Ralph," she said, "for you to speak of my relations as if they were my custodians or my patrons. I am completely removed from them as regards all responsibility, all independence. I wish to keep friends with them, of course; we are of the same blood, and quarrels between kinspeople are always in odious taste. But any very insolent opposition would make me break with them to-morrow."

"And also with your cousin, Courtlandt Beekman?" asked Kindelon, smiling, though not very mirthfully.

Pauline put her head on one side. "I draw a sharp line between him and the Poughkeepsies," she said, either seeming to deliberate or else doing so in good earnest. "We were friends since children, Court and I," she proceeded. "I should hate not to keep friends with Court always."

"You must make up your mind to break with him," said Kindelon, with undoubted gravity.

"And why?" she quickly questioned.

"He abominates me."

"Oh, nonsense! And even if he does, he will change in time . . . I thought of writing him to-day," Pauline slowly proceeded. "But I did not. I have put off all that sort of thing shamefully."

"All that sort of thing?"

"Yes — writing to people that I am engaged, you

know. That is the invariable custom. You must
announce your intended matrimonial step in due
form."

He looked at her with a pitying smile which she
thought became him most charmingly. "And you
have procrastinated from sheer dread, my poor
Pauline!" he murmured, lifting her hand to his
lips and letting it rest against them. "Dread of
an explosion — of a distressing nervous ordeal.
How I read your adroit little deceits!"

She withdrew her hand, momentarily counter-
feiting annoyance. "You absurd would-be seer!"
she exclaimed. "No, I'll call you a raven. But
you can't depress me by your ominous wing-flap-
ping! I thought Aunt Cynthia would drop in
yesterday; I thought most *certainly* that she
would drop in to-day. That is my reason for not
making our engagement transpire through letter."

"I see," said Kindelon, with a comic, quizzical
sombreness. "You didn't want to open your
guns on the enemy; you were waiting for at least
a show of offensive attack. . ."

But, as it chanced, Mrs. Poughkeepsie did
drop in upon Pauline at about two o'clock the
next day. She came unattended by Sallie, but
she had important and indeed momentous news to
impart concerning Sallie. As regarded Pauline's

engagement, she was, of course, in total ignorance of it. But she chose to deliver her own supreme tidings with no suggestion of impulsive haste.

"You are looking very well," she said to Pauline, as they sat on a yielding cachemire lounge together, in the little daintily-decked lower reception-room. "And, my dear niece," she continued, "you must let me tell you that I am full of congratulations at your not being made ill by what happened here the other evening. Sallie and I felt for you deeply. It was so apparent to us that you would never have done it if you had known how dreadfully it would turn out ... But there is no use of raking up old by-gones. You have seen the folly of the whole thing, of course. My dear, it has naturally got abroad. The Hackensacks know it, and the Tremaines, and those irrepressible gossips, the Desbrosses girls. But Sallie and I have silenced all stupid scandals as best we could, and merely represented the affair as a capricious little pleasantry on your part. You have n't lost caste a particle by it — don't fancy that you have. You were a Van Corlear, and you 're now Mrs. Varick, with a great fortune; and such a whim is to be pardoned accordingly."

Pauline was biting her lips, now. "I don't want it to be pardoned, Aunt Cynthia," she said, "and I don't hold it either as a capricious pleasantry or a whim. It was very serious with me. I told you that before."

"Truly you did, my dear," said Mrs. Poughkeepsie. She laughed a mellow laugh of amusement, and laid one gloved hand upon Pauline's arm. "But you saw those horrible people in your drawing-rooms, and I am sure that this must have satisfied you that the whole project was impossible . . . *en l'air*, my dear, as it unquestionably was. Why, I assure you that Sallie and I laughed together for a whole hour after we got home. They were nearly all such droll creatures! It was like a fancy-ball without the mask, you know. Upon my word, I enjoyed it after a fashion, Pauline; so did Sallie. One woman always addressed me as 'ma'am.' Another asked me if I '*resided* on *the* Fifth Avenue.' Still another . . . (no, by the way, that was n't a woman; it was a man) . . . inquired of Sallie whether she danced the Lancers much in fashionable circles. . . . Oh, how funny it all was! And they did n't talk of books in the least. I supposed that we were to be pelted with quotations from living and dead authors, and asked all kinds of radical questions as to what we had read. But they simply talked to us of the most ordinary matters, and in a *very* extraordinary way . . . However, let us not concern ourselves with them any more, my dear. They were horrid, and you know they were horrid, and it goes without saying that you will have no more to do with them."

"I thought some of them horrid," said Pauline, with an ambiguous coolness, "though perhaps I found them so in a different way from yourself."

Mrs. Poughkeepsie repeated her mellow laugh, and majestically nodded once or twice as she did so.

"Well, well, my dear," she recommenced, "let us dismiss them and forget them . . . I hope you are going out again. You have only to signify a wish, you know. There will not be the slightest feeling in society — not the slightest."

"Really?" said Pauline, with an involuntary sarcasm which she could not repress.

But her aunt received the sarcasm in impervious good faith. "Oh, not the slightest feeling," she repeated. "And I do hope, Pauline," she went on, with a certain distinct yet unexplained alteration of manner, "that you will make your *rentrée*, as it were, at a little dinner I shall give Sallie next Thursday. It celebrates an event." Here Mrs. Poughkeepsie paused and looked full at her niece. "I mean Sallie's engagement."

"Sallie's engagement?" quickly murmured Pauline. The latter word had carried an instant personal force of reminder.

"Yes — to Lord Glenartney. You met him once or twice, I believe."

"Lord Glenartney!" softly iterated Pauline. She was thinking what a gulf of difference lay, for the august social intelligence of her aunt, between the separate bits of tidings which she and Mrs. Poughkeepsie had been waiting to impart, each to each.

"Yes, Glenartney has proposed to dear Sallie," began the lady, waxing promptly and magnificently confidential. "Of course it is a great match, even for Sallie. There can be no doubt of that. I don't deny it; I don't for an instant shut my eyes to it; I consider that it would justly subject me to ridicule if I did. Lord Glenartney .was not expected to marry in this country; there was no reason why he should do so. He is immensely rich; he has three seats, in England and Scotland. He is twice a Baron, besides being once an Earl, and is first cousin to the Duke of Devergoil. Sallie has done well; I wish everybody to clearly understand, my dear Pauline, that I *think* Sallie has done brilliantly and wonderfully well. A mother always has ambitious dreams for her child . . . can a mother's heart help having them? But in my very wildest dreams I never calculated upon such a marriage for my darling child as this!"

Pauline sat silent before her aunt's final outburst of maternal fervor. She was thinking of the silly caricature upon all manly worthiness that the Scotch peer just named had seemed to her. She was thinking of her own doleful, mundane marriage in the past. She was wondering what malign power had so crooked and twisted human wisdom and human sense of fitness, that a woman endowed with brains, education, knowledge of right and wrong, should thus exult (and in the sacred name of maternity as well!) over a union of this wofully sordid nature.

"I—I hope Sallie will be happy," she said, feeling that any real doubt on the point might strike her aunt as a piece of personal envy. "Curiously enough," she continued, "*I*, also have to tell you of an engagement, Aunt Cynthia."

Mrs. Poughkeepsie raised her brows in surprise. "Oh, you mean poor dear Lily Schenectady. I've heard of it. It has come at last, my dear, and he is only a clerk on about two thousand a year, besides not being of the *direct* line of the Auchinclosses, as one might say, but merely a sort of obscure relation. Still, it is said that he has fair expectations; and then you know that poor dear Lily's freckles *are* a drawback, and that she has been called a *spotted* lily by some witty persons, and that it has really become a nickname in society, and " —

" I did not refer to Lily Schenectady," here interrupted Pauline. " I spoke of myself."

The mine had been exploded. Pauline and Mrs. Poughkeepsie looked at each other.

" Pauline ! " presently came the faltered answer.

" Yes, Aunt Cynthia, I spoke of myself. I am engaged to Mr. Kindelon."

" Mr. Kindelon ! "

" Yes. I am sure you know who he is."

" Oh, I know who he is." Mrs. Poughkeepsie spoke these words with a ruminative yet astonished drawl.

" Well, I am engaged to him," said Pauline, stoutly but not over-assertively. She had never looked more composed, more simply womanly than now.

Mrs. Poughkeepsie rose. It always meant something when this lady rose. It meant a flutter of raiment, a deliberation of readjustment, a kind of superb, massive dislocation.

"I am horrified!" exclaimed the mother of the future Countess Glenartney.

Pauline rose, then, with a dry, chill gleam in her eyes. "I think that there is nothing to horrify you," she said.

Mrs. Poughkeepsie gave a kind of sigh that in equine phrase we might call a snort. Her large body visibly trembled. She rapidly drew forth a handkerchief from some receptacle in her ample-flowing costume, and placed it at her lips. Pauline steadily watched her, with hands crossed a little below the waist.

"I do so hope that you are not going to faint, Aunt Cynthia," she said, with a satire that partook of strong belligerence.

Mrs. Poughkeepsie, with her applied handkerchief, did not look at all like fainting as she glanced above the snowy cambric folds toward her niece.

"I — I never faint, Pauline . . . it is not my way. I — I know how to bear calamities. But this is quite horrible . . . it agitates me accordingly. I — I have nothing to say and yet I — I have a great deal to say."

"Then don't say it!" now sharply rang Pauline's retort.

"Ah! you lose your temper? It is just what

I might have thought — under the circumstances!"

Pauline clenched her teeth together for a short space, to keep from any futile disclosure of anger. And presently she said, with a shrill yet even directness, —

"What, pray, *are* the circumstances? I tell you that I am to marry the man whom I choose to marry. You advised me — you nearly *forced* me, once — to marry the man whom it was an outrage to make my husband!"

"Pauline!"

"What I tell you is true! He whom I select is not of your world! And, by the way, what is your world? A little throng of mannerists, snobs, and triflers! I care nothing for such a world! I want a larger and a better. You say that I have failed in my effort to break down this barrier of conservatism which hedged me about from my birth . . . Well, allow that I *have* failed in that! I have not failed in finding some true gold from all that you sneer at as tawdry dross! . . . Tawdry! I did well to chance upon the word! What was that gentlemanly bit of vice whom you were so willing I should marry a few years ago? You 've just aired your tenets to me; I 'll air a few of mine to you now. We live in New York, you and I. Do you know what New York means? It means what America means — or what America *ought* to mean, from Canada to the Gulf! And that is — exemption from the hateful bonds of self-glorifying snobbery which have disgraced Europe for centuries! You call yourself an aristocrat. How dare you do so? You dwell in a land which was washed with the blood, less than a century ago, of men who died to kill just what you boast of and exalt! Look more to your breeding and your brains, and less to your so-called caste! I come of your own race, and can speak with right about it. What was it, less than four generations ago? You call it Dutch, and with a grand air. It flowed in the veins of immigrant Dutchmen, who would have opened their eyes with wonder to see the mansion you dwell in, the silver forks you eat with! *They* dwelt in wooden shanties and ate with pewter forks . . . Your objection to my marriage with Ralph Kindelon is horrible — that and nothing more! He towers above the idiot whom you are glad to have Sallie marry! What do I care for the little 'lord'? You bow before it; I despise it. You call my project, my dream, my desire, a failure . . . I grant that it is. But it is immeasurably above that petty worship of the Golden Calf, which *you* name respectability and which *I* denounce as only a pitiful sham! The world is growing older, but you don't grow old with it. You close your eyes to all progress. You get a modish milliner, you keep your pew in Grace Church, you drop a big coin into the plate when a millionaire hands it to you, and you are content. Your contentment is a pitiful fraud. Your purse could do untold good, and yet you keep it clasped — or, if you loose the clasp, you do it with a flourish, a vogue, an *éclat.* . . . Mrs. Amsterdam has done the same for this or that asylum or hospital, and so you, with fashionable acquiescence, do likewise. And you — you, Cynthia Poughkeepsie, who tried to wreck my girlish life and almost succeeded — you, who read nothing of what great modern minds in their grandly helpful impulse toward humanity are trying to make humanity hear — you, who think the fit set of a patrician's gown above the big struggle of men and women to live — you, who immerse yourself in idle vanities and talk of everyone outside your paltry pale as you would talk of dogs — *you* dare to upbraid me because I announce to you that I will marry a man whom power of mind makes your superior, and whom natural gifts of courtesy make far more than your equal!"

As Pauline hotly finished she saw her aunt re-
cede many steps from her.

"Oh, this — this is frightful!" gasped Mrs.
Poughkeepsie. "It — it is the *theatre!* You will
go on the stage, I suppose. It seems to me you
have done everything but go on the stage, already!
That would be the crowning insult to yourself —
to your family!"

"I shan't go on the stage," shot Pauline, "because I have no talent for it. If I had talent,
perhaps I would go. I think it a far better life
for an American woman than to prate triumph-
antly about marrying her daughter to a titled
English fool!"

Mrs. Poughkeepsie uttered a cry, at this point.
She passed from the room, and Pauline, overcome
with the excess of her disclaimer, soon afterward
sank upon a chair . . .

An almost hysterical fit of weeping at once
followed . . . It must have been a half-hour later
when she felt Kindelon's face lowered to her own.
He had nearly always come, since their engagement, at more or less unexpected hours.

"Some hateful thing has happened," he said
very tenderly; "whom have you seen? Why do
you sob so, Pauline? Have you seen *her?* Has
Cora Dares been here?"

Pauline almost sprang from her chair, facing him. "Cora Dares," she cried, plaintively and with passion. "Why do you mention her name now?"

Kindelon folded her in his strong arms. "Pauline," he expostulated, "be quiet! I merely thought of what you yourself had told me, and of what I myself had told *you*? What is it, then, since it is not she? Tell me, and I will listen as best I can."

She soon began to tell him, leaning her head upon his broad breast, falteringly and with occasional severe effort.

"I— I was wrong," she at length finished. "I should not have spoken so rashly, so madly . . . But it was all because of you, Ralph — because of my love for you!"

He pressed her more closely within the arms that held her.

"I don't blame you!" he exclaimed. "You were wrong, as you admit that you were wrong . . . but I don't blame you!"

XIII.

THAT night was an almost sleepless one for Pauline, and during the next morning she was in straits of keen contrition. Theoretically she despised her aunt, but in reality she despised far more her own loss of control. Her self-humiliation was so pungent, indeed, that when, at twelve o'clock on this same day, Courtlandt's card was handed to her, she felt a strong desire to escape seeing him, through the facile little falsehood of a "not at home." But she concluded, presently, that it would be best to face the situation at once, since avoidance would be simply postponement. Courtlandt was as inevitable as death; he must be met sooner or later.

She met him. She did not expect that he would offer her his hand, and she made no sign of offering her own. He was standing near a small table, as she entered, and his attention seemed much occupied with some exquisitely lovely roses in a vase of aerial porcelain. He somehow contrived not wholly to disregard the roses while he regarded Pauline. It was very cleverly done, and with that unconscious quiet which stamped all his clever doings.

" These are very nice," he said, referring to the roses. He had a pair of tawny gloves grasped in one hand, and he made an indolent, whipping gesture toward the vase while Pauline seated herself. But he still remained standing.

" Yes," she replied, as we speak words automati cally. " They are rare here, but I know that kind of rose in Paris."

" Did your future husband send them ? " asked Courtlandt. His composure was superb. He did not look at Pauline, but with apparent carelessness at the flowers.

" Yes," she said; and then, after a slight pause, she added : " Mr. Kindelon sent them."

Courtlandt fixed his eyes upon her face, here. " Was n't it rather sudden ? " he questioned.

" My engagement ? "

" Your engagement."

" Sudden ? Well, I suppose so."

" I did n't expect it quite yet."

She gave a little laugh which sounded thin and paltry to her own ears. " That means you were prepared for it, then ? "

"Oh, I saw it coming."

"And Aunt Cynthia has told you, no doubt."

"Yes. Aunt Cynthia has told me. I felt that I ought to drop in with my congratulations."

Pauline rose now; her lips were trembling, and her voice likewise, as she said: —

"I do hope that you give them sincerely, Court."

"Oh, if you put it in that way, I don't give them at all."

"Then you came here to mock me?"

"I don't know why I came here. I think it would have been best for me not to come. I thought so when I decided to come. Probably you do not understand this. I can't help you, in that case, for I don't understand it myself."

"I choose to draw my own conclusions, and they are kindly and friendly ones. Never mind how or what I understand. You are here, and you have said nothing rude yet. I hope you are not going to say anything rude, for I have n't the heart to pick a quarrel with you — one of our old, funny, soon-healed quarrels, you know. I am too happy, in one way, and too repentant in another."

"Repentant?"

"Yes. I said frightful things yesterday to Aunt Cynthia. I dare say she has repeated them."

" Oh, yes, she repeated every one of them."

" And no doubt with a good deal of wrathful embellishment!" here exclaimed Pauline, bristling.

" Do you think they would bear decoration? Would n't it be like putting a cupola on the apex of the Trinity Church steeple?"

" Not at all!" cried Pauline. "I might have said a great deal worse! Oceans and continents lie between Aunt Cynthia and myself! And I told her so!"

" Really? I thought you were at pretty *close* quarters with each other, judging from her account of the row."

" There was no *row!*" declared Pauline, drawing herself up very finely. "What did she accuse me of saying, please?"

" Oh, I forget. She said you abused her like a pickpocket for not liking the man you 're engaged to."

Pauline shrugged her shoulders, in the manner of one who thinks better of the angry mood, and handsomely abjures it. "Positively, Courtlandt," she said, "I begin to think you had no purpose whatever in coming here to-day."

His sombre brown eyes began to sparkle, though quite faintly, as he now fixed them upon her. "I certainly had one purpose," he said. She saw that his right hand had thrust itself into the breast of his coat, as though it searched there for something. " I wanted to show you this, as I imagined that you don't see the horrid little sheet called 'The Morning Monitor,'" he proceeded.

" 'The Morning Monitor'!" faltered Pauline, with a sudden grievous premonition, as she watched her cousin draw forth a folded newspaper. " No, I never heard of it."

" It has evidently heard of you," he answered. " I never read the vilely personal little affair. But a kind friend showed me this issue of to-day. Just glance at the second column on the second page — the one which is headed ' The Adventures of a Widow '—and tell me what you think of it."

Pauline took the newspaper with unsteady hand. She sank into her chair again, and began to read the column indicated. The journal which she now held was one of recent origin in New York, and it marked the lowest ebb of scandalous newspaper license. It had secured an enormous circulation; it was already threatening to make its editor a Crœsus. It traded, in the most unblushing way, upon the curiosity of its subscribers for a knowledge of the peccadilloes, imprudences, and general private histories of prominent or wealthy citizens. It was a ferret that prowled, prodded, bored, insinuated. It was utterly lawless, utterly libellous. It left not even Launcelot brave nor Galahad pure. It was one of those detestable opportunities which this nineteenth century, notwithstanding a thousand evidences of progress, thrusts into the hands of cynics and pessimists to rail against the human nature of which they themselves are the most melancholy product. It had had suits brought against it, but the noble sale of its copies rendered its heroic continuation possible. Truth, crushed to earth, may rise again, but scurrilous slander, in the shape of " The Morning Monitor," remained capably erect. It fed and throve on its own dire poison.

Pauline soon found herself reading, with misty eyes and indignant heart-beats, a [illegible] of baleful biography of herself, in which her career, from her rash early marriage until her recent entertainment of certain guests, was mercilessly parodied, ridiculed, vilified. These pages will not chronicle in any unsavory details what she read. It was an article of luridly intemperate style, dissolute grammar, and gaudy rhetoric. It bit as a brute bites, and stung as a wasp stings, without other reason that that of low, dull spleen. It mentioned no other name than Kindelon's, but it shot from that

one name a hundred petty shafts of malign innu-
endo.

"Oh, this is horrible!" at length moaned Pauline. She flung the paper down; the tears had
begun to stream from her eyes. "What shall I
do against so hideous an attack?"

Courtlandt was at her side in an instant. He
caught her hand, and the heat of his own was like
that of fever.

"Do but one thing!" he said, with a vehemence
all the more startling because of his usual unvaried
composure. "Break away from this folly once
and forever! You know that I love you — that I
have loved you for years! Don't tell me that you
don't know it, for at the best you've only taught
yourself to forget it! I've never *said* that I
loved you before, but what of that? You have
seen the truth a hundred times — in my sober
way of showing it! I've never thought that you
returned the feeling; I don't even fancy so now.
But I'm so fond of you, Pauline, that I want you
to be my wife, merely liking and respecting me.
I hate to shame myself by even speaking of your
money, but you can sign that all away to some
hospital to-morrow, if you please — you can get it
all together and throw it into the North River, as
far as I am concerned! Send Kindelon adrift —

jilt him! On my soul I beg this of you for your own future happiness more than anything else! I don't say that it will be a square or right thing to do. But it will save you from the second horrible mistake of your life! You made one, that death saved you from. But this will be worse. It will last your lifetime. Kindelon is n't of your *monde*, and never can be. There is so much in that. I am not speaking like a snob. But he has no more sense of the proprieties, the nice externals, the way of doing all those thousand trifling things, which, trifling as they are, make up three-quarters of actual existence, than if he were an Indian, a Bedouin, or a gypsy! Before Heaven, Pauline, if I thought such a marriage could bring you happiness, I 'd give you up without a murmur! I 'm not fool enough to die, or pine, or even mope because of any woman on the globe not caring for me! But now, by giving me the right to guard you — by making me so grateful to you that only the rest of my life can fitly show my gratitude, you will escape calamity, distress, and years of remorse!"

It had hardly seemed to her, at first, as if Courtlandt were really speaking; this intensity was so entirely uncharacteristic of him; these rapid tones and spirited glances were so remote from his accustomed personality. Yet by degrees she recognized not alone the quality of the change, but its motive and source. She could not but feel tenderly toward him then. She was a woman, and he had told her that he loved her; this bore its inevitable condoning results.

And yet her voice was almost stern as she now said to him, rising, and repelling the hand by which he still strove to clasp her own, —

"I think you admitted that if I broke my engagement with Ralph Kindelon it would not be — I use your own words, Court — the square or right thing to do . . . Well, I shall not do it! There, I hope you are satisfied."

He looked at her with a surpassing pain. His hands, while they hung at his sides, knotted themselves. "Oh, Pauline," he exclaimed, "I am *not* satisfied!"

She met his look steadily. The tears in her eyes had vanished, though those already shed glistened on her cheeks. "Very well. I am sorry. I love Ralph Kindelon. I mean to be his wife."

"You meant to be Varick's wife."

"It is horrible for you to bring that up!" she cried. "Here I commit no mistake. He is a man of men! He loves me, and I love him. Do you know anything against him — outside of the codes and creeds that would exclude him from one of Aunt Cynthia's dancing-classes?"

"I know this against him; he is not true. He is not to be trusted. He rings wrong. He is not a gentleman — in the sense quite outside of Aunt Cynthia's definition."

"It is false!" exclaimed Pauline, crimsoning. "Prove to me," she went on, with fleet fire, "that he is not true — not to be trusted. I dare you to prove it."

He walked slowly toward the door. "It is an intuition," he said. "I can't prove it. I could as soon tell you who wrote that villainous thing in the newspaper there."

Pauline gave a laugh of coldest contempt. "Oh," she cried, "in a moment more you will be saying that *he* wrote it!"

Courtlandt shook his head. The gesture conveyed, in some way, an excessive and signal sadness.

"In a moment more," he answered, "I shall be saying nothing to you. And I don't know that I shall ever willingly come into your presence again. Good-by."

Pauline gave no answer, sinking back into her seat as he disappeared.

Her eye lighted upon the fallen newspaper while she did so. Its half-crumpled folds made her forget that her cousin was departing. She suddenly sprang up again, and caught the sheet from the floor. A fire was blazing near by. She hurried toward the grate, intending to destroy the printed abomination.

But, pausing half-way, she once more burst into tears. A recollection cut her to the heart of how futile would be any attempt, now, to destroy the atrocious wrong itself. That must live and work its unmerited ill.

"And to this dark ending," she thought, with untold dejection, "has come my perfectly honest ambition — my fair and proper and wholesome plan!" And then, abruptly, her tearful eyes began to sparkle, while a bright, mirthless smile touched her lips.

"But I can at least have my retort," she decided. "*He* will help me — stand by me in this miserable emergency. I will send for him, — yes, I will send for Ralph at once! He will do just as I dictate, and I know what I *shall* dictate! Miss Cragge wrote that base screed, and Miss Cragge shall suffer accordingly!"

XIV.

SHE sent for Kindelon at once, but before her message could possibly have reached the office of the "Asteroid," he presented himself.

He had recently seen the article, and told her so with a lover-like tenderness that she found balsamic, if not precisely curative.

"It is fiendish," he at length said, "and if I thought any man had done it I would thrash him into confessing so. But I am nearly sure that a woman did it."

"Miss Cragge?"

"Yes."

"You can't thrash her, Ralph. But you can punish her."

"How?"

"Through your own journal — the 'Asteroid.' You can show the world just what a virago she is."

"No," he replied, after a reflective pause, "that can't be."

"Can't be!" exclaimed Pauline, almost hysterically reproachful. "The 'Asteroid' can call the 'Herald,' the 'Times' and the 'Tribune' every possible bad name; it can fly at the throats of politicians whom it does n't indorse; it can seethe and hiss like a witch's caldron in editorials about some recent regretted measure at Albany! But when I ask it to defend me against slanderous ridicule it refuses — it "—

" Ah," cried Kindelon, interrupting her, " it refuses because it is powerless to defend you."

" Powerless!"

" *Qui s'excuse s'accuse.* Any attempted vindication would be merely to direct the public eye still more closely upon this matter. All evil things hold within themselves the germ of their own destruction. Let this villainy die a natural death, Pauline; to fight it will be to perpetuate its power. In the meanwhile I can probably gain a clue to its authorship. But I do not promise, mind. No, I do not promise!"

" And this is all!" faltered Pauline. " Oh, Ralph, according to your argument, every known wrong should be endured because of the notoriety which attaches to the redressing of it."

He looked very troubled and very compassionate as he answered her. " The notoriety is in many cases of no importance, my love. If I were coarsely assailed, for instance, I should not hesitate to openly confront my assailant. But with a pure woman it is different; and with *some* pure women — yourself I quote as a most shining example of these latter — it is unspeakably different! The chastity of some names is so perfect that any touch whatever will soil it."

"If so, then mine has been soiled already!" cried Pauline. "Oh," she went on, "you men are all alike toward us women! Our worst crime is that you yourselves should talk about us! To have your fellow-men say, 'This woman has been rendered the object of a scandalous insult, but has retaliated with courage,' is to make her seem in your eyes as if the insult were really a deserved one! Whenever we are prominent, except in a social way, we are called notorious. If our husbands are drunkards or brutes who abuse us, and we fly to the refuge of the divorce-court, we are notorious. If we go on the stage, no matter how well we may guard our honest womanhood there, we are notorious. If we turn ministers, doctors, lecturers, philanthropists, political agitators, it is all the same; we are observed, discussed, criticised; hence we are notorious. Now, I 've never rebelled against this finely just system, though like nearly all other yoked human beings I have indulged certain private views upon my own bondage. And in my case it was hardly a bondage. . . . Except for certain years where discontent was in a large measure remorse, I have been lifted by exceptional circumstance above those pangs and torments which I have felt certain must have beset many another woman through no act of her own. But now an occasion suddenly dawns when I find myself demanding a man's full justice. To tell me that I can't get it because I am a woman is no answer whatever. I want it, all the same."

Kindelon gazed at her with a sort of woe-begone amazement. "I don't tell you that you can't get it, as far as it is to be had," he almost groaned. "I merely remind you that this is the nineteenth century, and neither the twentieth nor the twenty-first."

Pauline gave a fierce little motion of her shapely head. "I am reminded of that nearly every day that I live," she retorted. "You fall back, of course, upon public opinion. All of you always do, where a woman is concerned, whenever you are cornered. And it is so easy to corner you — to make you swing at us this cudgel of 'domestic retirement' and 'feminine modesty.' I once talked for two hours in Paris with one of the strongest French radical thinkers of modern times. For the first hour and a half he delighted me; he spoke of the immense things that modern scientific developments were doing for the human race. For the last half-hour he disgusted me. And why? I discovered that his 'human race' meant a race entirely masculine. He left woman out of the question altogether. She might get along the best way she could. When he spoke of his own sex he was superbly broad; when he spoke of ours he was narrower than any Mohammedan with a harem full of wives and a prospective Paradise full of subservient houris."

Kindelon rose and began to pace the floor, with his hands clasped behind him. "Well," he said, in a tone of mild distraction, "I'm very sorry for your famous French thinker. I hope you don't want me to tell you that I sympathize with him."

"I'm half inclined to believe it!" sped Pauline. "If my cousin Courtlandt had spoken as you have done, I should have accepted such ideas as perfectly natural. Courtlandt is the incarnation of conventionalism. He is part of the rush in our social wheelwork, and yet he makes it move more slowly. He could no more pull up his window-shades and let in fresh sunshine than you could close your shutters and live in his decorous *demijour!*"

Kindelon still continued his impatient pacing. " I'm very glad of your favorable comparison," he said, with more sadness than satire. He abruptly paused, then, facing Pauline. " What is it, in Heaven's name, that you want me to do?"

" You should not ask; you should know!" she exclaimed. Her clear-glistening eyes, her flushed cheeks, and the assertive, almost imperious posture of her delicate figure made her seem to him a rarely beautiful vision as he now watched her. " Reflect, pray reflect," she quickly proceeded, " upon the position in which I now stand! I attempted to do what if I had been a much better woman than I am it would not at all have been a blameworthy thing to do. The result was failure; it was failure through no fault of my own. I found myself in a clique of wrangling egotists, and not in a body of sensible co-operative supporters. Chief among these was Miss Cragge, whose repulsive traits I foresaw — or rather you aided me to foresee them. I omitted her from my banquet (very naturally and properly, I maintain), and this is the apple of discord that she has thrown." Here Pauline pointed to the fatal newspaper, which lay not far off. " Of course," she went on, with a very searching look at Kindelon, " there can be no doubt that Miss Cragge *is* the offender!   I, for my part, am certain of it; you, for yours, are certain as well, unless I greatly err. But this makes your refusal to publicly chastise her insolence all the more culpable!"

"Culpable!" he echoed, hurrying toward her. "Pauline! you don't know what you are saying! Have I the least pity, the least compunction toward that woman?"

Pauline closed her eyes for an instant, and shook her head, with a repulsing gesture of one hand. "Then you have a very false pity toward another woman — and a very false compunction as well," she answered.

"How can I *act*, situated as I am?" he cried, with sharp excitement. "You have not yet allowed our engagement to transpire. What visible or conceded rights *have* I to be your defender?"

"You are unjust," she said. . "I give you every right. That article insinuates that I am a sort of high-bred yet low-toned adventuress. No *lady* could feel anything but shame and indignation at it. Besides, it incessantly couples your name with mine. . . . And as for right to be my champion in exposing and rebuking this outrage, I — I give you every right, as I said."

"I desire but one," returned Kindelon. His voice betrayed no further perturbation. He seated himself at her side, and almost by force took both her hands in the strong grasp of both his own.

"What right?" she questioned. Her mood of accusation, of reproach, was not yet quieted; her eyes still sparkled from it; her restless lips still betrayed it.

"The right," he answered, "of calling you my wife. As it is, what am I? A man far below you in all worldly place, who has gained from you a matrimonial promise. Marry me!—marry me at once!—to-morrow!—and everything will be different! Then you shall have become mine to defend, and I will show you how I can defend what is my own!"

"To-morrow!" murmured Pauline.

"Yes, to-morrow! You will say it is too soon. You will urge conventionalism now, though a minute ago you accused *me* of urging it! When you are once my wife I shall feel empowered to lawfully befriend you!"

"Lawfully!" she repeated. "Can you not do so manfully, as it is?"

"No—not without the interfering claims and assertions of your family!"

"I *have* no real family. And those whom you

call such are without the right of either claim or
asscrtion, as regards any question of what I choose
or do not choose to do!"

He still retained her hands; he put his lips
against her check; he would not let her withdraw, though she made a kind of aggrieved effort
to do so.

"They have no rights, Pauline, and yet they
would overwhelm me with obloquy!   As your
husband—once as your wedded, chosen husband,
what should I care for them all?   I would laugh
at them!   Make it to-morrow!   Then see how I
will play my wife's part, and fight her battle!"...

They talked for some time after this in lowered
tones . . . Pauline was in a wholly new mood
when she at length said,—

"To-morrow, then, if you choose."

"You mean it?   You promise it?"

"I mean it—and I promise it, since you seem
so doubtful."

"I am doubtful," he exclaimed, kissing her,
"because I can scarcely dream that this sudden
happiness has fallen to me from the stars!" . . .

When he had left her, and she was quite alone,
Pauline found her lips murmuring over the words,
in a sort of mechanical repetition: "I have promised to marry him to-morrow."

She had indeed made this vow, and as a very sacred one.   And the more that she reflected upon it the more thoroughly praiseworthy a course it seemed.   Her nearest living relations were the Poughkeepsies and Courtlandt.   She had quarrelled with both — or it meant nearly the same thing.   There was no one left to consult.   Besides, even if there had been, why should she consult any third party in this affair, momentous though it was?   She loved; she was beloved.   She was a widow with a great personal, worldly independence.   She had already been assailed; what mattered a little more assailance?   For most of those who would gossip and sneer she had a profound and durable contempt ; . . . Why, then, should she regret her spoken word?

And yet she found herself not so much regretting it as fearing lest she might regret it.   She suddenly felt the need, and in keenest way, of a near confidential, trustworthy friend.   But her long residence abroad had acted alienatingly enough toward all earlier American friendships.   She could think of twenty women — married, or widows like herself — who would have received her solicited counsel with every apparent sign of sympathy.   But with all these she had lost the old intimate sense ; new ground must be broken in dealing with them; their views and creeds were what her own had been when she had known and prattled platitudes with them before her dolorous marriage: or at least she so chose to think, so chose to decide.

"There is one whom I could seek, and with whom I could seriously discuss the advisability of such a speedy marriage," at length ran Pauline's reflections. "That one is Mrs. Dares. Her large, sweet, just mind would be quite equal to telling me if I am really wrong or right . . . Still, there is an obstacle — her daughter, Cora. Yet that would make no difference with Mrs. Dares. She would be above even a maternal prejudice. She is all gentle equity and disinterested kindliness. I might see her alone — quite alone — this evening. Neither Cora nor the sister, Martha, need know anything. I would pledge her to secrecy before I spoke a word . . . I will go to her! I will go to Mrs. Dares, and will ask her just what I ought to do."

This resolve strengthened with Pauline after she had once made it. The hour was now somewhat late in the afternoon. She distrusted the time of Mrs. Dares's arrival up-town from her work, and decided that the visit had best be paid at about seven o'clock that same evening.

A little later she was amazed to receive the card of Mr. Barrowe. She went into her reception-room to see this gentleman, with mingled amusement and awkwardness; she was so ignorant what fatality had landed him within her dwelling.

"I scarcely know how to greet you, Mr. Barrowe," she said, after giving a hand to her guest. "You and I parted by no means peacefully last night, and I — I am (yes, I confess it!) somewhat unprepared " . . .

At this point Mr. Barrowe made voluble interruption. His little twinkling eyes looked smaller and acuter than before, and his gaunt, spheroidal nose had an unusual pallor as it rose from his somewhat depressed cheeks.

"You need n't say *you* are unprepared, Mrs. Varick!" he exclaimed. "I am unprepared myself. I had no idea of visiting you this afternoon. I had no idea that you would again give me the pleasure of receiving me. Handicapped as I am, myself, by visits, letters, applications, mercantile matters, I have insisted, however, on getting rid of all — yes, *all* trammels."

Here Mr. Barrowe paused, and Pauline gently inclined her head, saying, —

"That is very good of you. Pray proceed."

"Proceed!" cried Mr. Barrowe. He had already seated himself, but he now rose, approached Pauline, took her hand, and with an extravagant gallantry which his lank body caused closely to verge upon the ludicrous, lifted this hand ceremoniously to his pale lips. Immediately afterward he resumed his seat. And at once he recommenced speaking.

"I feel that I — I owe you the most profound of apologies," he declared, with a hesitation that seemed to have a sincere emotional origin. "Handicapped as I am by a hundred other matters, besieged as I am by bores who want my autograph, by people who desire me to write for this or that journal, by people who desire consultation with me on countless literary or even commercial subjects, I nevertheless have felt it a question of conscience to pay you this visit."

"A question of conscience?" said Pauline, suavely.

"Yes, Mrs. Varick. I — I have seen that stringently objectionable article in the . . . ahem . . . the 'Morning Monitor.' May I ask if you also have seen it? And pray be sure that when I thus ask I feel confident you *must* have seen it, since bad tidings travel quickly, and " . . .

"Yes, Mr. Barrowe, I have seen it," said Pauline, interrupting another thin, diplomatic sort of cough on the part of her visitor. "And I should be glad if you could tell me what devoted foe wrote it."

Mr. Barrowe now trembled with eagerness. "I — I *can* tell you!" he exclaimed. "It — it was that unhappy Miss Cragge! I had no sooner read it, in my office this morning, than I was attacked by a conviction — an absolute conviction — that *she* wrote it. Handicapped, besieged as I am . . . but let that pass " . . .

"Yes — let that pass," softly cried Pauline, meaning no discourtesy, yet bent upon reaching the bare fact and proof. "You say that you are sure that Miss Cragge wrote the article?"

"Positively certain," asseverated Mr. Barrowe. "I went to the lady at once. I found her at her desk in the office of — well, let us not mind *what* newspaper. I upbraided her with having written it! I was very presumptuous, perhaps — very dictatorial, but I did not care. I had stood up for the lady, not many evenings ago, at the risk of your displeasure."

"The *lady!*" repeated Pauline, half under her breath, and with a distinct sneer. "Go on, please, Mr. Barrowe. Did Miss Cragge confess?"

"Miss Cragge *did* not confess. But she showed such a defiant tendency *not* to confess — she

treated me with such an overbearing pugnacious-
ness and disdain, that before I had been five
minutes in her society I had no doubts whatever
as to the real authorship of the shocking article.
And now, Mrs. Varick, I wish to offer you my
most humble and deferential apologies. I wish to
tell you how deeply and sincerely sorry I am for
ever having entered into the least controversy
with you regarding that most aggressive and venomous female! For, my dear madam, besieged and
handicapped though I may be by countless " . . .

"Don't offer me a word of apology, Mr. Barrowe!" here struck in Pauline, jumping up from
her seat and seizing the hand of her guest. "It
is quite needless! I owe you more than you owe
me! You have told me the name of my enemy,
of which I was nearly certain all along." And
here Pauline gave the gentleman's bony and ca-
daverous face one of those glances which those
who liked her best thought the most charming.

"I had been told," she went on, with a very
winning intonation, "that you have a large, warm
heart!"

"Who — who told you that?" murmured Mr.
Barrowe, evidently under the spell of his hostess's
beauty and grace.

"Mr. Kindelon," Pauline said, gently.

"Kindelon!" exclaimed Mr. Barrowe, "why he is my worst enemy, as — as I fear, my dear madam, that Miss Cragge is yours!"

"Oh, never mind Miss Cragge," said Pauline, with a sweet, quick laugh; "and never mind Mr. Kindelon, either. I have only to talk about *you*, Mr. Barrowe, and to tell you that I have never yet met a good, true man (for I am certain that you are such) who stood in his own light so persistently as you do. You have an immense talent for quarrelling," she went on, with pretty seriousness. "Neglect it — crush it down — be yourself! Yourself is a very honest and agreeable self to be. I am always on the side of people with good intentions, and I am sure that yours are of the best. A really bitter-hearted man ruffles people, and so do you. But your motives for it are as different from his as malice is different from dyspepsia. I am sure you are going to reform from this hour."

"Reform?" echoed Mr. Barrowe.

Pauline gave a laugh of silver clearness and heartiest mirth. As often happens with us when we are most assailed by care, she forgot all present misery for at least the space of a minute or so.

"Yes," she cried, with a bewitching glee quite her own and by no means lost upon her somewhat susceptible listener, "you are going to conform the Mr. Barrowe of real life to the Mr. Barrowe who writes those brilliant, judicial, and trenchant essays. Oh, I have read them! You need not fancy that I am talking mere foundationless flattery such as you doubtless get from many of those people who . . . well, who handicap you, you know . . . And your reformation is to begin at once. I am to be your master. I have a lot of lessons to teach !"

" When are your instructions to begin ? " said Mr. Barrowe, with a certain awkward yet positive gallantry. "I am very anxious to receive them."

" Your first intimation of them will be a request to dine with me. Will you accept ?— you and your wife of course."

"But my wife is an invalid. She never goes anywhere."

" I hope, however, that she sometimes dines."

" Yes, she dines, poor woman . . . incidentally."

" Then she will perhaps give me an incidental invitation to break bread . . . Oh, my dear Mr. Barrowe, what I mean is simply that I want to know you better, and so acquire the right to tell you of a few superficial faults which prevent all the world from recognizing your kindly soul. I . . ."

But here Pauline paused, for a servant entered

with a card. She glanced at the card, and made an actually doleful grimace.

"Mr. Leander Prawle is here," she said to her visitor.

Mr. Barrowe gave a start. "In that case I must go," he said. "I once spoke ill of that young gentleman's moŝt revered poem, and since then he has never deigned to notice me."

"But you will not forget the dinner, and what is to follow," said Pauline, as she shook hands.

"No," Mr. Barrowe protested. "If you cleave my heart in twain I shall try to live the better with the other half of it."

"I should not like to cleave it in twain," said Pauline. "It is too capable and healthy a heart for that. I should only try to make it beat with more temperate strokes . . *Au revoir*, then. If you should meet Mr. Prawle outside, tell him that you are sorry."

"Sorry? But his poem was abominable!"

"All the more reason for you to be magnanimously sorry . . Ah, here he is!"

Here Mr. Leander Prawle indeed was, but as he entered the room Mr. Barrowe slipped past him, and with a suddenness that almost prevented his identification on the part of the new-comer . .

"Mrs. Varick," exclaimed Leander Prawle,

while he pressed the hand of his hostess. "I came here because duty prompted me to come."

"I hope pleasure had a little to do with the matter, Mr. Prawle," said Pauline, while indicating a lounge on which they were both presently seated.

Mr. Prawle looked just as pale as when Pauline had last seen him, just as dark-haired, and just as dark-eyed; but the ironical fatigue had somehow left his visage; there was a totally new expression there.

"I suppose," he began, with his black eyes very fixedly directed upon Pauline's face, "that you have heard of the . . the 'Morning Monitor's' outrageous . . ."

"Yes, Mr. Prawle," Pauline broke in. "I have heard all about it."

"And it has pained you beyond expression!" murmured the young poet. "It must have done so!"

"Naturally," replied Pauline.

"It . . it has made *me* suffer!" asserted the new visitor, laying one slim, white hand upon the region of his heart.

"Really?" was the answer. "That is very nice and sympathetic of you."

Mr. Prawle regarded her with an unrelaxed and

very fervid scrutiny. He now spoke in lowered and emotional tones, leaning toward his hearer so that his slender body made quite an exaggerated curve.

"My whole soul," he said, "is brimming with sympathy!"

Pauline conquered her amazement at this entirely unforeseen outburst.

"Thanks very much," she returned. "Sympathy is always a pleasant thing to receive."

Mr. Prawle, still describing his physical curve, gave a great sigh. "Oh, Mrs. Varick," he murmured, "I should like to kill the man who wrote that horrible article."

"Suppose it were a woman," said Pauline.

"Then I should like to kill the woman!.. Mrs. Varick, will you pardon me if I read you .. a few lines which indignation com——yes, combined with reverence — actual reverence — inspired me to write after reading those disgraceful statements? The lines are — are addressed to yourself. With — with your permission, I — I will draw them forth."

Without any permission on Pauline's part, however, Mr. Prawle now drew forth the manuscript to which he had referred. His long pale fingers underwent a distinct tremor as he

unrolled a large crackling sheet of foolscap. And
then, when all, so to speak, was ready, he swept
his dark eyes over Pauline's attentive countenance. "*Have* I your permission?" he falteringly inquired.

"It is granted, certainly, Mr. Prawle."

After a slight pause, and in a tone of sepul-
chrally monotonous quality, the young gentleman
read these lines:—

> "White soul, what impious voice hath dared to blame
>   With virulent slander thine unsullied life ?
>   Methinks that now the very stars should blush
>   In their chaste silver stateliness aloft !
>   Methinks the immaculate lilies should droop low
>   For very shame at this coarse obloquy,
>   The unquarried marble of Pentelicus
>   Deny its hue of snow, and even the dawn
>   Forget her stainless birthright for thy sake !
>   Curséd the hand that wrote of thee such wrong;
>   Curséd the pen such hand hath basely clasped;
>   Curséd the actual ink whose . . ."

"My dear Mr. Prawle!" exclaimed Pauline, at
this point; "I must beg you not to make me the
cause of so terrible a curse! Indeed, I cannot
sanction it. I must ask you to read no more."

She was wholly serious. She forgot to look
upon the humorous side of Mr. Prawle's action;
his poem, so called, addressed her jarred nerves

and wounded spirit as a piece of aggravating impudence. The whole event of his visit seemed like a final jeer from the sarcastic episode recently ended.

He regarded her now with a sorrowful astonishment. "You — you wish me to read no more!" he exclaimed.

"Yes, if you please," said Pauline, controlling her impatience as best she could.

"But I — I wrote it especially *for* you!" he proceeded. "I have put my soul into it! I consider it in many ways the most perfect thing that I have *ever* done. I intended to include it in my forthcoming volume, 'Moonbeams and Mountain-Peaks,' under the title of 'Her Vindication.' Even the grossly material poetic mind of Arthur Trevor, to whom I read it a few hours ago, admitted its sublimity, its spirituality!"

"I will admit both, also," said Pauline, whose mood grew less and less tolerant of this self-poised fatuity. "Only, I must add, Mr. Prawle, that it would have been better taste for you to have left this exasperating affair untouched by your somewhat saintly muse. And I shall furthermore request that you do not include the lines in your 'Moonbeams and Hill-Tops,' or" —

"Mountain-Peaks!" corrected Mr. Prawle, rising with a visible shudder. "Oh, Mrs. Varick," he went on, "I see with great pain that you are a most haughty and ungenerous lady! You — you have smitten me with a fearful disappointment! I came here brimming with the loftiest human sympathy! I believed that to-day would be a turning-point in my existence. I confidently trusted that after hearing my poem there would be no further obstacle in my career of greatness!"

Pauline now slowly left her seat. Unhappy as she was, there could be no resisting such magnificent opportunities of amusement as were now presented to her.

"Your career of greatness?" she quietly repeated. "Did I hear you properly, Mr. Prawle?"

Her guest was refolding his manuscript with an aggrieved and perturbed air. As he put the paper within a breast-pocket he rolled his dark eyes toward Pauline with infinite solemnity.

"You doubt, then," he exclaimed, "that I am born to be great — supremely great? Ah, there is no need for me to put that question now! I had thought otherwise *before* . . when you smiled upon me, when you seemed to have read my poems, to be familiar with my growing fame!"

"You mistake," said Pauline: "I never meant

to show you that I had read your poems. If I smiled upon you, Mr. Prawle, it was from courtesy only."

"Horrible!" ejaculated the young poet. He clasped his hands together in a somewhat theatrically despairing way, and for an instant lowered his head. "I — I thought that you were prepared to indorse, to assist my genius!" he soon proceeded, levelling a look of strong appeal at Pauline. "I thought that you had separated my poetic veracity from the sham of Trevor and Corson! I — I thought, Mrs. Varick, that in you I had found a true worshipper!"

Pauline was at last amused. "I usually reserve my worship for divinities, Mr. Prawle," she said, "and I have found but a few of these in all the history of literature."

"I see!" cried her companion, "you mean that I am *not* a genius!"

"I did not say so. But you have given me no proof of it."

"No proof of it! What was the poem I have just read?"

"It was .. well, it was resonant. But I objected to it, as I have told you, on personal grounds." As she went on, Pauline tried to deal with a rather insubordinate smile of keen, sarcastic enjoyment.

"So you really think," she continued, "that you possess absolute genius?"

"I am certain of it!" cried Mr. Prawle.

"That is a very pleasant mental condition."

"Do *you* doubt it? . . . Ah! I see but too plainly that you do!"

"Frankly," said Pauline, "I do."

Mr. Prawle flung both his hands towards the ceiling. "It is Kindelon's work," he cried, with an effect of very plaintive lamentation. "Kindelon is among those who yet oppose me."

"Mr. Kindelon is not responsible for my opinions," said Pauline. "However, you probably have other opponents?"

"Their name is legion! But why should I care? Do you join their ranks? . . . Well, Shelley almost died because of being misunderstood! I had hoped that you would assist me in — yes, in the publication of my book of poems, Mrs. Varick. I do not mean that I wrote to you, for this reason, the poem which you have just refused to hear me read. Far from it! I only mean that I have cherished the idea of securing in you a patron. Yes, a patron! I am without means to bring forth 'Moonbeams and Mountain-Peaks.' And I had hoped that after hearing me read what I have already told you is my most nobly able creation, you would . . . consent, as a lover of art, of genius, of . . . "

" I understand," said Pauline. " You wish me to assist you in the publication of your volume." She was smiling, though a trifle wearily. " Well, Mr. Prawle, I will do it."

" You will do it ! "

" Yes.   You shall have whatever cheque you write me for " . . She approached Prawle and laid her hand upon his arm. " But you must promise me to destroy ' Her Vindication ' — not even to think of publishing it. Do you ? "

" Yes . . if you insist."

" I do insist . . Well, as I said, write to me for the amount required."

Prawle momentarily smiled, as if from extreme gratitude. And then the smile abruptly faded from his pale face. " I will promise ! " he declared. " But . . oh, it is so horrible to think that you help me from no real appreciation of my great gifts — that you do so only from *charity !* "

" Charity is not by any means a despicable virtue."

" From a great millionaire to a poor poet — yes ! The poet has a sensitive soul ! He wants to be loved for his verses, for his inspiration, if he is a true poet like myself ! "

"And you believe yourself a true poet, Mr. Prawle?"

"I?"

It is impossible to portray the majesty of Mr. Prawle's monosyllabic pronoun. "If I am not great," he enunciated slowly, "then no one *has* been or ever *will* be great. I have a divine mission. A truly and positively divine mission."

Pauline gave a little inscrutable nod. "A divine mission is a very nice thing to have. I hope you will execute it."

"I *shall* execute it!" cried Mr. Prawle. "All the poets, on every side of me, are singing about The Past. I, and I alone, sing of The Future. I set evolution to music . . what other poet has done that? I wrest from Buckle, Spencer, Tyndall, Huxley — from all the grand modern thinkers, in fact — their poetic and yet rationalistic elements! If you had heard my poem to yourself *through* — if you had had the patience, I — I may add, the kindliness, to hear it through, you would have seen that my terminus was in accord with the prevailing theories of Herbert Spencer's noble philosophy " . . .

"Shall I ever cling to or love Herbert Spencer again?" thought Pauline, "when I see him made the shibboleth of such intellectual charlatans as this?"

"In accord," continued Mr. Prawle, "with every-thing that is progressive and unbigoted. I finished with an allusion to the Religion of Humanity. I usually do, in all my poems. That is what makes them so unique, so incomparable!"

Pauline held out her hand in distinct token of farewell.

"Belief in one's self is a very saving quality," she said. "I congratulate you upon it."

Mr. Prawle shrank offendedly toward the door. "You dismiss me!" he burst forth. "After I have bared my inmost soul to you, you *dismiss* me!"

Pauline tossed her head, either from irritation or semi-diversion. "Ah, you take too much for granted!" she said, withdrawing her hand.

Mr. Prawle had raised himself to his full height. "I refuse your assistance!" he ejaculated. "You offer it as you would offer it to a pensioner — a beggar! And you — *you*, have assumed the right of entertaining and fostering literary talent! I scarcely addressed you at your last reception . . I *waited*. I supposed that in spite of Kindelon's known enmity, some of your guests must have told you how immense were my deserts — how they transcended the morbid horrors of Rufus Corson, and the glaring superficialities of Arthur

Trevor. But I discover, plainly enough, that you are impervious to all intellectual greatness of claim. I will accept *no* aid from you!—none whatever! But one day, when the name of Leander Prawle is a shining and a regnant one, you will perhaps remember how miserably you failed to value his merits, and shrink with shame at the thought of your own pitiable misjudgment!"...

"Thank Heaven that monstrosity of literary vanity has removed itself!" thought Pauline, a little later, when Leander Prawle had been heard very decisively to close the outer hall-door. "And now I must dwell no longer on trifles—I must concern myself with far weightier matters."

The coming marriage to Kindelon on the morrow seemed to her fraught with untold incentive for reflection. "But I will not reflect," she soon determined. "I will at once try to see Mrs. Dares, and let her reflect for me. She is so wise, so capable, so admirable! I have consented because I love! Let her, if she shall so decide, dissuade me because of experiences weightier than even my own past bitter ones!"

The hour of her resolved visit to Mrs. Dares had now arrived. In a certain way she congratulated herself upon the distracting tendency of both Mr. Barrowe's and Mr. Prawle's visits. "They have prevented me," she mused, "from dwelling too much upon my own unhappy situation. Mr. Barrowe is a very sensible fool, and Mr. Prawle is a very foolish fool. They are both, in their way, taunting and satiric radiations from the dying bonfire of my own rash ambition. They are both reminders to me that I, after all, am the greatest and most conspicuous fool. Some other woman, more sensible and clever than I, will perhaps seek to establish in New York a social movement where intellect and education are held above the last Anglomaniac coaching-drive to Central Park, or the last vulgarly-select *cotillon* at Delmonico's. But it will be decades hence. I don't know how many .. but it will be decades .. All is over, now. I face a new life; I have ended with my *salon.* Only one result has come of it — Ralph Kindelon. Thank Heaven, he is a substantial result, though all the rest are shadow and illusion!"

Pauline soon afterwards started on foot for the residence of Mrs. Dares. It was nearly dusk. She had determined to set before this good and trusted woman every detail of her present discomfort, and while confessing her matrimonial promise as re-garded the marriage with Kindelon on the morrow, to exhort counsel, advice, guidance, justification. Being a woman, and having made up her mind, justification may have been the chief stimulus of her devout pilgrimage.

The great bustling city was in shadow as she rang the bell at Mrs. Dares's residence.

A strange, ominous, miserable fear was upon her while she did so. She could not account for it; she strove to shake it off. She remembered her own reflections: "All is over now. I face a new life."

But she could not dismiss the brooding dread while she waited the answer of her summons at Mrs. Dares's door.

XV.

THE tidy young negress opened the door soon afterwards. Pauline asked for Mrs. Dares. The answer came that Mrs. Dares was at home.

"I wish to see her alone," said Pauline.

"Miss Cora's got a gent'man in the back room," came the answer, "but there's nobody right here."

Between "right here" and the "back room," Pauline was soon shown the difference. As she sat in a little prettily-furnished apartment, awaiting the appearance of Mrs. Dares, she readily apprehended that some sort of a chamber lay behind. This was, reasonably, the Dareses' dining-room. But she heard voices from beyond the rough decorative woollen tapestry which intervened in heavy concealing folds.

At first, seated quietly and thinking of just what she should say to Mrs. Dares, Pauline quite disregarded these voices.

"I shall tell the plain, unvarnished truth," she

reflected. "I shall not leave a single detail. I shall trust her judgment absolutely."

A moment later she started, with a recognizing sense that she had heard a familiar tone from one of the voices behind the tapestry. Evidently a man was speaking. She rose from her seat. She had approached the curtain instinctively before realizing her act. A new impulse made her withdraw several steps from it. But the voice had been Kindelon's, and she now clearly heard Kindelon speak again.

"Cora!" she heard him say, "there are certain wrongs for which no reparations *can* be given. I know that the wrong I have done you is of this sort. I don't attempt to exculpate myself. I don't know why I came here to bid you this farewell. It was kind of you to consent to see me. Hundreds of other women would have refused, under like conditions. But you have often said that you loved me, and I suppose you love me still. For this reason you may find some sort of consolation hereafter in the thought that I have made an ambitious marriage which will place me high in the esteem of the world, which will give my talents a brilliant chance, which will cause men and women to point to me as a man who has achieved a fine and proud success. . . Good-by,

Cora . . . Let me take your hand once — just once — before I go. I 'll grant you that I 've behaved like a scamp. I 'll grant everything that can be said in my own disfavor. Good heavens! don't look at me in that horribly reproachful way, you — you make me willing to renounce this marriage wholly! Cora, I will do so if you 'll pardon the past! I 'll come back to you, I 'll devote my future life to you! only tell me that you forgive and forget!"

"No, no," Pauline now heard a struggling and seemingly agonized voice reply. "There is no undoing what you have done. Keep your promise to *her,* as you have broken your faith with *me.* I do not say that my love is dead yet; I think it will not die for a long time . . . perhaps not for years. But my respect is wholly dead. . . I will not touch your hand; I will not even remain longer in your presence. I — I have no vengeful feeling toward you. I wish you all future happiness. If you shine hereafter as your talents deserve, I shall hear of your fame, your triumph, with no shadow of bitterness in my soul. And my chief hope, my chief anxiety, will be for the woman whom you have married. I know her enough to know that she is full of good impulses, full of true and fine instincts. You will go to her with an aching conscience and a stained honor. But I pray that after she has lifted you into that place which you seek to gain through her, she may never know you as I have known you — never wake to my anguish of disappointment — never realize my depths of disillusion!"

Pauline waited to hear no more. She thrust aside the drapery of the doorway and passed into the next room.

Cora uttered a swift and smothered cry. Kindelon gave a terrible start. Then a silence followed. It seemed to Pauline a most appreciable silence. She meant and wished to break it, yet her speech kept defying her will, and resisted her repeated effort at due control. But at length she said, looking straight at Kindelon, —

"I have heard — I did not mean to hear — I don't want you to say a single word — there is nothing for you to say. I simply appear before you — before you both! I — I think that is enough. I know every thing now. You . . must have been certain that if I had previously known — that if you had not told me a falsehod I . . I . . should never " . . .

And then poor Pauline reeled giddily, putting forth both hands in a piteous, distraught way . . . When Kindelon caught her she had already lost consciousness. . . .

The sense of blank was a most acute one when she awoke. Her first clear thought was, "How long have I been unconscious?" . . . And then came remembrance, and with remembrance the pain of a deep-piercing hurt.

No one was near by except Mrs. Dares. Pauline lay upon a lounge; she felt the yielding of cushions beneath her head and shoulders. Her first audible sign of revived consciousness was a little tremulous laugh.

"That's you, Mrs. Dares?" she then said. "I— I must have fainted. How funny of me! I—I never fainted before."

Mrs. Dares put both arms about her, and kissed her twice, thrice, on the cheek.

"My poor, dear, unhappy lady!" she said. " I am sorry — so miserably sorry."

Pauline repeated her tremulous laugh. She was beginning to feel the reassertion of physical strength. " I — I came here to see only you, Mrs. Dares," she now said, "but it was fated otherwise. And . . . and yet it has all been better — far better." Here she laughed again, and a little hysterically. "Oh, how superb a failure I 've made of it, have n't I? I thought the 'Morning Monitor' had dealt me my last *coup*. But one other still remained!"

She lay silent for some little time, after this, and when Mrs. Dares presently spoke to her the lids which had dropped over her eyes did not lift themselves. It was so sweet, so tender, so exquisitely gentle a voice that it brought not the slightest exciting consequences.

"He is greatly to blame. I do not excuse him any more than you will. But you must not think the worst of him. You must think him weak, but you must not think him entirely base. I look at his conduct with impartial eyes. I try to look at everybody with impartial eyes. He was far below you in the social scale — that is the phrase which means inferiority nowadays, and I am afraid it will mean inferiority for many a year to come. He had engaged himself to my dear Cora. He meant to marry her. Then he met you. Everything about you dazzled and charmed him. It was yourself as much as your position, your wealth, your importance. He cared for you; he was enchanted by you; his nature is not a deep nature, though his intellect is large and keen. He is almost the typical Irishman, this Kindelon — the Irishman who, in statesmanship, in governance, in administrative force, has left poor Ireland what she is to-day. He meant well, but he had not enough *morale* to make this well-meaning active and cogent. The temptation came, and he yielded at once. There was no premeditated dishonor. The strain was put upon him and he could not bear the strain — that is all. Such men as he never can bear such a strain. There was not a hint of coldbloodedness in his conduct — there was none of the fortune-hunter's deliberate method. There was, indeed, no method at all; there was nothing except an inherent moral feebleness. Brilliant as he is, exceptional as he is, he can no more help consent and acquiescence in any matter which concerns his personal, selfish desires, than the chameleon can help taking the tints of what surrounds it. And I do not believe that he knows, at this hour, whether he loves you or my poor Cora the best. That is he — that is Kindelon — that is the fascinating, distressing race that he represents. He loved you both; his big, expansive Irish heart was quite capable of doing that. But his insecure, precarious conscience was incapable of pointing to him the one straight, imperative path. Hence your own sorrow, my dear, ill-used lady, and hence the sorrow of my poor unfortunate Cora!"

Pauline's eyes slowly unclosed as Mrs. Dares's last words were spoken.

"You speak like a sybil!" she murmured.

"But you speak too late. If I had only talked with you a little sooner! I should have been so prepared for such words *then!* Now they only come to me like mockery and . . . and sarcasm!"

Again Mrs. Dares stooped and kissed her.

"God knows," she said, "that I mean them for neither!"

"God help me from believing that you do!" answered Pauline. She raised herself, and flung both arms about Mrs. Dares's neck, while a sudden paroxysm of sobs overmastered and swayed her.

XVI.

BY a little after nine o'clock, this same evening, Pauline was driven in a carriage to her own residence.

She alighted with excellent composure, rang the bell and was promptly admitted.

But she had no sooner entered the hall than she found herself face to face with Courtlandt.

He was in evening dress; he looked thoroughly his old self-contained self. Pauline passed at once into the little reception-room just off the hall. Courtlandt followed her. She sank into a chair, slowly untying the strings of her bonnet. A brisk fire crackled on the hearth; she stared into it.

"So you came to me," she said, with a kind of measured apathy.

"Yes," said Courtlandt. "I obeyed the message that you sent me."

Pauline impetuously turned and looked at him. The fire-light struck her face as she did so, and he saw that her gray eyes were swimming in tears.

She made no attempt to master her broken voice. "O Court," she said, "it was ever so good of you to come! I almost doubted if you would! I should have remembered that you — well, that you cared for me in another than a merely cousinly way. But there was no one else — that is, no one near me in blood. It is wonderful how we think of that blood-kinship when something dreadful happens to us. We may not recall it for years, until the blow comes. Then we feel its force, its bond, its claim . . . I want you to sit down beside me, Court, and quietly listen. You were always good at listening. Besides, you will have an immense satisfaction, presently; you will learn that your prophecies regarding *him* were correct. My eyes are open — and in time. I shall never marry him. I shall never marry any one again. And now, listen." . . .

For a long time, after this, Courtlandt showed himself the most patient of auditors. But he was silent for a good space after his cousin had at length ended, while the fire sputtered and fumed behind the silver filigrees that bordered its hearth, as though it were delivering some adverse, exasperated commentary upon poor Pauline's late disclosures.

But presently Courtlandt spoke. "I think you

have had a very fortunate escape," he said. "And I hope you mean, now, to come back and be one of us, again."

"What a way of putting it!" she exclaimed, with a great quivering sigh.

"There's no other way to put it. Theory's one thing and practice another. As long as the world lasts there will be a lot of people in every land who are better and hold themselves better than a huge lot of other people. One can argue about this matter till he or she is black in the face; it's no use, though; the best way to get along is to take things as you find them. You and I did n't make society, so we'd better not try to alter it."

Pauline gave a weary little smile. Her tears had ceased; she was staring into the fire with hard, dry, bright eyes.

"O Court," she said, with a pathetic little touch of her old cruelty, "I'm afraid you don't shine as a philosopher. You are better as a prophet; what do you say of Cora Dares and *him?* Will they marry?"

"Yes," returned Courtlandt unhesitatingly. "And I dare say he will make her an excellent husband. Did n't you tell me that she was an artist? . . . Well, he's an editor, a sort of general scribbler, so they will be on a delightful equality. They'll marry. You say I'm a prophet; depend upon it, they'll marry sooner or later."

"You make me recall that you are Aunt Cynthia's nephew," said Pauline, with another weary smile. She was in a very miserable mood. Her wound still bled, and would bleed, as she knew, for many a day.

Courtlandt's preposterously trite and commonplace little axiom had already begun to echo itself in a kind of rhythmical mockery through her distressed brain: "The best way to get along is to take things as you find them."

Was it the best way, after all? Was thinking for one's self and living after one's own chosen fashion nothing but a forlorn folly? Was passivity wisdom, and individualism a snare?

The fire crackled on. There was more silence between the two cousins. The hour was growing late; outside, in the streets, you heard only the occasional rolling of carriage-wheels.

"By the way, speaking of Aunt Cynthia, Court, — will she ever notice me again?"

"Certainly she will."

"Is n't she furious?"

"That newspaper article has repressed her fury. She's enormously sorry for you. Aunt Cynthia

would never find it hard, you know, to be enormously sorry for a Van Corlear; she came so near
to being one herself; a Schenectady is next door
to it."

" Yes, I understand," mused Pauline. She was
still staring into the fire. " There is that clannish
feeling that comes out strong at such a time . .
Court, I will write to her."

" Do, by all means."   .

" Not an apology, you know, but a . . well, a
sort of pacific proposal."

" Do, you 'll find it will be all right, then.
Aunt Cynthia would never put on any grand airs
to one of her own race; she has too much respect
for it." . . .

The longest silence of all now ensued.   The fire
had ceased to crackle; its block of crumbled coal
looked like the fragments of a huge crushed ruby.
Pauline did not know that Courtlandt was watching her when she suddenly heard him say, —

" You 're going to have a hard fight, Pauline,
but you 'll come out of it all sound — never fear.
I suppose he *was* the sort of chap to play the mischief with a woman, if she once gave him a
chance."

" O Court," came the melancholy answer, " I
was n't thinking of *him*, just then. I was think-

ing of what my life has meant! It seems to me, now, like a broken staircase, leading nowhere. Such a strange, unsatisfactory life, thus far!"

"All lives are that, if we choose to look on them so," returned Courtlandt. "It is the choosing or not choosing to look on them so that makes all the difference . . Besides, you are young yet."

"Oh, I am seventy years old!" she cried, with a little fatigued moan.

"In a year from now you will have lapsed back into your normal age."

"I can't believe it!"

"Wait and see."

"Ah, I shall have to do a good deal of waiting — for nothing whatever!"

"I too shall wait," said Courtlandt grimly.

She suddenly turned and scanned his face. "For what?" she sharply questioned.

"For you."

Pauline threw back her head, with a brief, bitter laugh. "Then you will have to wait a long time!" she exclaimed, with sorrowful irony.

"I expect to do that," answered Courtlandt, more grimly still. "And I am a good prophet. You told me so."